SAM TENNEY

RYAN GATTIS
Kung Fu High School

Ryan Gattis is the author of *All Involved* and, most recently, *Safe*, a literary thriller about a freelance safecracker trying to atone for a dark past. He lives in Los Angeles.

KUNG FU HIGH SCHOOL

KUNG FU HIGH SCHOOL

RYAN GATTIS

MCD × FSG ORIGINALS

NEW YORK

MCD × FSG Originals
Farrar, Straus and Giroux
18 West 18th Street, New York 10011

Printed in the United States of America
Originally published in 2005 by Hodder and Stoughton, Great Britain
Originally published in the United States in 2005 by Harcourt, Inc.
First FSG Originals paperback edition, 2017

Library of Congress Cataloging-in-Publication Data
Names: Gattis, Ryan, author.
Title: Kung Fu High School / Ryan Gattis.
Description: First Farrar, Straus and Giroux paperback edition. |
   New York : Farrar, Straus and Giroux, 2017.
Identifiers: LCCN 2017005065 | ISBN 9780374182267 (pbk.) |
   ISBN 9780374716639 (e-book)
Subjects: CYAC: Drug traffic—Fiction. | Murder—Fiction. |
   Gangs—Fiction. | Martial arts—Fiction. | High schools—Fiction. |
   Schools—Fiction.
Classification: LCC PZ7.G22737 Kun 2017 | DDC [Fic]—dc23
LC record available at https://lccn.loc.gov/2017005065

Designed by Richard Oriolo

Our books may be purchased in bulk for promotional, educational, or business
use. Please contact your local bookseller or the Macmillan Corporate and
Premium Sales Department at 1-800-221-7945, extension 5442, or by e-mail at
MacmillanSpecialMarkets@macmillan.com.

www.fsgbooks.com • www.fsgoriginals.com
www.twitter.com/fsgbooks • www.facebook.com/fsgbooks

1   3   5   7   9   10   8   6   4   2

This novel is very respectfully dedicated
to the memories of:

李
小
龍
(Bruce Lee)

and

Robert Cormier

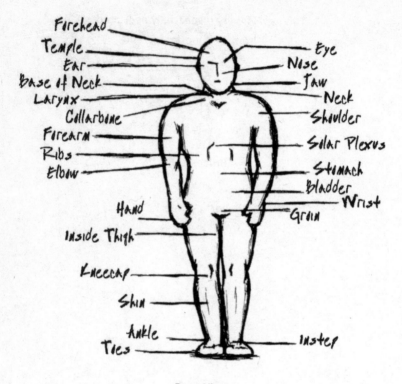

Front View

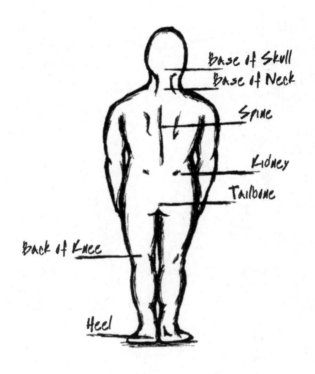

Base of Skull
Base of Neck
Spine
Kidney
Tailbone
Back of Knee
Heel

Back View

I dreamt of so many good things happening for me here.
Now, there is nothing. Everything is finished, gone.

—Cheng Chao-an, *Tang Shan da Xiong/Fists of Fury*

Bunting nodded. Continued to stare into space. Not wanting
to look at Janza now or anybody or anything. Staring into
the future, next year, beyond. Him, Bunting, in command of
the entire school. Stooges at his beck and call. An army at
his disposal. No rules except for those he made up. The
boss. More than that. Like a dictator, for crissake.

Beautiful.

—Robert Cormier, *Beyond the Chocolate War*

'Tis gone!
We do it wrong, being so majestical,
To offer it the show of violence;
For it is, as the air, invulnerable,
And our vain blows malicious mockery.

—William Shakespeare, *Hamlet*, Act I, Scene i

INTRODUCTION

I WAS IN LONDON, CALLING LOS ANGELES, WAITING FOR A response to my question. I was on the phone with James, a survivor of the Columbine High School shootings, and one of my former roommates at Chapman University. I'd just asked him what he thought about me writing a novel about high school violence and right then I was bearing his silence. As he thought about how to respond,

I heard low voices in the background. It sounded like a party. And I ruined it.

After a long pause in which I was certain we might not even be friends anymore, James surprised me.

"Just make it art," he said.

Just make it art. To this day, these are the most profound words about writing and pain I've ever heard, and they have guided my writing career, such as it is, ever since. Would it not have been so much better that day in Littleton, I thought, if the gunmen who truly wanted to do such terrible things actually had to suffer in order to commit them? This is how the idea of King High School first came to me. Instantly I knew the students in my story would not have guns. All violence would be hand-to-hand, face-to-face. It would be consequential, it would require commitment and willingness to sacrifice, and, perhaps most important, it would mirror my own understanding of the body in pain as a survivor of violence myself. It would not be like a Hollywood action film where the main character is shot in the lung and carries on running just as fast, it would be as true as I could possibly make it. I dashed off an e-mail then, asking my good friend Dr. William Peace if he'd be the medical advisor on the book—if he'd read my work and make certain that every act of violence (and medical treatment) in fiction was exactly how it would be in life.

I didn't wait for his reply. I already had an idea. If I framed my story in the context of a martial arts tale, a vengeance story, it might give me the distance I needed to make it art. Only one thing made sense: kung fu. It seems much of my formative pre-Internet years were spent filling out VHS mail order forms for Hong Kong martial arts films. Those who are now household names brought up bewildered glances when I babbled on about how great they were back then: Jet Li, Jackie Chan, Michelle Yeoh. There was only ever one favorite for me, though—an American, Bruce Lee. I loved *The Big Boss*, but something upset me about its story: the female cousin was nothing more than a plot device, someone who, when in peril, inspired the hero's violence. I decided then that in my tale, she would not only be the narrator, she would be the hero.

When I started writing, it was the voice of this young woman, a survivor, that came to me. She understood what pain was and was willing to risk it in order to protect those closest to her. I knew even then that not every reader would be able to understand her, much less relate to her. To some, she might seem cold, standoffish. Good. These were her survival tactics. Not to feel. To do. This is what consistent violence does to those who must bear it. It makes them wary, tired. One gets eyes for it. Its patterns become comprehensible and must be planned for. Emotions, on the other hand, can become the enemy. Only order makes consistent combat endurable. And here she was, Jen B., a disciplined, intelligent, intellectual fighter who deeply understood every ounce of negative touch—punches, kicks, chokeholds—but couldn't, for the life of her, understand a hug or romantic love. It broke my heart to tell her story, so I wrote it as fast as I could.

The first draft was done in two weeks, and when I got to the other side, I was not the same writer I had been when I started.

KUNG FU HIGH SCHOOL

THE PROMISE, A.K.A. THE PROLOGUE

YOU GOT THE STOPWATCH? GOOD. RESET IT. WE'LL TIME this. No, no, don't push that start button yet. Just wait. Now the way I hear it, it all began when Thug #1 punched Jimmy as he was walking on the road that went through the woods that Jimmy was known to walk every day after school. Well, not exactly punched Jimmy but tried, came up hard behind him and threw an awkward, crooked-wristed fist in his general direction. Completely sloppy technique—okay—now push the button.

Jimmy ducked, turned, and twisted while pivoting on his standing leg and delivered a forearm throat chop to Thug #1, incapacitating the ever-living shit out of the guy and hurtling his body backward onto the concrete.

Stop the clock. What's it say?

"Not even one full second. Well, almost a second."

Start it again.

Thug #2 comes out from behind a tree and has a shovel over his head like he's going to tomahawk Jimmy with the edge of it. Bad idea. Thug #2 obviously hasn't seen a single kung fu movie in his whole damn life because he still has a surprised look on his face when Jimmy straight leg kicks him in the gut, which makes Thug #2 catapult forward, doubling over, but while Thug #2 is trying to bring the shovel down on Jimmy and regain his breath, Jimmy leg sweeps him with so much force that he goes up into the air backward. Now, Jimmy—get this—comes up out of the leg sweep, stands up, and extends his right leg backward into an "L" at the knee and actually clips the guy at the base of the neck with a kick that knocks him out and then, Jimmy doesn't stop there, he actually catches this guy by the back of the neck with the bottom of his foot. Completely cushions him, because, you know, the guy was out like a light, if he let him drop, his skull would've just gone smush.

"I can't even picture that. What do you mean?"

I mean he caught him with his foot. He held up the weight of a full-grown man with his leg extended backward in that "L" shape. Like the guy's head was an inflated ball.

"I still can't see it."

Dammit, give me that pen. That napkin too. Okay, here:

4

The Napkin

See? On partial extension, knee at a ninety-degree angle point-ing backward while standing on one leg, Jimmy knocked the guy out with an aimed kick to the base of the skull, then he CAUGHT Thug #2 by the back of the neck with the sole of his foot. Then he grabbed the shovel with his left hand and just stayed in that position. STAYED!

"What?! No fucking way. That's not even possible. Physics and shit. Man, Jet Li couldn't do that WITH wires."

Serious. Jimmy just did it for show. To scare everyone watching. Now stop that clock. Time?

"Counting Thug #2's running toward Jimmy and not our little argument, that would be 4 seconds total—4.3 to be precise."

Start it again and keep it running this time.

Because Thug #3 comes running at Jimmy and before he even gets close, he gets smashed in the shins with the shovel head. See, Jimmy pushed passed-out Thug #2 back up to standing real quick, took one giant step, and swung the shovel so that it cracked #3's shins, then turned back around and caught #2 AGAIN but with his instep this time just as #2 was falling back over and before his head even hit the ground. Meanwhile, Thug #4 takes a flying leap at Jimmy, as he is supposedly busy trying to keep #2's skull from cracking but still man-ages to find time to block Thug #4's kick with the shaft of the shovel and then swat him out of the air like a lobbed baseball. BANG. After all that, Jimmy just lays #2 down on the ground gently like his body was some balloon attached to a soccer-ball head.

"I'm still not seeing it."

Ayight, just flip that napkin over. Here:

The Other Side of the Napkin

Got it now?

"I mean, yeah, I got it. I just don't believe it. There is no way that would ever, ever happen."

You don't know Jimmy.

"Yeah, guess I don't. So, what happened after that?"

Jimmy walks to the nearest pay phone and calls an ambulance. The ambulance shows up with the cops and he gets booked for assault and all kinds of other things. Anyway, his mom bails him out of jail that night with the last of his fighting prize money and extracts a sacred promise from Jimmy. She looks deep into his eyes and makes him swear on the soul of his father that he will never fight again.

"Wait, what?"

She made her son promise never to fight again.

"And he did? He promised?"

He did.

"And he meant it?"

He did.

"Whoa."

Yeah. That was the beginning of the end. Oh, so what you got on that stopwatch?

"Time elapsed, 9.6 seconds to send four nameless and faceless bad guys to the hospital. Hero doesn't even get scratched. Just like the movies."

Yeah, like the first part of the finale, right before the big boss, but then our hero gets well and truly fucked up.

KUNG FU HIGH SCHOOL

THE GOOD REVEREND DOCTOR MARTIN LUTHER KING HIGH School, that's the block-letter official name chiseled into the three-foot-thick concrete sign that sits in the dying yellow weeds in front of the cluster of buildings that was my school. First, it got called M.L. King or MLK, simple enough. Then there was King Junior to be more precise and that was because he started having a national holiday all to his posthumous self, but the word was never officially added to the title because everyone thought it would lead to confusion and people would think we were a junior high. That didn't stop us from calling it King Junior anyway. King Joony followed not long before it was mercifully shortened to King Joo. It never was KJ and I don't know why that is. But I do know that by the time Ridley was running drugs out of the school cafeteria, people in the city just knew us as Kung Fu.

Wasn't really surprising that Kung Fu High School was a name someone from the outside came up with first. It was supposed to be an insult because there were so many Asian American kids attending but that was a bullshit reason. We didn't have any more Asians than anywhere else. Us students didn't care though. We liked it. It was Bruce Lee tough, a gory stamp of approval that featured a clenched fist crushing the blood right out of a still-beating heart. That was how we saw it in our minds. That was what the nickname meant to us, that Kung Fu.

The way most everybody talks about it though, you'd think it was the evilest place on earth. They don't even talk about us like we're humans because of what happened. Senseless animals, I've heard. Wild beasts, I've heard. Monsters? Demons? Heard those too and I've heard even worse. There are more rumors and stories about us than could ever be written down. Every single one made up because the brutal truth could never be released to the public. Not like it mattered. Nobody wanted to believe it was real anyway. That a school like ours could actually exist and that it could really go off the way it did. That so many people could be murdered. I guarantee the whole thing was easier for them to deal with if what actually happened stayed in their horror-packed imaginations and didn't occur in a regular old high school.

It was like this: main building was a four-story building, a giant box with minimal windows, connected to the two-story gym by a

9

cake-wedge corner of bi-level cafeteria built long after the original plans. The central quad was marked out in huge rectangles of flat concrete. In front of the gym, a two-foot-high, six-foot-wide box, poured of the same concrete so that it looked like it was rising up out of the ground, was spaced between every three rectangles. Those solid things were supposed to be for sitting on, but that was a damn rare occurrence. On the east edge of campus was the other main building. Long and only one level, it housed the auto shop, home economics, and what passed for art studios on one end, while the special education center took up the other. Across from the gym was the theater and band building. Built on the original grade of the hill, the tiered theater angled down the small mound and the bottom, where the stage was, bordered the parking lot. It blocked off the quad from streetview. That was all KFHS was: five faded redbrick buildings plus a couple of disused portable classrooms, surrounding a dirty gray quad. Not so scary, not so special, and definitely not the seventh circle of hell. Long before our "gangbanger" Armageddon went down though, we had a reputation.

Don't even go there, they'd say when the talk first went around town. Haven't you heard that that one guy died there? It's true too. Robert W. Lewis, nicknamed Robbie, aged sixteen, did die here, right in front of his locker, #126, but it wasn't because he was stabbed or shot or kicked in the chest so hard that it turned his rib cage to dust and liquefied all his internal organs so powerfully that he vomited all his innards onto the laminate floor that was missing more than a few grayish white tiles. That shit isn't even possible. What actually happened was Robbie had a bad heart and Robbie had a heart attack after Robbie took some cocaine during Robbie's study hall period then Robbie got dead while reaching for Robbie's chemistry book. He wasn't the first person to die here, just the first white one with rich parents to make a fuss. So that was the story that got the status ball rolling but it was much worse than one white kid OD'ing and that incident certainly didn't stop anything.

The circle was in effect Monday through Friday and if you got challenged, you had to fight. No choice. Two hundred people circle you up and sling you into the middle against Bruiser Calderón and you ain't going anywhere but at his throat or balls. Don't even waste time with his knees or those tiny eyes hidden under that caveman brow. Keep that chin down and cover those ears. Head butt if you can sneak one but focus on his soft points and don't get distracted.

For reals though, why the nickname Kung Fu? Personally, I think it was because 99.5 percent of our student body knew one form or another of martial arts. Serious. If it weren't for a few people that could only hold their own because of how big they were, the number would've been 100 percent. Dojos all over the city were booked out with kids from our high school who wanted to learn self-defense tactics fast. So then Express Dojos sprang up. Like kung fu kapitalism. They specialized in one-week intensive courses in anything you wanted: those popular Japanese forms, Karate, Sumo, Judo, Aikido, Jujitsu, Ninpo/Ninjitsu, Chinese styles of kung fu but specific ones like Hung, Kui, Lee, but never Mo, don't know why, then there was Wing Chun, all kinds of Korean Leg Fighting, Hapkido, Tae Kwon Do, Hwa Rang Do, Kuk Sool Won, Hup Kwon Do, the ill kind of Muay Thai where all the kids got yellowed shinbones from kicking stumps until the scar tissue prevented any kind of feeling apart from invincibility, and there was Kuntao, Indonesian Silat, Filipino Escrima, some dance-y Capoeira, Front-Foot Boxing, Vanilla Kickboxing, Krav Maga, even some styles most people thought long dead, I mean Tibetan, Mongol, some Nigerian craziness, all started popping back up too, but various mixtures always reigned.

Usually the big circle winners knew two or three real well and could switch up on you in the time it took to button your collar.

Happy hybrids, everything was everything, even the type of shit that people only ever saw in movies was in our big house: animal styles like snake, eagle claw, and monkey, fists of the elements, seriously everything. Authentic? Not authentic? It didn't matter. So long as it worked, we stole it. We stole it all. I mean, that's the real American Way, right? Gee, Hawaii looks nice, we're fuckin' taking it, right? Roll over it, dress it up, or put a flag in it, just claim it as your own. All them fusions got crazy too. But no one ever saw that. It was all just a tall tale unless you experienced it for yourself.

But Robbie dying, that was fact and after that the other rich kids started getting transfers to other schools, prestigious public or private ones in different districts so they didn't have to show up for classes in the rundown part of the city anymore. The state threatened to pull our funding, which didn't help because the total population was almost three thousand mostly bad kids that had nowhere to go but to infect good schools, or so everyone thought. Besides, Ridley would've just found another high school to operate out of. Didn't matter where really.

It was the perfect cover and it was even better when all the rich kids with clean faces took off and the only dirty-faced white kids who were left might as well have been black, brown, red, or yellow too. So that was it. Asian, Latino, European, African, Indian, and every other American thing in between became one big mix. The only dress code in our world was instituted by us and it was just this: make damn sure you looked like everybody else. Giant-sized work coat with no shape to it, block-color wool hat keeping you warm over a button-up shirt, khaks or jeans, and a pair of boots. Any and all logos got taped over or torn out. Used to be a time when everyone wore 'em, no longer. Those kinds of identifiers could bring trouble down on you. The hard truth was, we were all targets. We were all the color of poor and just trying to survive the same sinking ship. For real. Can't say that the Kung Fu rep isn't deserved though.

If it was your first week at KFHS, I pitied you. On my first Friday, my brother pulled me aside before the welcome assembly and we watched from the brick pillars in front of the gym as all the freshmen got surrounded. Didn't matter if you were a guy or a girl. You got kicked in. You learned the hard way who ruled the school. By the time your next year rolled around, you couldn't wait for some ignorant freshmen to walk through the courtyard with color-coded binders clutched to their chests and fear in their eyes.

And you kicked them in the chin too. When they were prone on the ground, you lifted their arms up out of that crybaby fetal position and unloaded on the armpit lymph node because you weren't really kicking them so much as the kids that kicked you the year before. You broke bones, aimed for joints. You spat on split faces. You took tufts of hair as partial scalps and pressed them in the clear plastic folders meant for science reports and then hung them up inside your locker so no one would fuck with you. It was the only way not to be next.

Violence wasn't just for us though. It was for everyone who ever came near. Other high schools would send their sports teams but no fans when it came time to play us on the athletic schedule. North High School had a hired security team on hand the day they beat us by twelve points on our court but it didn't matter. In a rare showing of school spirit, every player on their basketball team, the security guys with their sheathed clubs, and the coaches with their clipboards, all got various vertebrae kicked in by our "fans," who were really just there to roll and not for any other reason. We were suspended from all athletic competitions for a year after that and were only let back in after Principal Dermoody agreed to hold games without any fans at all, just to keep up pretenses. Then floodlight-equipped helicopters had the habit of flying overhead on game days, lighting up the quad, and the kids that sat in ambush and hid in the trees with their belts wrapped around their knuckles had to duck low into the branches and make like bird nests to avoid getting spotted.

So why didn't anything get solved by the powers that be? Why weren't the bad guys caught, tried, and sent to jail? Truth, justice, and more of that awesome American Way, where was all that shit? Situated squarely behind greed, I guess. Let's start with the food chain:

algae/students → protists/teachers → squid/administration →
seals/cops → walruses/lawyers & judges & media →
killer whale/Ridley

Students didn't matter, next to worthless. You were in or you were out. If you were in, expect some early morning dope runs before hockey practice. If you were out, you were fair game at all times. If you didn't know how to defend yourself, either leave or find someone who could watch your back 24–7. Impossible, right? Those were just a few unwritten regulations.

Teachers there to protect you? Yeah, right. Nobody cared about the teachers. Either they were passionate believers in the power of teaching to change the disenchanted youth, who got in nice cars at the end of the day and went back to cookie-cutter houses in the suburbs, or they were deadbeats, ex-cons who slipped through the cracks without a background check. And all of 'em were on Ridley's payroll. Except for Mr. Wilkes, the chemistry teacher. He'd been there longer than anyone's oldest brothers and sisters can even remember.

The Administration? That's a joke too. From what I hear, Principal Dermoody was the one who masterminded the restructured school lunch program so that Ridley could run his drugs out of the shipping trucks. In: frozen pizza, freeze-dried potatoes, and horse-burger. Out: Champa, Spillback, Razorhead, Warped, Mixit, Agrenophene, Smoke, EX-O, Tapwap, and Giggledust.

The cops didn't count either. Well, they counted, but different than you think. They caught a thick kickback on every shipment that went by the precincts. I'm talking percentages here. Probably in the realm of 12 percent and trust me when I say that they knew about every single shipment and how much it carried; they made sure to get their 12 percent on every ounce.

Lawyers, judges, media? You aren't getting it yet, are you? Everyone was in on it. Everyone. It's no coincidence that old white dudes that used to be driving Cadillacs and Mercurys started driving Benzes and Beemers, and the rich fools that were driving Benzes and Beemers upgraded to Porsches and whatever else the next level was. If none of that connects the dots for you, believe this: Ridley even had regular dinners at the mayor's house as a welcome and invited guest. The poached salmon with garlic and herb sauce, that was his most favorite meal there.

So, how could something so rock solid, so positively fuckin' entrenched go wrong? A complex, well-supported system like that couldn't possibly be wiped out in one day, could it? In a word, yes. But really, I can sum it up in two: Jimmy Chang. He was the rebel (if refusing to fight in a cauldron of fighters can be called that) when he came to Kung Fu HS halfway through my sophomore year and he wasn't any hero then. He was just my cousin.

UNINVITED GUEST

THE DAY JIMMY CAME, ME AND DAD WERE IN THE KITCHEN.
He didn't knock. He just walked right in through the front door. It
really was our fault that it wasn't locked. Didn't matter though.
Jimmy didn't have time to say hello because Kyuzo caught him by
the throat and slammed him against the near wall in the entryway,
putting an imprint into the dirty old deco wallpaper. Dad and I

didn't see it, but we heard it. More like we heard the breaking of the wooden wall-hanging my parents got in Germany all those years ago when they lived there. It was a carved likeness of some tiny city with a river through it, can't remember which, but in two pieces it was just a city on one side and a bridge and river on the other.

Dad used to be in the Air Force and they were stationed there in Deutschland. Believe it or not, Kyuzo was born at Spangdahlem Air Base. I still call him a fuckin' nazi if I get mad enough, just to get under his skin. He's named after the swordsman character in *The Seven Samurai* because Dad loved that movie so much, but I just call him by his nickname, Cue. Because Kyu = Cue, or Cue Ball, on account of his shiny bald head. Dad loved Japan always. He used to be stationed there too, once.

It's generally rare for any business to follow us home from Kung Fu, but it's happened before. I got up slow and brought two knives with me into the hallway but they were unnecessary because Cue and Jimmy were already laughing super loud and it echoed into the kitchen. I couldn't put them back though. Habit.

"Jen, Dad, *Jimmy's* here!" Cue yelled too loudly. "Oh, man, what the hell are you doing here? Can't you at least ring the bell?"

Just hearing his name, I felt my mother's disavowing ice pick of a look all over again. I felt the hidden part of me that still was that defiant, cold girl returning her gaze and making ice cubes in between. Like I'd grown up completely encircling that hidden, staring me—left her intact like a nested Russian doll down deep. As untouched as the pencil mark on the kitchen entryway to measure my height at twelve. I fought that emotional old shit though. Pushed it down, all five feet and eight straggling inches of me. Below that.

I took the corner and just held the knives out naively, like a cheerleader offering up her pompoms for the home team. The city part of the wall-hanging was on the floor and the bridge half hung crookedly above it, still on the wall. Funny how the exterior was a dark brown but the inside was just normal, aged-looking wood. Untouched by the stain, it looked like yellowy bone, marrow even. Percussive though. It had sounded like claves when it hit the tile. Just once, like TAC.

"Are those knives for me?" Jimmy had his arm around Cue and with his other hand, he rubbed at the growing red spot at the base of his neck.

"Dinner, crazy boy. Hope Cue taught you good not to walk right into people's houses without ringing the doorbell."

That's all that came out of my mouth and I'm lucky it did. I mean, at least it wasn't garbled or anything. And at least I didn't stammer or just stop talking altogether. Because I hadn't seen Jimmy in years and he was gorgeous. Even with the farmer-boy mop on his head, the thick black strands couldn't hide his light brown eyes. I felt a twinge in my stomach when he pushed his hair off his forehead and leaned his head back into the weak hall light.

Yup, his brown eyes were just as light as they'd ever been. Like bright sunlight passing through label-less brown beer bottles, they shined at me. Mental note: NOT allowed to feel sexual attraction to cousin. The best part was, non-embarrassment-wise, I didn't drop the knives when I led the boys into the kitchen. They just pushed past me into the dining room anyway. A waist-high, partition-type wall separated the two rooms.

"Uncle B.—what happened?" Jimmy asked as Dad, tired as he was, tried to push himself up on his walker.

"Shit, your mom didn't tell you? Modern construction. Can you believe it? Always wear your helmet, son."

Dad shook Jimmy's hand and smiled his halfway smile that had sat on his face ever since the accident. I could tell he was smiling for real though because the vein in his neck twinged and that only happened when he meant it to.

"Foreman Dad took his helmet off for a water break and a brick fell on him."

I said it as I took the pasta noodles off the boil. They were a little soft because I'd left the pot on the burner. If they complained, I'd blame it on Jimmy.

"It was damn hot that day. What do you want from me, *mi angelita*?"

Dad put his hands in the air. Insert canned laugh track. I didn't turn around, didn't react to his little drama, just told the draining noodles my answer all low: *nada. Nada*, I said, to that full sieve. The literal translation in the dictionaries is always one word: nothing. But to me, when I breathed the accented syllables into the steam, pushing a coat of fog onto the window, it meant less/more than nothing at the same time. A push/pull kind of nothing. A go-away-but-don't-go-away kind of nothing. A please die/don't die kind of nothing. It always canceled itself out.

"What the heck is you doing here, stealthy? Why the big bag?" Cue's voice broke my thoughts like he knew them, then made sure to change gears. "You know, I heard you when you passed the mailbox. If you want to sneak up on me again, don't wear cowboy boots."

The hick. The big shitkicker. Jimmy didn't have an answer. He just looked at me like he was a lost puppy while I shredded the cheese into the smallest bowl we had. Thank god for self-control. I almost told them both that he could sleep in my bed right then.

"So, what? You're living here?"

I could see Cue putting two and two together from all the way across the kitchen, over the partition, and inside the dining room beside the packed bookcase. He sat down at the table and motioned for Jimmy to do the same.

"No. I mean, yeah, if I can and that's cool with you guys and Uncle B.," Jimmy said, adding, "You didn't get the letter?"

He had to push a stack of old newspapers out of the way before he could pull a chair out and sit down between Dad and Cue.

"Sure we did. Blue envelope. Marin still has great handwriting, like your *mamá*'s used to be." Dad said it like me and Cue had forgotten. Jimmy kind of nodded. I didn't say shit, only tore the last of the lettuce harder.

"Oh yeah, we heard you got in trouble but we figured it was no big deal. I mean, not compared to what we go through, Farm Boy. Besides, you probably just slapped somebody." With that said, Cue smacked Jimmy lightly across the cheek, rolled his eyes, and made a little girly scream to accompany it, "Ay!"

"I got in a fight." Jimmy actually lowered his head when he said it.

Cue and I just laughed at that, at the words, at his shame, at everything. I was setting the salad and cheese bowls on the table and Cue looked me up and down with his wide silly smile before poking me right in my splenectomy scar. I squirmed but spilled nothing. Only he knew where it was. Got that ruptured from a body blow. Good thing it's out now. Only way to make sure it'll never happen again. Surgery sure sucked though. I mean, everything in my torso was tender for weeks and weeks. Everything. I could barely eat. Lost thirteen pounds and I even got a cold when I was recovering too. Coughing was like getting beaten up all over again. Total nightmare.

"Yeah, well, it was completely Mom's idea, which was why she wrote the letter. I had to promise her I'd never fight again though."

Probably for the first time since Jimmy had walked in, the house was completely quiet. Even though the big pot was off the boil and empty of noodles, a few bubbles rolled to the surface of the splash of water left in it and popped. I just watched them, scooping pasta onto the plates without looking down. The letter hadn't said anything about that.

Cue laughed the silence right out the door.

"What, like *The Fresh Prince of Bel-Air* meets *Fists of Fury*? You be a cross between Will Smith and Bruce Lee? You're fuckin' lying to me! Hey, Jen, you finally got something to write about!"

Cue had the biggest smile on his face I'd seen in a long time. He always did when he was teasing me about my notebooks. Genuinely though, he was excited. He was convinced it was a joke, and a good one too. Because he knew. I knew. Hell, even Dad knew that Jimmy was the best fighter in the whole family. Always had been. With him fighting too, the Waves would win the Grand Championships again. No doubt.

"Dead serious, man. I promised my mom. No more fighting. None."

Maybe it's because I've been hit so many times that it makes you harebrained but I'm more sensitive to things like changes in temperature ever since I made a habit of acquiring broken bones and, honestly, the temperature in the room lowered when Jimmy said those words. Fahrenheit five degrees easily, and I was standing in front of the stove.

"Well, you in trouble then, *primo*, cuz if you expect to come to the Fu, you gotta roll."

Cue flexed and his black wife-beater shuddered. Trap muscles grew up next to his neck like pyramid ramps to his head made out of that dinosaur capsule stuff that expands when you put it in water. His biceps rolled over onto themselves like snowballs becoming snowboulders rolling too fast down a powdery hill and the scar on his left pectoral muscle made a sidewinding motion like the desert snake. That was Cue's move too. The Sidewinder.

"The Fu?" Just after he said it, Jimmy patted his stomach and gave me a look that said he approved of my cooking, or the smell of it at least. Bless him.

"Kung Fu High School, kid," I said.

Cue just made a face at me. And that was okay. We'd take it outside later.

"Now that's a joke, right?"

"Maybe it used to be but it ain't anymore," I said as I put two plates down, one in front of Jimmy and one in front of Dad.

"Thank you." Dad said it soft.

"Yeah, thanks," Jimmy said, clapping his hands once.

"Ah, you'll be alright though. You're legacy. You're a Wave, baby, just like me and Jen."

Cue spun me around and pulled my loose T-shirt up to show Jimmy the Yakuza-style tattoo that covered my entire back. I fidgeted a little as he pulled down my bra strap to show Jimmy the tan fishing boat between my shoulder blades. The whole thing had taken four visits to complete. We'd got some old Japanese guy in Little Ginza to do it for a hundred bucks and it looks real good too with its waves that look like rounded fish scales crashing into the center meridian of my back. Big puffy-faced clouds blow looping visible wind from my shoulder blades onto the surface of the water from both sides, so that it traps the fisherman in his boat.

"It's the storm of all storms," Cue said before tapping the outline of the fisherman on my spine, "and it only comes for one at a time."

He was almost as proud of it as I was. Jesus, did it take a long time to heal though. The guy said one month but it was more like two because I kept rolling over on my back at night when I was asleep and rubbing the lotion off with the sheet. I didn't mean to, just happened. It was a damn good thing I got the work done in the summer and not during the school year. That would've been trouble.

"Just what're you guys into?"

Quiet as he always was during such conversations, Dad even laughed when Jimmy said that. There were a few things he needed to be told.

THE SURVIVAL LIST

THERE ARE A NUMBER OF THINGS ALL KIDS SHOULD KNOW before they attend Kung Fu High School. Unfortunately, they don't always get it. It comes too slowly or it comes the hard way, too fast to duck. But here they are, the seven rules to go along to get along:

1. Get Kicked In

This is unavoidable. Try to look at it as a necessary evil for continued existence. It happens at one point or another to everyone at Kung Fu. My brother couldn't protect me forever. The day after the cops picked him up for menacing, I got circled. But it wasn't a one on one. Everyone knew I hadn't caught it during the freshman warm-up so I got it double. They knew I was right-handed so they snapped my right wrist and broke three fingers including my pinkie. I had to learn to write left-handed after that. They wrecked six of my ribs and my right eyelid was sliced almost in half after someone decked me with thick class rings on their fingers. That one took forever to heal. It still droops a little. I got a hairline clavicle fracture to match my dislocated shoulder. I had internal bleeding. I was bedridden for two weeks. My chin got split open and you could see my lower gums through the hole that needed six stitches to close. Now I got this habit of rubbing the flat semicircular scar underneath my lip every time I'm thinking. I can only feel it when I press kind of hard because the nerves never grew back or reconnected.

2. Don't Complain, a.k.a. Shut Up, Part 1

It helped that I couldn't open my mouth for two weeks after that. This is real important. Whatever you do, do not open your big fat mouth and tell everyone how unfair it is that you got kicked because it doesn't work that way. You're new? You lose. It's that simple. Don't get too heartbroken. You're guaranteed not to be the only one. Everybody loses.

3. Join a Family, Stay Loyal to Your Family, NO MATTER WHAT

This is how the family system works. There are six families at Kung Fu. Each family has a Pop, Mom, and a council of Aunts and Uncles. Everyone else is a kid. Four families are affiliated with Ridley but hate each other; those are: Runners, Whips, Fists, and Blades. The other two have no beef with Ridley but sure as hell aren't beholden to him. They just don't care (at least, not outwardly). Those are the Wolves and Waves. Nobody bothers them because generally the best fighters are Wolves or Waves. The families aren't something you can join or not join, like some club. My brother's a Wave, so I'm a Wave. That's how it works. Legacies don't get drafted, they're automatic pickups. In every instance, your family chooses you. You cannot choose your family. Each year after the freshman warm-up, the draft takes place. Each family has done its research on you, more than you know. They know if you can't punch high or feint left. They know if you struggle on footwork or suck at defense. They know everything. And since nothing at Kung Fu is fair, the draft order is determined by whoever won the school Grand Championships the previous year. Blades got sixth place? Sixth pick. Waves won last year? Number one. There is no bickering, that's how it goes. If your family struggles, they will eventually be cannibalized by another family. There used to be ten families. All sprouted up in the time since Ridley got here. The Wrecks, Goons, Muds, and Saws? All gone. Only six left.

Something else about families, no outward show of family affiliation is made. No colors, no similar clothes, haircuts, or sign language. The rule is to look the same as everyone else. Everybody knows whose side who is on. Word gets around. They see who you hang with when school is out. Mainly, the families make sure to blend so that Principal Dermoody can't identify us. Like we're all arms and legs of a big chameleon, changing at the same time. He would just love to isolate and scapegoat a family, blame them as responsible for everything going wrong at Kung Fu—everything from low test scores to creating an unsafe school zone. He'd hand them over to the cops who'd hand them over to the judges who'd hold them up to the media and that would be that. Lots of handshaking and congratulations and they'd say how Kung Fu was safe now, but really, nothing would change. It would get worse. It's *been* getting worse. Families have been disappearing for years, and each time it happens, Ridley gets stronger. Everybody wonders who is next to go down. His own families aren't even safe. That's the real scary thing, nobody ever knows. Only a matter of time though. We've learned to count on it.

Beyond all that, I can say Kung Fu's probably the most equal place in the whole world, real egalitarian. It don't matter what you look like or where you're from or what your religion is. It don't matter if you're a girl or a boy or if you like boys or girls or both. Nobody cares. Just don't shove it in anyone's face. Can you fight? Good, because that's all that matters. You might as well make it a conscious decision. Make it easy on yourself.

Of course, ALWAYS travel with a family member wherever you go.

4. Learn How to Sew

Home economics is probably the most popular class at Kung Fu. No joke. No class saved more lives last year. Got a sturdy vest? Sew some Kevlar into it. Reinforce all daily-use clothing with padding and plating. The lighter the better, the stronger the better. Steel is stupid, too heavy. Aluminum is best because it's durable and light. Thick turtlenecks with molded throat protection are standard. Reinforce those earmuffs you got lying around. It's easy. Remove the outer layer and pull out all the cotton filling. Replace it with aluminum cut to fit. Voilà! That's arts and crafts the Kung Fu way. Sweatshirts and vests lined with serious internal organ protection are prized. The people who are best with the needle are usually put to work making garments for the whole family. They're called sew masters. Everyone wears a cup, even a modified version for girls. The pubis breaks easily. Get used to it.

Of course, the armor can backfire. Ronny from the Blades was wearing a wool hat lined with aluminum when he got chopped in the skull and the metal sewn into the lining nearly took his ears off. It would have too, if he didn't luck into such a good surgeon.

5. Shut Up, Part 2

Don't ever talk to anyone outside your family. Forget about all that Romeo and Juliet, two lovers from opposing families bullshit. Don't ever approach a member of another family unless you got a problem or a challenge. I've seen some nasty circles get started out of nowhere and it's all because some boy thought some girl was giving him eyes and maybe they could hook up. Next thing he knows, she's tearing him up in the round. You want sex or love? Get it from inside your family. If not, wait 'til you leave Kung Fu, if you can.

6. Pick a Fight Here, Start a Fight There, but Also Know Your Strengths and Weaknesses

This is crucial. It's impossible to be invisible at Kung Fu. Ridley has everyone ranked. So you have to fight someone sometime and since you do, do your absolute best to pick your battles. Always go through your family Mom or Pop and have them set it up, never take someone on yourself and never fight someone you don't know. Know your opponent and know yourself. Got a weak chin? Fight someone who brings it to the body. Just be smart, simple, and unafraid. It takes real skill, intelligence, toughness, and courage to face up to someone a foot taller and forty pounds heavier than you and still crack them a solid one before you have to go to the hospital for a well-earned vacation. ALSO: don't be too good. Be just good enough. The closer you are to the middle of the pack, the less likely it is that anyone'll be shooting for you.

There's a seventh rule though, even if nobody ever really talks about it: Always Avoid Principal Dermoody and Cap'n Joe. You get called down to Dermoody's fortress for skipping class or vandalizing the girls' bathroom, DO NOT GO. Sure, you want to go, you want to trust him, but don't. Show the pass to the head of your family. They will take care of it for you. ALSO: if you see Dermoody's bodyguard, Cap'n Joe, walk the other way fast. Do not get within his reach for any reason. Be smart always.

FAMILY STATS

I GUESS IT'S REAL HARD TO KNOW ANYTHING ABOUT THE school unless you know something about the families. Most of this stuff is just my opinion and came from one of my old notebooks so don't get too excited. Of course, I'm gonna be biased as hell and I'm sure lots of people probably disagree with me. The numbers might be wrong as well. Too bad.

I rated everything out of eight, not ten. Don't know why really, it just seemed right. The stats part I took from a video game at that one arcade, Jerry's Cosmic Dungeon. It's on Winnick Avenue, just off the downtown loop if you wanna go see for yourself. Couldn't think of any other way to do it really and that seemed good enough for this. Roll over it. Dress it up. Put a flag in it. Here goes:

RUNNERS

GRAND CHAMPIONSHIP VICTORIES: 2 (Counting 1 as Muds)
MEMBERS: 402, I think
FAVORED STYLES: Leg fighting
TOP FIGHTER: Donnie K.
POWER: 4
STAMINA: 6
COURAGE: 4
SPEED: 7
CHIN/BODY (DEFENSE): 6
CUTS (CHANCE TO BE CUT AND OPEN CUTS ON AN OPPONENT): 6
SPECIAL MOVES: Hurricane Jump, Liquid Legs, Golden Griffin Kick

See, they got their name from running drugs for Ridley back when he first came to Kung Fu. They absorbed the Muds four years ago. Although they aren't very good fighters on the whole, they're pretty damn loyal to Ridley because he stopped the Wolves from cannibalizing them two years back. Stuff like that doesn't get forgotten at Kung Fu. Serious.

WHIPS

GRAND CHAMPIONSHIP VICTORIES: 1
MEMBERS: 363
FAVORED STYLES: Varies, although they prefer elusive types of combat techniques
TOP FIGHTER: Bruiser C.

POWER: 3

STAMINA: 7

COURAGE: 5

SPEED: 7

CHIN/BODY (DEFENSE): 5

CUTS (CHANCE TO BE CUT AND OPEN CUTS ON AN OPPONENT): 5

SPECIAL MOVES: Dragon Claw Tackle, Sizzling Sling, Shark Fin Suplex

Whips run interference for Ridley. Always have, really. If he needs a disturbance caused across town to distract the cops' attention from an extra large shipment, he sends Whips. That's just how it is. No one questions it. They're a regular terror squadron: bombing out stores, tipping trucks over on the highway, doing whatever they got to do. Whips are probably the most dangerous of the families loyal to Ridley. Bruiser is a badass fighter.

FISTS

GRAND CHAMPIONSHIP VICTORIES: 3

MEMBERS: 320

FAVORED STYLES: Strong hand techniques only

TOP FIGHTER: Maria R.

POWER: 7

STAMINA: 3

COURAGE: 7

SPEED: 1

CHIN/BODY (DEFENSE): 7

CUTS (CHANCE TO BE CUT AND OPEN CUTS ON AN OPPONENT): 7

SPECIAL MOVES: Frozen Palm, Metacarpal Bomb, Windwalker

Typical foot soldiers: not real smart, courageous though, and pretty damn strong. I've personally seen Maria knock out plenty of chumps with one punch. Other than that, there isn't a whole lot to say about the Fists. They're pretty boring fighters because they fight like mad buck gorillas and don't exhibit much of a style.

BLADES

GRAND CHAMPIONSHIP VICTORIES: 2

MEMBERS: 463

FAVORED STYLES: Ninpo, Ninjitsu

TOP FIGHTER: Karl F-H.

POWER: 2

STAMINA: 6

COURAGE: 3

SPEED: 6

CHIN/BODY (DEFENSE): 4

CUTS (CHANCE TO BE CUT AND OPEN CUTS ON AN OPPONENT): 8

SPECIAL MOVES: Nail Gun Spin, Shadow Volcano, Nightfall, ??? (unknown attack)

Blades are one of the original families. That counts for something. They've pretty much remained unchanged through the years. Bandits, all of them. Still doing all the dirtiest work for Ridley. Nothing so glamorous as running the shipments or creating diversions, but more along the lines of cleaning up messes that inevitably happen in the drug trade. They know where the bodies are. They also know where the heads, arms, and legs to those bodies are, shit like that.

WOLVES

GRAND CHAMPIONSHIP VICTORIES: 2 (1 as Goons)

MEMBERS: 488

FAVORED STYLES: Varies, although they prefer elusive combat techniques

TOP FIGHTER: Melinda A.

POWER: 3

STAMINA: 7

COURAGE: 5

SPEED: 7

CHIN/BODY (DEFENSE): 5

CUTS (CHANCE TO BE CUT AND OPEN CUTS ON AN OPPONENT): 5

SPECIAL MOVES: Frostbite Cross Combination, Timber Claw Double Kick, Permafrost Punch

Wolves have always maintained their independent spirit, staying well clear of Ridley, even after combining with the Goons. Melinda is probably the smartest of the fighters at Kung Fu and is real good at picking her battles. The Wolves haven't won the Grand Championships in a few years and are a bit desperate to get another title.

WAVES

GRAND CHAMPIONSHIP VICTORIES: 5 (1 as Wrecks, 2 as Saws)

MEMBERS: 601

FAVORED STYLES: Primarily defensive, aikido and several lost kung fu styles

TOP FIGHTER: Kyuzo B.

POWER: 5

STAMINA: 5

COURAGE: 8

SPEED: 5

CHIN/BODY (DEFENSE): 8

CUTS (CHANCE TO BE CUT AND OPEN CUTS ON AN OPPONENT): 5

SPECIAL MOVES: Tsunami Uppercut, Tidal Throw, Ocean Floor Earthquake Kick, plus two other attacks I'm not allowed to name

The Waves started when the Wrecks and Saws came together about six years ago and became the most dominant family around, mostly because of superior numbers but also because of superior fighters and consistently winning the Grand Championships. Waves pretty much operate on a don't ask/don't tell policy regarding Ridley's drug operation. Kyuzo is by far the best fighter at Kung Fu, and winner of two straight Grand Championships in the solo division. Beyond badass, for real. Maybe that's just me though. He is my brother, after all. He's blood.

GETTING THERE

TAKES ME BETWEEN TWENTY AND THIRTY MINUTES TO GET dressed every morning. First I tie my hair back, that's if it's dry. If it isn't, I do it last, low and tight on my head. Then it's chonies, then leggings. I leave the sheath on my inner left calf empty today because I know Cue will be on high alert with Jimmy being new and all. I don't need to get overexcited and stab somebody on his watch, so it's best it isn't even there. I don't carry it much anyway, not anymore. The thing used to be my crutch back when I couldn't hold my own but things are different now. I'll be more than fine with fists, feet, and my big brother guarding my back. Khaks get put on next. I just got them back from our sew master, he put kneepad sleeves in so I can throw in light Kev padding for everyday use or aluminium pleated shunts for when I got a roll match. Shunts are the thin oval-shaped shields cut to fit in our clothing.

Nearly finished, I put on two T-shirts, both with reinforcement in the chest and shoulders and Cue always teases me because I always look way bigger than I am when everything's on. After that it's my hooded sweatshirt: straight kidney, rib, vital organ, and arm protection. On top of everything goes a flannel, for style. I got alum gloves and my boots have push-out quarter-inch nails in the toe if it gets real bad. The best part about them is that I pass the metal detector test every time because the guard guys in yellow jackets just assume it's the rivets and not the nails in the soles underneath. That's innovation at work, baby. So yeah, we do have metal detectors, but it's just for axes or knives, you know, blatant shit like that. They laugh about shunts all the time, call 'em our "metal shop projects," but that's assuming they even get noticed.

I passed Cue in the hall on his way to the shower and the same thought traveled in the air between our eyes: fighting or not, we got to get Jimmy some gear. He nodded and shut the door behind him but it didn't stick. It's hollow and the latch is crooked. Basically, it just hides nudity and that's about it. You can hear everything going on inside.

I was carrying a glass of water down to Dad's room when we did our telepathy thing. The sun was still down and I had to wake Dad up to give him his meds so I was late putting our lunches together when I got yelled at.

"Yo, let's go." Cue was the director every morning before school.

"Jen, grab them sandwitches, we don't need brown bags. We late! What the hell you thinkin'? We never use them. Damn, girl! Jimmy's ready. Let's gee-oh."

Always calling sandwiches sandwitches with a real hard "t" sound, Cue'd done it every day since we made up the story of the Sand Witch when we were in the Great Sand Dunes camping. That was when Mom was still alive. See, me and Cue didn't feel like hiking anywhere and the fact that these giant piles of sand were there wasn't too great either because we'd grown out of sandboxes and hadn't started our training back then. Wouldn't've mattered, you can't kick in the loose sand anyway. So we were just there, sat down, digging ourselves little holes into the clay underlayer to keep our feet cool and made up the story while we did it:

Once there was a Sand Witch that lived in a far-off temple and would fly around and pick up all the little boys that ever traveled the road alone. She would take them home and eat them. One day, a little girl with very short hair that looked like a little boy was walking along the path and the Sand Witch flew down and grabbed the little girl to take back to her corrupted temple. But when the Sand Witch found she was mistaken, that she had not grabbed a little boy, she didn't eat the little girl. Instead, the Sand Witch treated her like an apprentice and taught her all of her secrets, including how to fly. She said eating the little boys gave her the power of flight and, well, we didn't really have time to finish the story because Mom and Dad walked up and gave us ham-and-cheese sandwiches right after that.

That was the kicker. He and I got real excited and never called them anything else ever since. I'm still kind of working on a move called the Sand Witch but I haven't told Cue that yet because he'd laugh his ass off and then expect me to show him something great. So far though, it's just a leg sweep. No combo. Not worthy of competition.

In my own defense, the reason I never used paper bags for lunches was because we just chucked the food in plastic bags and then in our backpacks and hoped our books didn't squash it. We never bought nice little lunch-sized paper bags in their nice little packaging because they were a waste of money and usually we just got some of the plastic ones from the produce department or bigger paper ones for free at the grocery store when they packed our stuff. So that's what I was doing when he wanted to leave. I was trying to find the little ice-cream-box-sized paper bags to put sandwitches in so Jimmy wouldn't think we were weird or too poor.

Cue had a point though. We were "late" (late to Cue meant we wouldn't be thirty minutes early and have time to plan for the day) and that was bad because we had to walk to school in packs and getting left behind was a bad idea. I don't know why he even stressed it. Not like anyone was ever gonna leave without him.

Alfredo and the Hunters were already in our front yard, kicking their heels into the dirt and making holes where they shouldn't've been making holes. Alfredo was an Uncle in the Waves. He also ran the Hunters, a subfamily within our family. All families have little groups inside 'em. Cue trusted him because Alfredo saved his life once, but I've never trusted Alfredo. He's got corneyes. You know, the kind of eyes that never really have whites around the irises, just slightly yellow. Except for Alfredo, it's serious yellow, like he fell down in a field of corn and got corneye instead of pinkeye. That's the joke anyway.

I tossed Cue his sandwitch and handed Jimmy his and we were out. And damn if it wasn't the second I walked through that door that Alfredo put his corneyes on my tits, even before he looked at Jimmy. Yeah, that's the second reason I don't like him. He keeps thinking we can get together but he's dead wrong.

"Who dis?" Alfredo spat when he was done talking. Reason number three.

"This is Jimmy, he's my cousin." I knew it was Cue's place to talk but I couldn't resist.

"Cousin, huh?" Alfredo stepped up on Jimmy, all close too. That was Jimmy's turn to earn some respect and stare Alfredo in his beady little corneyes and let him know that he could tie him in a knot and roll him home to his *mamá*. But he didn't. He just stood there with a dumb smile on his face.

"Hi, nice to meet you," Jimmy said.

Damn, if Cue didn't laugh, we'd've had a roll on what used to be the lawn. We couldn't afford to water it anymore. Besides, that didn't make much sense in winter.

Of course, Alfredo got pissed anyway.

"What the fuck is that guy's problem, K?"

Everybody in the Waves called Cue, K. That or Pop. Poppa Don maybe, but that was pretty much it.

"Shut it, Corny," I said, "Jimmy'd roll your shit in a heartbeat."

I should've been the one shutting it but it was all right there for the taking. And nothing gets Alfredo's goat better than calling him Corny. Cue shot me a look over his shoulder as he led us down the street.

"Yeah? We'll see, little Jen-Jen. We'll see"—Alfredo raised his voice—"because I heard Chang was washed up. I heard Chang's gone softer than the Three Ninjas put together and yo, that's Rocky, Colt, AND Tum Tum!"

Alfredo turned his attention to Cue after getting some laughs from his Hunters. "Seriously, K, what use is this guy to us if he won't roll? He's strictly a liability. Strictly slack me and the Hunters gotta pick up. And you know we don't carry stragglers. Hunters don't truck with no bitches."

And then he licked his lips at me like he was LL Cool J or something, which he's not and never will be. All that guy's tired antics are straight out of the bad movies he was always referencing. I was about to tell him so too, but Jimmy put his hand on my shoulder and for a second I couldn't feel the ground underneath my feet.

"Enough!" Cue was thinking about something else already and I didn't blame him. He was brainstorming, not just how to keep Jimmy out of a fight today, but for good. He must've known it was impossible.

"I am finished. No more fighting," Jimmy said, then the little bastard smiled at me. It took an effort not to smile back too. Gravitas, that's what Jimmy had, gravitas. I learned that word in a Laurence Olivier documentary that I'll never, ever admit to having watched late one night on TV.

"See?" Alfredo was just spooning it on. "He really is a bitch."

I couldn't let that one go. Me and Cue both knew that Jimmy could tear Alfredo apart.

"You know what, 'Fredo? Keep talking like that and the only kiss you'll ever get from me will be the kiss of death like I'm Michael Fuckin' Corleone but I'll be the one breaking your heart—" I paused for effect, and Alfredo was about to jump in and say something but I talked over him—"when I pull it out your rib cage!"

There was even a chorus of "ooohs" from the Hunters on that one.

Usually, it was just talk. This wasn't. I would've rolled on him in the street and that just isn't smart. By far the worst place to ever roll is the street. The cops would steam in and pick you up, throw you in juvie, and you're done. In our neighborhood, they pick on you, they taunt you, and then they wait. They're like trapdoor spiders just hiding in their holes, waiting for us to make a mistake.

"Jen!" Cue spun around and lifted my whole body up off the ground. My feet were dangling before I even knew what hit me. His face loomed close to mine, but with eyes gone soft inside his sneer. When Cue's mouth turned up like that, his whole face followed: forehead, hairline, chin, everything. We have the same cheekbones. "Just stop right now. We don't need this. So save it." Big brother, always being the badass, dropped me on the ground instead of setting me back on my feet.

Thankfully, Alfredo laughed when he glared at me. That meant he could keep walking without losing face. Cue was smart like that. Turning, Alfredo pulled his trademark long black comb out of his back pocket, the one that was too big for his stupid pinhead, and surfed it through his hair. What a vain bastard. Reason number four. Not like I needed any more reasons.

Jimmy offered me a hand up and I forgot about everything else. Instead, I had to tell myself that I am not Sleeping Beauty. I am not Snow White. I am not a pretty princess. I am not the heroine. I do not get the guy in the end. The sooner I got used to it, the better.

We got to school fifteen minutes early, passed the metal check, and then Cue had plenty of time (but he'd never admit it) to iron out Jimmy's schedule and assign him a couple of Waves for each class: Period 1 Photography (7 Waves, easy class), Period 2 Earth Science (4 Waves), Period 3 Geometry (6 Waves), Period 4 Lunch (the back right corner of the cafeteria was sort of our section), Period 5 Gym (0 Waves), Period 6 English (4 Waves), Period 7 Study Hall (10 Waves, generally, it would mean Jimmy could skip out and go home, but not at Kung Fu—circles started at closing bell and you weren't allowed to leave early). We were the only family that I knew of that had chess-inspired classroom seating strategies (unwritten part of number three on the survival list: families weren't allowed to sit together, too easy to detect who was with who, Dermoody would be in on us in a flash). So the seating arrangements were like snapshots of opening chess moves that Cue thieved from some book. He'd look at the diagrams of the pieces set up and then he'd assign desks in the somewhat similar positionings of one side, always black. Roll over it. Dress it up. Put a flag in it.

Cue said he picked them all according to how many people were in each class. So it was funny to hear Cue explain to Jimmy that he was a bishop to N2 in the fianghetto in his science course, and rook to king's one, castling in English. They were all static. Not set up to continue a game, but just to spread us out. Secretly, I was a little sad I didn't have any classes with Jimmy, but he was a junior and I was a sophomore and that was the bad luck of the draw.

I hoped to god that he'd last until the final bell, but by lunchtime, everybody had heard that Jimmy was new and it was only curiosity that kept them off him. Like they thought his claim not to fight anymore was a lie, so they didn't go too close right away. I knew it would happen, everyone noticing him, I had just prayed it wouldn't. Word had spread fast. If he wasn't a legacy, the family with the last pick in the draft would've got him. That would've been the Blades. They knew who he was. Everyone knew who Jimmy Chang was. And it was well within their right to test him on closing bell.

We were in public so I couldn't give Jimmy a hug goodbye, I just gave him a shoulder clench instead. You know, how guys do. For someone who was supposedly done fighting, he was absolutely solid. He must still be training, I thought as I turned away and shuffled off to my Period 1 Civics (3 Waves, Hungarian Defense), where I was an unmoving bishop on the back row, the buried piece.

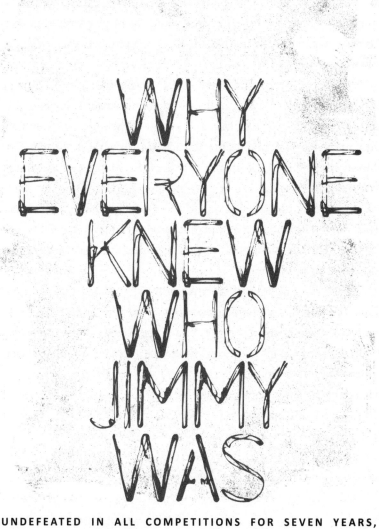

WHY EVERYONE KNEW WHO JIMMY WAS

UNDEFEATED IN ALL COMPETITIONS FOR SEVEN YEARS, that's why. That's never happened before so I'll just say it this way: undefeated forever and ever. In the United States, he was undefeated for five years. Officially a combined 882-0-0, he averaged nine major tournaments per year and the maximum number of fights per tournament, sometimes as many as three fights per day depending on seeding. Put it this way, Jimmy stopped collecting trophies. He didn't have room for them anymore. So he would either give them back, convince the organizers to make it a standing trophy with engraved names, or donate it to charity somehow. He probably even sold one or two for scrap.

By the time he was fourteen, Jimmy'd won five straight national championships and five straight world championships in three different disciplines: karate, judo, and kung fu. Then he won a scholarship to the most prestigious martial arts academy in Hong Kong: Fire Mountain School. It was in all the papers. They taught all the southern styles of kung fu. Had been doing it for hundreds and hundreds of years. Lots of people had no idea how difficult that must've been, relocating to HK after spending most of his life out on the plains. But Jimmy went, left his parents, moved halfway across the world, sucked it up, and went to work.

After training for six months within the school, Jimmy began competing on the local circuit in every tournament available. Same result. Not a single loss. He tore China up en route to two more world championships in FIVE different disciplines. And he would have won all the Chinese championships as well if not for the fact that he was barred from certain ones for not being a citizen. That didn't stop people from idolizing him, wanting to be near him, politicians from using him to curry favor with the masses. It must've been a crazy time. Jimmy found himself the national spokesman for a noodle company, and a cooking sauce company. They made sweet-and-sour sauces and stuff like that, put them in bottles and sold them for home use. He sent the money to his parents because rules at his school forbade the live-in members from earning. They were only there to train.

It probably goes without saying that Jimmy was the most famous kid in the world of martial arts. They even put his face on a Chinese edition Coke can without his permission. That's how famous Jimmy was: fifteen years old and the legend of all legends. Kids would play tournaments in their backyards and actually get into real fights over who could be Jimmy Chang, All American, All World, All Invincible.

So why did everyone at Kung Fu know him? Because Jimmy Chang isn't real. He's a myth: the kid who couldn't lose. You probably heard about piano prodigies who can start playing at four or some ridiculous age, well Jimmy was like that, except with martial arts. His dad started him out at three, training him in the fields. See, his dad was a farmer and a good one but somehow he found time to run a farm and train Jimmy at night. He started Jimmy out with simple Tiger Fist forms, just practice stuff to do in the morning and at night in the barn. Of course, it didn't take him long to progress. He was on to full contact by the time he turned six. So his dad taught him what he knew of Hung Gar and Yong Chun styles. By the time Jimmy was eight he was competing.

When he quit just before his sixteenth birthday, his record was 2,412–0–0. He was a ghost. Never been injured. Never even been thrown. And for his last full year on the mat in Hong Kong, NEVER EVEN BEEN HIT. Get your head around that. Not a single opponent scored a hit on him. All the scorecards are kept in the main tournament hall in HK. You can go look if you want. But that's not really necessary, because if you saw Jimmy's final fight to defend his world championship in the open category (any style was acceptable), you would've seen everything you'd ever need to see. That was the day he fought The Bulgarian.

Nobody I know knows The Bulgarian's real name and if they did they couldn't pronounce it, so everyone, even the TV announcers, just called him The Bulgarian. Supposedly he was the biggest-ever threat to Jimmy's domination of the sport. Cue and I didn't believe that for a second. We heard the same thing every year. It was all just hype. We knew Jimmy couldn't be defeated. It didn't matter that The Bulgarian had been stolen from his gypsy parents and taken off to

Mongolia when he was a kid and raised in the mountains like some wild, latter-day Genghis Khan warrior.

The World Championships were being held in London that year and there was this huge procession in front of Buckingham Palace and then down in front of Big Ben, I remember watching that. The best part though was the standing room only in the giant event hall. There must have been twenty thousand people in there. Serious. The atmosphere was ridiculous. People were even singing: "Hey throw that fellah / We said a-hey throw that fellah / Jimm-y throw that fellah / hey throw that fellah," to the tune of "Guantanamera." But Jimmy didn't throw that fellah. He looked disinterested for much of the match, and it was amazing to watch him avoid full-strength spinning kicks by centimeters, and hammer-throw punches by millimeters. The timed first and second rounds ended with no points scored and the third and final round was much the same until the last two seconds.

To this day, every person who saw that fight swears Jimmy somehow teleported himself behind The Bulgarian to score the hit that won it. They showed it on television for months on super-slow-motion replay but watching it was like watching a jumpy old movie that was missing frames somewhere. See, Jimmy was in front of The Bulgarian, not two inches from him, with his heels on the out-of-bounds line, as the big challenger opened his arms wide and was bringing them down on Jimmy. There was no way he could escape. There was really no room, nowhere to go. I remember grabbing Cue's leg in the shady bar we had snuck into to watch the match on pay-per-view at one in the afternoon. I knew he had had it. Cue knew it was over. Everyone watching knew it was over.

The announcers were even starting the sentence, "A remarkable run has finally en—," when Jimmy disappeared/reappeared behind The Bulgarian, extended his right leg, and executed a perfect kick to the back of his opponent's weight-bearing knee, sending him sprawling forward onto the out-of-bounds part of the mat. I'd love to be able to tell you that I jumped and screamed and shouted and was so happy that Jimmy won, but I didn't. My mouth was just as open as Cue's and we were trying to figure out how he did it. It was shocking for real.

The cameras timed it afterward. Jimmy literally disappeared for a thousandth of a second before reappearing and winning the match. This didn't go over too well. Back in China, a leading priest denounced Jimmy as a dark spirit and people really got scared.

His time at Fire Mountain School ended and Jimmy returned to the farm. His dad was real sick by then though, so Jimmy took care of him day and night for three months until he finally passed away. Lung cancer. His dad never went to the hospital because he said he didn't believe in it. That was less than a year before he came to live with us. Me and Cue talked about it once and in a way, we think that was Jimmy's first loss ever. Because after that, Jimmy went a little crazy and got in that brawl that forced his mother to make him promise never to fight again and also, to send him here.

So as far as any person at Kung Fu was concerned, Jimmy Chang was Count Dracula, Houdini, and Bruce Lee all rolled into one when Cue and me walked him out into the unusually bright sunlight for early winter to find that every single student at Kung Fu had circled up. Kids were packed in sixteen deep, all the way to the front of buildings. People had dragged tables out of the cafeteria and were standing on them. I could see that Ridley had positioned himself in the usual place so that he could look down on the circle from the second-floor bay windows of the main building, in what used to be the guidance office. Even Dermoody was on the far end of the quad with Cap'n Joe, just standing still and observing like they were Wyatt Earp and Doc Holliday. They knew this was Ridley's time. They wouldn't interfere with the circle. It was moving, as people pushed against shoulders and bodies, stuck their elbows in ribs to get a glance at

Jimmy, to size him up. I could tell the conclusion they were all coming to: he was so much smaller in real life.

From high enough above the Kung Fu quad, it must've looked like some kind of growing tropical storm rolling toward an unseen coast. These students, these fighters, just pinpoints of streaming cloud mass pushed by hurricane winds around a silent center, had been waiting.

THE TEST

THAT WAS THE QUIETEST I EVER HEARD KUNG FU. OUT IN
the open air of the quad, it was cold enough to snow but there were
no flakes. White clouds clotted up the sky like rough skin after the
old scab gets picked and it didn't look like they'd be dropping anything anytime soon. There was no wind, and I could smell one of the
last operating factories. Sulphur-y, but not as strong. It was harsher

than usual. For real though, I was surprised I even noticed. Everyone at Kung Fu was used to them after about two weeks.

When we got to the middle, you could just feel the stares of two-thousand-plus kids on me, Cue, and Jimmy. That was when I started to get nervous. Usually, I don't get nervous before rolls. Well, not my own anyway. After a while it's just like going to work. Nothing special. But I had this feeling in my gut that Jimmy wasn't going to fight back. I knew he wasn't. I hoped at least that he would dodge but I had a feeling that he wouldn't. Everyone making up the circle had no idea though. They thought Jimmy was the Prince of Darkness and when he smiled, it made it worse. Previously, fear was Ridley's territory. He must've felt threatened.

From up on his perch, the bastard was looking at me too. I could feel it. Whenever he did, it felt like I hadn't taken a shower in three days, just greasy. Anonymous hands were pushing us farther to the center as people tried to get closer, but not too close, to Jimmy. It wasn't just the reputation that drew eyes to him. It was something inside him that no one else had. Just as I could feel Ridley's eyes on me, I could feel when Jimmy was nearby.

When we broke through the mass of kids, Karl Fellar-Hahl was waiting in the circle, the Blades' Pop, big white guy with a shaved head. He wasn't so tough but he was a cutter and he was quick. The guy would fold if Jimmy threw a punch. He had almost no power but he picked his shots and made them count. A real TKO kind of guy, his strategy was always just to cut you, put your own blood in your eyes 'til you gave up or couldn't see where the next blow was coming from.

Karl was dangerous because he would fight dirty. Like after-it-was-over dirty, which isn't all that uncommon around here but Karl was probably the worst. If he got the upper hand on you, you better pray that your family had your back because if Karl lost it, got in a rhythm, he'd just keep going. He'd be all the sharks and the feeding frenzy too. Nine times out of ten it isn't a big deal because someone'd jump in and end it, but one time, Karl put a freshman in a coma. That was two years ago now. The kid is still in that coma.

In fact, they showed a picture of the kid in the newspaper last year in some plea to stop all youth violence. Clustered around the story were wicked pictures of the kid's head looking like a tennis ball with curving scars across the top. They had to remove pieces of his skull and put in a plate, then staple his scalp back on. His hair grew back all patchy because of it too. Kid has this weird circle of hair on his forehead now. That was all Karl's handiwork. He has the newspaper clippings in his locker. He'd show them to you if you asked him.

"Don't do it, Jimmy. Cue'll fight him for you, he'll rip that guy." I didn't grab his hand or get emotional.

"Don't worry, Jenny." That was all Jimmy said.

Don't worry, Jenny. The last time anyone called me Jenny was when Cue was stitching my stomach up and I was fidgeting. For some reason, I don't do so good with deep torso wounds. But before that, it was my mom. True. I was Mom's little Jenny. Of course, Jimmy couldn't've known that I had to turn away for that reason. Maybe he thought I was getting huffy or mad at him for needing to do this. I wasn't. I don't get like that when it's time to roll. I guess I just couldn't look in his eyes and hear him call me Jenny again.

See, I might start getting ideas. Ideas about getting out, with him. I hadn't slept much the night before. Thought too much about Jimmy, him sleeping out on the couch. You know, how much he'd be missing his mom and how tough it was with his dad gone. How small and cold that couch could be. Him on top of a rubbed-loose floral sheet stuffed into the back cushion creases, and did he sleep with a shirt on? In his underwear? Or was he naked there? Of course, stupid me, night is always when I think about that stuff. When my brain runs away with me for hours and I'm alone, visions lost on the ceiling while what's left of my consciousness puts together movie figments that will never be. The only power I have is a finger on the remote control, or two.

In daylight, I just switch off. I'm good at it. No feelings in. No feelings out. Which is exactly why I didn't appreciate Jimmy taking off his jacket and walking into the middle with no armor, just his tight little white V-neck undershirt and his palms out like he was Jesus about to get handed a free cross and crown. It just pissed me off. Cue could see it on me too. Damn brothers.

Jimmy didn't so much walk to the middle as he strolled into it. He didn't say a word when Karl backed up. Karl shuffled around him for a full minute, all the time getting pushed forward by the inner ring. Jimmy just stood there, palms out. And it was too quiet, from hundreds of kids locking gulps of air in their lungs. Finally, Karl juked and threw a weak jab. It hit Jimmy right in the nose, pushing his head back. Karl couldn't believe it. Neither could the crowd. Whispers sprang up and raced around the circle.

Cue and I had shifted to the right side of the inner ring so we could see Jimmy's face. He was bleeding. And the funny thing was, he looked interested as he touched his lips and looked at the blood on the end of his finger. He smiled, but not the Bruce-Lee-okay-you-got-your-one-shot-in-now-you're-dead wicked kind of smile, just a mystified one. Then he touched his nose and put his hand down, ready for more. I couldn't believe it. I looked at Cue but he was looking at Jimmy and the veins in his neck and forehead were bulging. There was nothing we could do to save him from himself.

When Karl hit Jimmy the second and third time, on a right cross to uppercut combination, the spell was broken. Whatever influence Jimmy's reputation had over the crowd was gone forever. He really was human, and, in the space of a few moments, it was fuckin' Thunderdome in that quad. Every single person was screaming something, just letting out all their pent-up fear, spitting it out into the air with vapor breath.

Karl ate those cheers up. By the time he figured out that Jimmy wouldn't be fighting back, he unleashed it. He opened up cuts on Jimmy's eyebrows, cheeks, and chin. He punched Jimmy in the side of the neck and tore a ragged line above the collarbone so fast that it was like the skin had been unzipped. Blood belly-flopped out the slashed epidermis, turning that white shirt dark red on impact. Then he worked the body. Karl was wearing his infamous gloves, the razor ones, and they were tearing Jimmy apart. If there was anything good about the beating, it was that Karl tried to lift Jimmy and give him the Nightfall throw but he couldn't pick Jimmy up. He tried twice. But he couldn't do it. Couldn't pick up a guy that was about half his size. Jimmy might as well have been a concrete statue. Those that knew what to look for were awed by the technique. He just stood there the whole time, not moving, taking his beating.

"That's enough!" It was Cue that screamed it.

Karl wasn't stopping. Poor Karl. He only had two seconds, if that. See, the guy really should've looked up earlier to see Cue rearing back, grabbing a fistful of black sweatshirt with one hand and bending his leg at the knee and hip so deeply that his whole body flexed like a pushed-down spring before he brought the Ocean Floor Earthquake Kick right down. Of course, Karl didn't look up until it was too late.

Cue's boot heel connected squarely on the left clavicle and powered downward through the sternum. All of us heard them give too because it'd gotten quiet when Cue moved forward: two quick snaps, like finishing off a buffalo wing and going for the marrow in the twiggy bones. The force of the blow sent Karl right out of his sweatshirt (Cue still had that in his hand) and his body came to a nasty, half-naked-and-face-first kind of splat on the freezing concrete. It was really unlucky that, instead of just splintering at the point of impact like a good little break, Karl's clavicle decided to crack clean and make a sharp left turn, shooting through his trap muscle and breaking out the skin in an open fracture worthy of some high-profile medical journal. It was weird because it kind of looked like a little kid's mouth blowing one of those red party-favor-uncurler things but getting stuck halfway, and oh, there was plenty of blood.

That Karl was a real complainer. He made the most awful wheezing sound when he rolled himself over and pointed to the shifted bone lump in his chest. He was an automatic human bellows with a hole in the accordion part. The Blades carried him off quick and leaped in the back of some kid's truck and raced to the hospital. At least he was alive. With that kind of force, he was lucky that busted breastbone didn't shank his heart. Not that I really cared about him at that point.

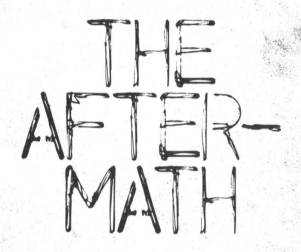

THE AFTER-MATH

MY FLANNEL WAS OFF AND I WAS WRAPPING JIMMY'S NECK
with it while Cue threw kid after kid away from us and back into the
crowd being formed by the breaking of the circle. Even the Hunters
had to get in on it. It was chaos. I was getting kicked while I tried to
hold the wound on Jimmy's neck closed. It pumped out blood in the

rhythm of his heart. Pressure, it needed more pressure! I couldn't see his eyes. They were completely swollen shut.

"It's gonna be okay, Jimmy, we're getting you out of here." I didn't know what else to say.

"Vas it, Jen!" On a scale of Cue angriness, this was about a nine out of ten. He meant the big neck cut, the one that was soaking my khaks all by itself.

"It's too big, Cue! We need Remo at the FC!" Did I just shout that at him? I guess I did. I mean, I did.

"I said fuckin' vas it right now!" Cue slammed a kid Blade in the face. Dropped him in one. Overeagerness is a rarely rewarded trait here. Essentially, that was the end of the crowd. People backed off, went their separate ways in a hurry, when they saw the kid roll up and blow away.

In Cuespeak, vas means Vaseline. That's another thing that you need at Kung Fu: your own personal first-aid kit. I was digging for mine in my pack but it was underneath my civics homework and I was getting the fill-in-the-blank take-home U.S. presidents test all bloody as I pulled for the dark blue satchel at the bottom. Got it.

Jimmy was breathing funny but I put my ear to his chest and I was pretty sure his ribs weren't broken. ABC: airways, breathing, circulation. Check, check, check. I tore open both five-by-nine sterile abdominal pads and I used the first one for the cut above the collarbone, skewing it at an angle before wrapping around his whole neck with all my red-striped gauze. Didn't stay red-striped for long though, that stuff is like a mini-sponge the way it soaks up blood. The second pad was just wide enough to wrap his forehead, over his eyes and part of his cheek. I vassed all the other cuts on his face. One, two, three, four, five, six, and left the top off the Vaseline and flung it back in the satch.

I looked up to see the quad empty, except for a few wounded stragglers, and Cue was next to me, tearing at Jimmy's shirt and putting pressure on his cousin's chest and he was talking. "No broken ribs, just some cuts, we're gonna have some serious fuckin' bruising on those abs but—" Cue's mind must've skipped a few steps because then he was yelling at me, "Lift, Jen, lift! Let's go!"

Once we had Jimmy up, Cue did the rest. He powered the three blocks to the free clinic and I had to run to keep up. Some drivers on the street must've seen us from their cars, but wounded people getting carried aren't that unusual a sight in this neighborhood. At the free clinic, we did our knock on the side door and Sally, the receptionist, let us in. She took us to the usual room next to the broom closet and closed the door behind her as she left.

"Put him on the table," I said.

Cue just glared at me. What could I do? I was feeling useless as it was and when that happens I just say whatever comes to mind.

"*Oye*, what do we got here?" Remo was next to the table before the door closed. I didn't even hear it open. That Sally sure was good to get him here so fast. By now, Remo's greeting was rhetorical, a joke between the three of us. Remo sized Jimmy up and decided to remove the abdominal pad on his forehead first.

"Hand me that squeeze bottle, Bruce," Remo asked, not looking away from Jimmy. He always played on my name. Bruce was short for Bruce Jenner, the gold medalist runner. I handed Remo the checkered water bottle.

It probably wasn't necessary but Remo soaked the whole pad down with water anyway. I'd seen him do it before. Just in case there was coagulation, he didn't want to rip a pad off even if it still appeared wet with blood. Gentle guy.

"Damn." Remo saw that Jimmy's eyes were both swollen shut. "What's his name?"

"Jimmy," Jimmy said.

"Ayight, Jimmy, you can obviously hear me, you're in a free clinic and I'm Dr. Rodriguez. I got some questions to ask you."

"Okay."

"Did you black out at all, is there anything you can't remember about being hit?" Remo was putting pressure on Jimmy's brow wound and rinsing the rest of his face.

"No, I remember everything."

"Okay, no stars, bars, or purple horseshoes at any time then? Are you dizzy or nauseated?" Remo peeled the other pad off Jimmy's neck. It wasn't bleeding anywhere near as bad as it had been.

"Nope, nope."

"The guy sounds together." Remo was cleaning the neck, chest, and stomach wounds. "Lucky for you guys most of this is cosmetic."

"What're you talking about? I've never seen anyone bleed that much." Cue was flexing.

"Calm down, Cue. Now, yeah, I know it's a lot of blood, and yeah, I do need to check for internal bleeding and wait for the eye swelling to go down before I can check those eyes but other than that, your boy looks like he can take a beating, and unless he's a hemophiliac, which I don't think he is, we'll get him fixed up good," Remo said, and I swear Jimmy smiled a little at the taking a beating part.

Overreaction. Remo was careful not to say the word but he thought it. I knew it.

"You did a great job, Jenner."

Jenner was the bad rat with the goatee in *The Secret of NIMH*. Remo loved his movies. Actually, his name isn't even Remo. That's just what Cue and I call him because he's a damn movie buff that looks like a young Fred Ward with blond hair. Remo's that light-skinned-Spanish kind of Latino. Same as my dad, but everyone thinks he's white because he doesn't really speak Spanish, just the odd word. Same as me. Like father like daughter.

"Thanks, Remo." I didn't feel like I had done a great job. Maybe he just meant I vassed the right wounds and put pressure on the right ones too.

"You're welcome. Chill here, keep that pressure on. I'll get my tools."

His tools. Remo was the best at wound stitching. Best I've ever seen anyway, and I've seen a few, most of it up close and personal. Anyway, he was so much better than anyone we had in the family, which was why we brought everything serious to him.

Back with his box, Remo set it on the rolling instrument stand near the table. Tweezers, specialist twine, clamps, scissors, he had everything in that box, even his initials on the inside of the lid.

"See? The ear wound is superficial. So the bleeding isn't coming from the canal. Good news, and"—Remo leaned in with his scope, first on the right, then the left—"both eardrums are *intacto*."

Superficial didn't mean all good. Jimmy's left ear had a hole torn in it big enough to stick your fingertip through. The outer ridge had pulled away from the ear just above the lobe. Kind of like the lid of a Tupperware container that won't close all the way on the lip. That'll stay as is. Remo told us never to stitch cartilage. Just let it heal, he always said. So I watched as the doc cleaned the drying blood off it and then wrapped and taped a bacitracin zinc–smeared gauze to Jimmy's ear.

He did have to stitch Jimmy's brow and neck though. No anesthetic and a total of twenty-three really tight stitches, all lined up, soldiers in a row. That was probably more than any other doctor would ever put in, but Remo was an artist and both wounds were going to heal well. Jimmy was going to have two real cute scars, one thin, one thick. That's when I knew I was starting to calm down. Thoughts like that one.

Mr. Unhittable's score for the day? Seventeen cuts, eight so deep that they required some stitching, resulting in forty total stitches, a torn ear, various bone bruises, assorted subdermal hematomas, and a wicked trachelematoma. Remo really was right, he got off light for the beating he took. It sure looked a hell of a lot worse. When Jimmy was all cleaned, stitched, and medicated, Remo handed a prescription paper to Cue.

"Take this to Fibber, and don't let him charge you more than ten bucks this time," he said. Fibber is the old pharmacist on Bleak Street. He's a big liar but he's also a good man. He's our connection for any meds. Shit, we owed Fibber; if it wasn't for him, Dad would've been out of stuff a real long time ago.

"Okay, ready? Blah, blah, blah, you know the speech so keep those wounds clean and bring him to my ma's house on Sunday night so I can check up on those *ojos* to make sure there aren't any detached retinas hiding behind those chunky blood oranges, aight?"

"Thanks, Remo." Cue was still all intense and he took Remo's hand in both of his mitts when he said it.

"Yeah, yeah, just bring that video you promised me last time." He was already turning away. "Got other patients, ya know. Check y'all later."

We didn't talk on the way home and we didn't stop by the Drugs & More on Bleak because Cue and I had plenty of painkillers for Jimmy to choose from. By now, Cue probably knew as much about them as anybody. So he just pocketed the prescription for a later date. That was standard procedure.

I would've carried Jimmy home but Cue didn't even ask me for my opinion, nearly picked Jimmy up like a sack of cat litter and put him on his back. Of course, Jimmy told us he could walk, just as long as Cue led. So I got stuck carrying all our book bags: mine and Jimmy's on one shoulder, Cue's on the other. I must've looked like the lady who wears four jackets and pushes that shopping cart everywhere.

If this had to happen, it's probably best that it happened on a Friday. At least that way Jimmy had two days to recover before he was doing it all over again. Cue and me both knew that he couldn't kick sternums in all semester, much less for the year. I mean, Cue was a senior, and with some luck, he was going to graduate and do his vet thing if a state school took a chance on him. He had good science grades and test scores. My life would've been so much easier if Jimmy would've fought, if he would've just knocked Karl out with one punch, or better yet, disappeared and reappeared on the top of the school just to freak everyone out. Something other than getting torn up, because if Jimmy Chang could get torched, then no one was safe. I knew it. Cue knew it. Ridley knew it. And everyone at Kung Fu knew it.

Crossing Common Street to Norman-Wide Avenue, I noticed that the trees didn't have leaves anymore. It was officially fuckin' winter. I was tired. Dad was late on his meds. Cue was pissed off. Between the fight and our time at the FC, white stuff was playing on the streets but hadn't started falling from the sky yet. Before, the last week even, everything had been brown. Extra sand strewn all over the asphalt, for wheel traction, so no cars slid off the roads. Of course, when the snow and ice melted, everything was just dirty.

But then, loaded down with packs, following the path the boys cut, I couldn't see any dirt anywhere, just the moving white stuff. See, I had this sensation that the flecks of dirt hadn't disappeared at all, hadn't been cleaned up, but, instead, had somehow got real old in two hours and had a change of hair color. Like miniature human heads with no bodies, too many to ever count: little *abuelos, abuelitas,* getting swept around in the wake winds of passing cars and floating on the air for a few seconds before settling again, then starting over. Forty-one whole years in a day.

SATURDAY

DAD ALWAYS SLEEPS LATE ON SATURDAYS SO JIMMY WAS Nurse Jen's first patient.

"Jimmy? You awake?" I pushed the door open to my room and nearly tripped over a damn box of schoolbooks that I forgot I put next to the closet.

"Sort of," Jimmy said with no trace of whine in his voice. Had to give the kid credit.

"Well, move your ass to the couch then. Time to clean those wounds up. You probably leaked all night."

"Can I sleep more first?" Jimmy asked as he was pushing himself up on his elbows. Facing away from me, he threw the sheet off. He had slept on his back all night. I could tell by the wrinkled sheet marks across his shoulders. He was only wearing his boxers. I had to turn around and face the hallway through the open door.

"Hell no, you'll sleep better if you don't get an infection." I said it like a joke but really, if he wasn't my cousin and hurt, he would've gotten kicked. I slept on the lumpy couch because of him. I got up at 8 a.m. to clean his wounds because he was swollen-eyed and incapable.

"Sorry. I'm coming."

I don't know how he does it, but that kid has got some kind of a sixth sense for my moods. Like he knows what I'm feeling. Then again, I've always worn my heart on my sleeve. If I don't like you, you know it.

After Jimmy got sweatpants tugged over his legs and one of Cue's button-up shirts on but not buttoned up, I helped him down the hall and into the living room. I kicked the tissue box out of the way and had him sit on a towel and lean back on the arm of the couch so that he was half reclining, like those Manet paintings I got shown in art class.

I can't help the tissue box thing. I always have to have it next to me when I sleep. I mean, ever since my nose was broken I've had sinus problems. I keep telling Remo that but he kids me, tells me I'm a liar and that a broken *nariz* has nothing to do with getting sinus infections. I'm no doctor but I do know that I never used to get the damn things before, but ever since my nose got smacked I get them five or six times a year. When that happens, my mucus goes all gloppy and neon yellow. I still swear there's a connection between the two.

It being a Saturday morning, I put the cartoons on. We luck out. It's an old episode of *G.I. Joe*. Shipwreck is mouthing off about something to Duke and Lady Jaye. It looked like they were right about to go into battle against Destro and those Cobra android super robots. It was one of the later episodes.

"Is this *G.I. Joe*?" Jimmy asked.

"Sure is." I answered him from the kitchen, where I got the usual supplies. I grabbed a bucket from under the sink, a couple of sterile towelettes, and some soap.

"Man, I haven't seen this in forever!" Jimmy was a smile monkey.

"Well, you still aren't seeing it. But maybe if you're real good and don't get in any fights, I'll let you see it next week." I put my mom voice on just to be silly but Jimmy didn't respond.

He wasn't reclining anymore, he was leaning forward on the couch but then he shifted back to his original position and put his legs up. I hadn't turned any lights on yet and the blinds were still shut so the light of the television threw all kinds of colors across his face as the familiar sound of laser gunfire filtered into the kitchen: blue, green, red, yellow, red, blue. I just stood there for a little bit and watched his face in the different colors. Blue suited him.

"You know nobody ever got shot on this show." I pushed his sprawled legs back toward him so I could sit down on the couch too. I set the bucket on the floor.

"Sure they did." Jimmy nodded toward the television as the sound of laser fire intensified, as if some pseudo-blind guy nodding toward the sounds would confirm what he said was true when all I could see was flashes across the screen and no one ever getting hit: twelve, thirteen, fourteen, fifteen straight with no hits, sixteen, number seventeen hit a tree and blew a branch off.

"No, people got hurt but mostly because they fell and had to be carried. Nobody ever died either."

"You got a problem with that?" He turned toward me as I said it and just then I could see his little iris peeping out from underneath the swollen flesh of his right eye socket. He could see.

"Just isn't real, is it?" I pulled the shirt corners to each side of his stomach and leaned down to soak a towelette in the bucket water as I prepared the soap. It was weird. Because Jimmy slept in my bed, I could smell my scent on his skin but I could also smell the different smell both of our scents made together, almost like licorice. The black kind, but more subtle though.

"So what's real?" He was looking at me again.

"Suffering. People get hurt every day. People die, Jimmy, that's real as fuck. What's the use in pretending that it doesn't happen?"

This was one of my pet subjects. I think he knew to back off, but he didn't. He just listened. That didn't happen to me very often so once the momentum was gone I just let it sit. Part of me worried I might've hit a nerve about his dad and all, but for what I'd been through, I was more than qualified to state something like that and not hurt a guy's feelings. I mean, he more than understood that I was right about death.

"So . . . how do you feel?" I had to ask the obligatory question before I got started on the stomach cuts.

"Sore," Jimmy said, and right after he said it, the television screamed, "Yo, Joe!"

We both laughed but I wasn't the one who groaned after I was done giggling. There it was. Complaint number one.

"And what did you think of your first beating?" I had to pop up and grab a dry, clean towel from the kitchen.

"It hurt." Jimmy plowed his fingers through his hair when he said it.

It was my turn to listen. I figured there was something else coming.

"I needed to feel it though."

He didn't need to further explain his point. I knew what he meant, especially when it came from a guy who had barely ever been hit in his life. Some things you just got to feel to understand. To be honest, I was just impressed that he didn't take it harder than he did. I mean, getting kicked in is about the most humbling experience there is.

THE REST OF the day was pretty slow. We just hung out. Dad took his pills on time and read his magazines. Cue made lunch for everybody though, which was good. He cooked up some steaks with his special beer technique and served whatever was left after the cooking on the side. I didn't drink any, just what got soaked into the steak, but Cue had a few and watched the baseball game and talked to Jimmy about Hong Kong.

I strained to listen to the stories but I was bleaching my civics homework in the kitchen sink and couldn't hear them over the announcers talking about a double play. That is a treacherous thing, I'm telling you. To get the blood out but to make sure the ink stays. For the most part, I had to go half and half. So later, after it dried, when I was answering questions about Monroe and "Manifes   tiny" I was still dodging light brown stains with my pen. Overall, I guess it was a pretty normal Saturday.

By evening, Jimmy was able to check his stomach and chest by himself. I took care of his face again though. His eyes were looking lots better and even his stitches looked great. The odd bag of ice was doing wonders for the swelling. His new ear hole was starting to knit itself back together. I asked him if his vision was fuzzy and he said no, so that was good too.

One unpleasant thing did happen in the evening though. Dad fell when using the bathroom so I had to pick him up and help him finish doing his business. Had to wipe him too. Stuff like that makes me sad. I mean, the guy used to be able to carry me on his shoulders and there I was, helping his naked rebelling body back onto the toilet and he said, "Thank you," and it didn't feel like an appropriate time to be saying it but I said, "You're welcome," so soft that he didn't hear me and I had to say it a second time, louder.

SUNDAY

JIMMY'S WOUNDS STOPPED SEEPING ON SATURDAY NIGHT
so I didn't have to get up early. Really, he just had to keep checking
the soon-to-be-scabs and swabbing them with the bacitracin zinc
Remo gave us and he should be good as new in a couple weeks. I slept
on the couch again but I didn't get to sleep late because Dad moved
into the front room to watch the early football game. Dad loves his

Broncos. Always has, ever since we left Denver. He took it real hard when Elway retired. Apart from Mom dying and his accident, that was the saddest I ever saw him. True.

So I woke to him screaming about a punt return for a touchdown. Not my favorite way to wake up, but it was what it was. Neither of us mentioned what happened in his bathroom the night before. Probably for the best. Underneath my blanket and in a half-sleepy haze, I watched the first quarter but didn't really follow it. I could tell that the Broncos were winning though because Dad was happy.

When I got my breakfast, I grabbed his pills.

"Can I have an extra pill today, *mi angelita*?" When Dad said that, I knew he wanted it pretty badly.

"I need it after my fall," he said.

"Are you bruised?" I asked. Dad went through a pretty rough time just after the accident where he got real dependent on his pills. Percocet mainly.

"Hey, Dad, does it feel like it's inside the bone or inside the muscle?" Cue strolled out from the hallway with just his towel on. Must've just had his shower because his hair was wet. We couldn't afford a blender so he got a special cup and lid thing to mix his protein shakes in and he was fixing one right then. All manual.

"In the bone." Dad had one eye on the television when he said it. The Raiders were punting again.

"Bone, huh? Half an Ib extra is probably going to help that best," Cue said. He knew I was soft when it came to Dad. He never minded being the bad guy. The punt was blocked.

Dad didn't argue because he was cheering at the TV. He just took the two and a half pills when I gave them to him with a glass of watered-down orange juice.

At about halftime, Jimmy was still sleeping so Cue and I left to go look for scrap wood. Cue was going to build Jimmy a bed and move it into his room so I didn't have to sleep on the couch anymore.

Cue built good beds but it all depended on how good a quality of wood we could salvage.

No snow again that day, which was good, but it was still the coldest it'd been in a while. The sky looked like one big cloud. Unfortunately, the night guy locked up the lumberyard so we couldn't walk off with any prime timber unless we scaled a nine-foot fence with razor wire at the top. Not even worth it. The department store shipping bays were empty and there was nothing left at the church where they were building a new playground. It had already been picked over. Someone even stole the swings, probably for the chains. We did luck out at the old brewery though. They had two stacks of shipping crates that were relatively intact. They were heavy as hell, and it sucked that Cue and I had to carry two of them all the way back to the house. It was about two miles.

We got back in time to see the Raiders kick a last-minute field goal and lose 42–3. Dad loved it and he mumbled something about the Super Bowl but I didn't respond. Cue cleared a space out behind the couch and we chucked all the wood down there on top of a plastic sheet because it was way too cold to work outside.

When the game was officially over we headed out for the grocery store. It was my day to cook too, so I brought the cookie-jar money that was left over from Dad's monthly disability check and I grabbed the food stamps too. With four people in the house now, I had to remember to get extra toilet paper with the real money because it never was included with the damn food stamps. Don't know why. Cue used to joke that we'd have to wipe our butts with soup can labels, but he doesn't laugh much about that stuff anymore. Sundays were generally a good day to go to the store because everyone else was just like Dad, watching the games, whatever ones were on. Cue got $6.48 for the cans he turned in for recycling. Without hesitation, he spent the money on protein powder.

I cruised the aisles packed with individual items but I mostly just bought stuff in bulk: giant bag of onions, giant bag of potatoes, giant bag of apples, three-pound bag of frozen peas, tons of hot dogs, five pounds of minced beef, multipack of boxed pasta. One of our Waves was running the register we picked so we got double coupons on everything even though we didn't have any coupons. He just opened the drawer and ran a bunch of previously used coupons again, overrode the computer error, then put them back in the drawer. With the money we saved, Cue took half to buy more protein powder and the other half for screws and brackets for Jimmy's bed.

We got back with the groceries and it felt like the heat was off. Dad was still in the front sitting chair, draped in five old afghans. Jimmy was sitting on the couch, wearing Dad's old ski hat and a scarf and the two of them were talking about Hong Kong too and that's when I got kind of jealous because I still hadn't heard anything about that damn city yet. Of course, it was then that I realized it really was just as cold inside as outside. I checked to make sure Cue closed the door behind us.

"Gas got turned off," Dad said.

"You'd think they'd at least turn it off on a Monday. Shit, I can't believe they pay a guy to go in to work on a Sunday and turn people's gas off." Cue moved over to the couch to sit next to Jimmy. "At least the electricity's still on." Yeah, and good thing we had an electric oven too.

As the lone female in the house, it was my job to put away the groceries apparently. I used to think there wasn't much worse than two guys in the house that I had to clean up after, cook for, and medicate but no, three was worse, even if the third was cute, the fact that he was related made it just as bad. The whole thing just gave me empathy for Mom. I pulled down the oven door and turned it on to 450 degrees to get some heat in the house. When it got up to about 300 and the coils turned orange, I turned the fan on so it would blow the heat toward the living room.

I pulled the box of noodles out of the first paper bag to put in the cabinet and then Jimmy was standing next to me. His left eye looked almost normal now. Buried in his discolored socket, it was no longer bloodshot, and the lid only sagged a little. Kind of like mine.

"Need any help?" He gripped the pack of toilet paper football-style. Like he was going to fade back to pass.

"Only if you feel up to it." I didn't put the generic macaroni and cheese back. That was for dinner.

"Yeah."

"Okay then, those go in the hall closet across from the bathroom." I turned to see that Cue was done watching television with Dad and was in the process of lining up the wood we'd put behind the couch. He'd also grabbed the paper bags when I was done with emptying them and he'd slit them up the side so he could lay them out flat underneath the wood but on top of the plastic. Then he started sanding.

"Hey, Daniel-san, while you're at it, sand the floor." I'd put the frozen peas and jumbo-pack hot dogs on the counter too. They both needed to thaw anyway. Milk got set aside as well. We didn't have any butter.

"Ah, Jen, you are about the funniest girl I know—so witty!" Cue plugged in the little electric sander, Dad's old one, circa 1982. It was red-orange and looked like one of the super bikes that left walls trailing behind them in *Tron*, but it worked and that was all that mattered.

"Gee thanks, Cue Ball," I said.

He didn't respond. He was already sanding down the first chunk of wood. It sounded like a squeaky electric razor being powered by a hamster wheel. Thanks to the oven, the house was finally heating up.

"What else?" Jimmy was behind me again.

"Boil six hot dogs in—" I was pointing to a small pot but the sander stopped abruptly and I got interrupted by Cue.

"Eight hot dogs, you know I need my protein!" The sander started right back up again. Sneaky bastard had the best ears of anyone I knew.

"Okay, eight, and just leave those two extra out for Cue's plate. The rest get chopped up and put in the mac, okay?"

With Jimmy and I both working on dinner, it went pretty quick. I accidentally dumped some paprika in the mixture and later Dad said it was the best I ever made so there you go.

After dinner, I got Dad to bed early and we didn't have any recurrence of bathroom problems. I checked and made sure that he didn't need my help and he said he was fine. So Jimmy borrowed some of Cue's warm clothes and we all walked out the door to Remo's mom's house. I made sure the oven was off and closed the door fast behind us to keep the heat in, then locked it tight.

SUNDAY NIGHT MOVES

IT WAS GETTING DARKER AND COLDER AS THE THREE OF US
walked the two blocks to the Rodriguez house. Remo wouldn't mind
us being a little late. We didn't go out in the open. Cue led. Jimmy and
I followed him as he cut through Mr. Hampton's yard, up onto the pic-
nic table, over the fence, and through Mrs. Johnson's rock garden. She
had it done up in a Zen motif and Cue said she'd be sure to notice our

footprints next morning so I had to go get her special rake leaning against the house and rescrape everything in a big oval after we walked through. I made Jimmy hold the tamales that I had made for Remo's mom, then I had to take a running leap at Mrs. Johnson's unfinished six-foot-high fence. Of course I got a bunch of splinters when I clung onto the top. But it was that or rake again, and I didn't feel like it.

Once I was over the fence we followed the rut in the field all the way to Tell Hill. You can actually see a huge chunk of the spreading suburbs from there because the whole thing got developed on an incline: all yellow dots of light with the occasional blinking red from the new power plant towers. A quick right and we were on the cul-de-sac, then another right. Almost lost Jimmy though and I had to grab him by the belt to make sure he didn't walk off into the dark in the wrong direction. It was Cue's belt and it was too big, so when I grabbed it, I got a lot of it in my hand. Like pulling back a slingshot but only getting slack.

When we got to the front door, I stood in front but Cue knocked. He had our backs. Until we were in the house, we weren't safe. That was the general rule of thumb: no relaxing until inside, until you could lock a door. Once you were inside you could do whatever you wanted, you could be yourself again, but not outside. You never knew who could follow.

When Remo opened the door I said, "Meals on Wheels," and pushed past him into the warm living room. Their heat hadn't gotten turned off. Lucky bastards.

"Yeah, yeah, come on in. Hey, Jimmy, looking good out there but come into the light here so I can check you out." Remo was wearing his black Green Lantern T-shirt, with just the symbol on it that looks like a white circle around a green "O" but with a horizontal line at the top and bottom. He always looked skinnier without his white lab coat on. I think he was trying to grow a beard too.

"Any concussion signs on this guy, Jenner?" Remo shut the door behind us and locked all three locks: both deadbolts and the chain. He pulled out his penlight and looked in Jimmy's eyes, then made Jimmy follow his finger left, right, before he was satisfied.

"Nope," I said. Remo looked at the green bowl I was holding and the little flecks of blood on it. Then he looked at my hands.

"Damn, Cue, why don't you rake for once? C'mere, Jenner." Remo set my covered bowl down on the hall table. "You know you can clear that jump better than she can."

"You worry about your own business. My sister can take care of herself." Cue winked at me after he said it. When he talked like that, it was hard not to feel a little pride at being worse for the wear. That was just one of the qualities that made him our leader.

"Ma, can you get me a bowl of hot water please?" Remo grabbed Jimmy and Cue's coats, tossed them onto a chair. Well, they were both Cue's coats, but it didn't matter to Remo.

All the walls in the house were painted a dusty tan color, even the wooden trim on the doorways. Here and there, hung up on the walls, they had these great Aztec relics. Well, replica relics of masks and stuff but they were really cool. Better than our house. We just have movie posters and sports stuff up.

"Huh?" Remo's mom was watching a dubbed version of *Matlock* on Telemundo and not really listening to us. She's the cutest old lady in the world.

"*¡Mamá, tráigame un tazón de agua caliente!*"

"*Sí, sí.*" Mrs. Rodriguez shuffled into the kitchen and came back with a yellow bowl but no water, warm or otherwise.

"Sit," Remo said to me and went to fill the bowl himself. By the time he came back with it, his mom had discovered the food.

"*¡Ay los tamales! Gracias, señorita.*" She clapped her hands together when she said the words and then did a kind of dance where she dipped and swayed at the knees. Like I said, so cute.

I always make my dad's mom's tamale recipe for Mrs. Rodriguez when we come to visit. I know that she doesn't eat too good with Remo always cooking. Sometimes I bring over two meals a week, but usually at least one. Tamales are one of the only things I can do well though, so I've had to be good with experimenting or else it would get too boring. I made tuna tamales once but that was a disaster. I mostly just stick to ground beef or chicken, but I make pork when we can afford it.

Remo's mom has early onset Alzheimer's. She'd be asking me who I was in ten minutes. You get used to it eventually. Her condition is why Remo lived at home still. He was probably twenty-six when she got diagnosed. He'd definitely be married and super rich and successful by now if he didn't insist on staying at the free clinic and taking care of his mom.

"So I hear there's a guy *en el hospital* who needed some real TLSC." Remo was looking right at Cue. "Tender loving sternum care."

"Really?" Give Cue credit. He genuinely sounded surprised.

"Dr. Vanez got called in. Saved the kid's life, as per usual." Remo looked at Jimmy, who was sitting down on the arm of the chair I was sitting in.

"That's good. I've heard of Vanez. He's the best supposedly." Cue knew Vanez real well. The guy was an orthopedic surgeon and a legend. When we still had a mom and a family insurance policy because of her teaching job, Vanez rebuilt Cue's shoulder. He did an amazing job too. Unless I'm a foot or two away from his skin, I can't see the scars. They blend real well.

"Indeed he is," Remo said, "indeed he is."

. He made me soak my hands in the hot water. It was almost too hot. Then he took out his tools and sterilized one of the needles before picking out the splinters. Total: five, but one big one underneath a fingernail. That hurt, but as far as splinters went, it was pretty good for me. Last time it was seven. Remo didn't stop with just the removal though. He dried my palms with a towel and then rubbed this real dark brown stuff on my hands. It smelled like tequila and evergreen trees but it looked like mud.

"What the hell is this?" I asked. He'd picked splinters out of my hands before but never used brown stuff to salve it.

"Good Mexican medicine, just keep your palms up until they dry. Then rinse it off." Remo went to put his tools away.

"Just as long as it isn't shit," I said, and I heard Remo laugh from down the hall but he didn't contradict me. Great. It probably was shit, part of it anyway.

We said goodnight to Mrs. Rodriguez as she got shepherded back to her own room to watch the rest of her show. I did always wonder if she could keep up with those mysteries. I mean, *Matlock* was an hour long so I'm sure she'd forgotten everybody by the time they figured out who the killer was.

"So, what did you bring for me today? Jeunet *y* Caro? A little *Delicatessen*?" Remo was anxious but probably because he thought we forgot to bring a video again.

"Warm. Better than that though." Cue pulled a video out of his back pocket. It was wrapped in brown paper. Jimmy and I moved over to the couch and just waited for their little dance to end. Disappointingly, he didn't smell like licorice anymore. I brushed by him to check, dragged the flat of my knee across his, not too slowly, just as I sat down next to him but made real sure to leave a few inches in between in case he thought I was doing it on purpose.

"*Dogme 95*?" Remo shouted it from the kitchen. He had put popcorn on the stovetop.

"Colder. Better than that crap." Cue squeezed in between Jimmy and me. Bastard.

"What is it, man? Just tell me."

Pop.

"*Hate*."

Pop. Pop.

"*Hate?*"

Pop.

"Yeah, *La Haine*. It's French."

Pop. Pop. Pop.

"Is it any good?"

Pop. Pop.

I could hear Remo pull his popcorn off the burner early. He was a weird guy. For some reason he liked his popcorn really underdone and he'd eat the kernels all the time, real loudly, always during the most tense moments in the movie too.

"*Jusqu'ici, tout va bien . . . mon ami . . . jusqu'ici, tout va bien . . .*"

"What the hell is that supposed to mean? I asked if it was any good."

"So far so good."

"Well, put it in, I got to see this."

Mrs. Rodriguez had a VCR from like 1986. It was a top loader. Bad as it was though, it was better than nothing. We didn't even have one. We had to come over to the Rodriguez house to watch anything. That is, if we hadn't already seen it at the video store on Bleak while some Wave was working.

Well, normal me, quiet Jimmy, loud Cue, and popcorn-crunching Remo finally shut up and watched the movie and Remo ended up loving it. The little French wannabe gangsters getting sucked into something so much bigger than them because of a lost gun that they found and how all the time they were looking for revenge when one of their buddies got hurt by the cops, he loved all of that. In fact, even though it was just a copy the video clerk gave us, he bought it for five bucks.

"Take the car," he said when we were getting our coats on to leave. "I'm too tired to drive you."

"No, that's cool, Remo. It's not too late. And we got three." Mr. Cue, always the tough guy. I wouldn't've minded a ride in a warm car.

"The way I hear it, you got two and a half." Remo didn't need to look at Jimmy this time. "Just leave the keys under the mat, I'll pick it up in the morning."

ALFREDO LOVED HIS KINFÉ, PROBABLY SLEPT NEXT TO IT too. When we pulled up outside of our house, he was standing there, playing with it. We don't call them knives here because they're so much more than knives. For one, they're smaller. Two, they're sharp on all four sides, sort of like an awl but longer and with a different blade. Always homemade, but not like a prison shiv that's just made out of anything hard enough to sharpen. It takes a whole lot more to make a kinfé and you got to pronounce it right too. Kinfé, like kin-fay, right? I've seen kids beaten up for saying it all wrong: ka-nee-fay. You ever hear someone call it that, it's usually followed by a good smack.

When making one, you got to find the right metal, or the right knives. The easiest ones to make come from just stripping four knives of their blades, cutting them in half and then taking the cutting edges and welding or fusing them together, edges out, so that the whole thing looks like an extended tip of a Phillips head screwdriver and sharp all around. It takes skills to make good ones but there's plenty of crap out there. I heard some guys in the Whips make theirs to be disposable and just put them together with sharpened plastic and superglue, then they use duct tape for the handles. The Hunters though, they take theirs real seriously. Most take about a week to make and even have a special name. Their type of kinfé is called the fleshhook.

"What's wrong?" Cue got out of the car and left the door open. He was all business when he walked toward Alfredo. I could see seven Hunters in various positions overlooking the house. They didn't move.

"We were guarding," Alfredo said. "We got a buzz that the Blades was coming after you tonight because of what you did to Karl Fuck-Head. You know we got your back."

"What's going on?" Jimmy asked me. All three of us had been squeezed into the front seat of Remo's 1962 whatever-it-was. Nobody knew what make or model it used to be. It had had so much body-work done over the years that it didn't have the tailfins it once had because they got knocked off when Remo backed into a garbage truck. It didn't have the logos and insignias and writing either because all of that had been stolen. There was a trend a couple years ago when the coolest thing was to have the rarest hood ornaments and names off of cars, so Remo's didn't last long. But it was a good car. It had a big couch of a front seat and I liked that I stayed pressed up against Jimmy even after Cue had got out.

"Looks like fuckin' Alfredo's got some news. He does this all the time. Shows up with some Hunters and makes a big deal out of something. If I had to guess, he's talking about Blades wanting to kill us because of Karl." I said it, then I yawned.

I could see Alfredo talking and making everything real dramatic but we couldn't hear him, so I just watched his mouth and put on my best Alfredo voice for Jimmy and just dubbed over him: "Blah blah, yeah, Karl got worse at the hospital today so a bunch of Blades decided it was time to nil you for jumping in on that fight with Jimmy but we showed up and they must've decided not to mess with us blah blah blah."

Jimmy only laughed because he was surprised how well my made-up words fit in with Alfredo's flapping mouth. Cue's back was to us. They were both standing in the headlight glow, just to the side, not quite lit up all the way. The conversation looked to be over because Alfredo nodded and the Hunters started leaving.

"It's okay," Cue turned and said. He motioned for me to pull the keys out of the ignition. We were pretty much parked on the curb in front of the house anyway. Remo'd just grab it in the morning.

Cue was walking toward me and then he stopped, fell forward. He made a sound like he usually does when he's kidding. Like a thud in the lungs. Like UHH! He makes that sound by hitting his chest with his fist so it sounds real. I swear I thought he was just playing because Cue doesn't do that stuff unless it's for a laugh. And I laughed. I leaned over, took the keys out, popped the lights off with the push of the extended knob. Like pushing in the shooter on a pinball machine. I looked to my right and Jimmy was getting out of the car so I shifted over in the seat and got out on the driver side, through the open door.

"Ayight, stop playing, I get it," I said. It was late. I really wanted to go to sleep on the couch, or feign sleep and pretend that Jimmy was next to me. I'd raid the laundry basket and grab one of the shirts he wore and I'd put it over one of the cushions and then scrunch up against it fetal or just hide it under the blanket.

I slipped. I was walking toward Cue, who was still on the ground but no longer hamming it up, and I slipped but I didn't fall.

"Fuckin' ice!" I didn't say it that loud. Natural reaction. Then I realized it was definitely cold enough for ice to be forming on the road but it wasn't wet enough. Too dark to see. I put my hand down on it. It was warm, wet. I could smell it. I licked my finger to make sure. It wasn't quite blood but it was close. Later, the coroner told me that it was part blood, part spinal fluid. 'Fredo and the Hunters were long gone.

I just sat down right there next to him. I couldn't breathe so good. He was still warm, everywhere but his ears. His big old ears that he'd had to grow into were freezing so I took my hat off and put it on him. He had something sticking out of his lower back. 'Fredo had shoved the kinfé between vertebrae and severed his spinal cord right above his hips if I had to guess. Really, I had no idea how he got that much force up without rigging some kind of air-powered gun to sling it, but that's possible and I wouldn't put it past 'Fredo. Just to make sure though, the next kinfé had gone right through my brother's temple, shattering that greater wing of sphenoid that pokes out along the coronal suture of a border like Switzerland squeezed in next to the frontal bone of France and the parietal bone of Germany and the temporal bone of Italy. Remo explained it like that to me once when I had a slight fracture of the frontal: your skull is Europe, he had said, your temple is a landlocked country.

Funny what kind of shit sticks in your mind at moments when control goes right out the window for good. My brother died before he hit the ground. There was no way to bring him back. And there never would be. Not with screaming ambulances and hyper paramedics with needles and drooping bags filled with see-through fluid, not with paddles to shock his heart into beating again, not with bandages to stop the bleeding. It didn't matter if Jimmy got Remo or Vanez or anybody. Nobody could put my big brother's spine and his brain back together again. Kyuzo was still warm under my hand. Maybe his soul was still inside. Tidying up some papers on its desk before it jetted for good?

I don't remember what Jimmy said. But Remo's car sped off. So he must've been in it. That big old land boat.

"Oh, Cue," I said, and it was so quiet around me. "Oh, Mister Cue. Baldhead. Baldy . . ."

I pushed my hat hard against his scalp, held my hand there on the woolly ridges, fingers spread out where his cowlick was, and with my other hand, I yanked the kinfé free. It took two tries, as hard as I could, to get it all the way out. I tried not to move it much, tried to pull it clean. More bone broke off though, chips maybe. But I didn't look down, looked at my window in my house as I heard the dripping, the splash, and felt something drop warmly onto my calf and slide into the puddle growing under us. My peripheral vision told me it looked like a fig in the dark. A big fig. Mom used to love those. I flattened my hat down over the hole in his head, covering it. Because it was too cold out and I didn't want him to get frostbite. Ever.

"This is all going to end badly now. You know that, right? So don't go tripping off to heaven with that soul just yet. I need you to watch over me. Watch over Jimmy. We'll see you soon enough." They weren't my words but they came from my throat, pushed by my lungs, sounds carved out by my tongue.

It must've just been wind in the trees, but I'm sure I heard an "okay." It nestled in my ear. So I just kept sitting, smoothing the hat down, stroking his bald head through it, imagining Cue's spirit in the trees of Mrs. Johnson's yard, waiting for a moment before it went to wherever spirits go, just to watch me and see how I reacted to this change, this shock. Maybe he would stay a little longer and keep watching. Maybe even follow.

And then the car was back. Ground yacht docking. Headlights so bright in my face it might as well've been daytime. Then Remo was next to me and he was checking my pulse. He must've thought I was hurt too, from all the blood on me. But it was my big brother's. My big invincible brother spilling out vincible all over my splinter-less hands and khaks and soaking me to the bone, getting me colder as I held him. It was changing in the night air, his blood. On me, it was freezing to solid. We were crystallizing together on our street. The one we truly grew up on.

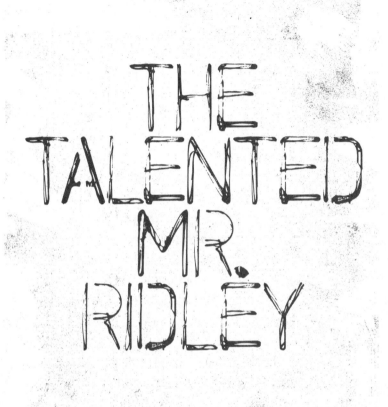

THE TALENTED MR. RIDLEY

I DIDN'T KNOW HOW LONG I'D BEEN SITTING ON THE COUCH
when my alarm went off. Hours and hours, easily. It helped that
I couldn't feel anything. Not pins or needles. Not the need to cry.
Couldn't feel my body sitting. Still couldn't breathe so good and it
felt like I had a snow-thick cloud in my chest but it helped that
I didn't see his face in my memory, hadn't looked down at him when

the lights were on us. So that was good, saying goodbye with my fingers. Not needing anything else to confirm that Cue was gone, at least he was whole as he could be, wearing a hat, frostbiteless in my remembering. My forearm muscles cramped, triceps spasmed. I'd probably been holding fists since I first sat. Please understand, anger was all I had left.

To not show up to Kung Fu the next day would've been a mistake. Would've been a huge sign of weakness. Even though I hadn't slept, I got ready as usual. Leaned on my routine. But when I put on my leggings, I put my kinfé in its sheath (I'd be avoiding the metal check and sneaking in through a side door). Barbie Bloodclot was her name and I even did a carving on the hilt of a curvy, normal-girl-looking Barbie with claws, not a stupid skinny one. I've only ever used her once to cut. He deserved it. Tried to rape me. Didn't get very far though, and what was worse was that he had to deal with Cue later. That guy's body is buried in the landfill now. Maybe it's weird, but I can't even remember his name. I used to know him.

With any luck, I'd get a shot at 'Fredo but the chances of that happening were about as likely as Dad waking up with no pain. When I buttoned up my flannel over my hooded sweatshirt I was mostly just hoping that I wouldn't be forced to use her because I couldn't be held responsible for what I would do to him.

I tried to give Dad his meds but he didn't want them. I knew he'd been crying. He was in his shell again. He did it every time something went real bad. Happened when Mom died. Happened when he had his accident too. I had to be the one to tell him how it went down. He didn't believe me until he heard the cop cars out front. I left his meds and a glass of water on the TV dinner tray that doubled as a bedside table. He'd take them on his own if it got bad enough.

The cops wanted the murder weapons but they couldn't find them. They wanted to search the house because they knew who Cue was. I wouldn't let them and they didn't have any warrants. They told me they'd be back. But the cops didn't care who killed Cue. If they had searched the house they would've found 'Fredo's kinfés in the yellow bucket in the kitchen, under the sink. It wouldn't've mattered. They knew it wasn't their score to settle. I pulled the blades out of the bucket and put them in my backpack. It was odd to feel them so dry.

Jimmy was still in bed fifteen minutes before we had to leave.

"Let's go, Jimmy. School." It was the most I got out while trying to drink my orange juice. I spilled some on the carpet too.

"What? You're going?" He sat up in my bed. I'd been on the couch again. Neither one of us had been able to face the prospect of sleeping in Cue's bed.

"Have to," I said. I didn't realize my glass was empty until I tried to drink again. It didn't matter really, because I couldn't taste it. The faint saltiness of Cue's blood felt like it had seeped into the depths of my tongue, into the core. It was my only taste.

"How can you be so normal?" Jimmy was just looking at me.

"Business needs to be handled. Grab everything that fits you from Cue's stash. Gear up good." I couldn't look at him, so I turned and walked up the hall.

No one was waiting for us outside the house. Actually, that was a good sign, but it also meant that we had a day to sort everything out. I mean, with Cue gone, the Waves'd need a new leader. Guaranteed, 'Fredo had already taken care of that and named himself as our new Pop. The long walk alone to school was just time to let it sink in. It was our temporary reprieve.

I had a class with Ridley: first period civics. Usually, he never showed up. He didn't have to. Paperwork always gets filed and cataloged and he just barely missed out on graduating year after year. Officially, he was a fifth-year senior and twenty-three years old. It wasn't that Ridley was stupid. Just the opposite really, he kept working the system to stay in control. Most of the time, he was invisible yet always around, but not that day. That day, Ridley was standing on the far side of the room as I walked in. He was wearing one of his trademark polo shirts. Today it was blue, red, and yellow in horizontal stripes. Ridley also had new glasses, must've bought them over the weekend because he was cleaning them and being extra careful. He'd been waiting for me.

"Class dismissed," he said. Didn't even look up.

Everyone left too, fast. The teacher didn't blink, just packed up her little folders, put them in her bag, and walked straight to the teachers' lounge to have a cigarette. She knew what was good for her.

"Good morning, Jennifer. Oh, I'm sorry, you do prefer Jen." The way he said it required no return of the greeting.

I started looking for my out. I could go out the window but it'd be more than a two-story drop and I'd be lucky not to break something, depending on how I landed. I could cross into the adjoining room and head for the fire exit but Ridley probably had people waiting there. I sure as hell couldn't go back out the room door because that was guarded, no doubt. I was caught. Spine tight, I leaned on one of the desks. If I was going down, Barbie and I were going to take someone with me.

Of course, Fred was with Ridley. That would be Ridley's little brother. Fred had mental retardation, only mildly though. It wasn't fair that he happened to be the nicest guy at Kung Fu. Everyone liked Fred, even if they had to. Fred was Ridley's favorite person in the whole wide world. Maybe it was because Fred lacked the capacity to see the beast in his brother.

Strange but true: Kung Fu has the best special education program in the state. In fact, it's probably the only legitimate reason why they haven't shut us down. That special ed program is all because of Ridley and he did it all because of Fred. Everyone knows that Ridley pulled the strings to get the best teachers, transportation, and training programs. Our track record for graduating kids from special education to real paying jobs (if they wanted 'em) was basically 100 percent. So when other parents were struggling to get their "normal" kids transferred away from Kung Fu, parents of mentally disabled children were putting their kids on the waiting list. Welcome to irony.

There's a little story about that too. Four years back, someone wanted to get to Ridley by going through his pet project and they took a few hostages. Bad idea. When all was said and done, Ridley had meaty parts of the perpetrators carved up and mailed to their own grandparents in those really expensive mail order steak packages with a note saying that they had won them. Probably all of them got eaten. That was what made his reputation as a genuinely evil guy.

Jimmy got pushed into the room by Mock, one of Ridley's bodyguards. It amazed me that he still let people push him around. That he still took that promise to his mom so seriously.

"Freddy, can you leave please? I'll see you at lunchtime and I'll bring the pickles." Ridley was tender when he said it, quiet but firm.

"Okay!" Fred said, and obeyed the request, leaving the room and saying goodbye to Mock on the way out. This was a bad sign. With Fred gone, Nice Ridley was gone too. Anything could happen.

He finally looked over at me.

"I know you want revenge, Jen, and you have every right to. I don't like how this came about. I don't like it one bit. In fact, just to make up for it, I'll take care of Alfredo for you," Ridley said. "Traitors are such despicable people. How can they possibly be trusted again once they've betrayed someone?"

Just then, 'Fredo walked in. He wasn't wearing any body armor. I could tell. Arrogant bastard thought he had nothing to fear from Ridley or me. Thought he was untouchable. He was flaunting it in my face, gloating. That's when it all came together: 'Fredo had killed my big brother all to get in good with Ridley. Maybe it went even deeper. Nothing else mattered. Promises *had* been exchanged, and

'Fredo, that stupid sap, had believed every single one of them. The whole meeting was a setup from the word go.

"Speak of the devil." Ridley gestured toward 'Fredo and he just grinned.

"But you're in a most difficult position now, Miss Jen. With Cue gone, who will protect you and Jimmy? Indeed, what will happen to your family if Alfredo is gone? The Waves will be cannibalized. If you're lucky, it will be by the Wolves. If not, one of mine. Are you willing to take that risk? Many family members could be lost either way, by defections, or accidents. And it would be all your call." Ridley was right.

'Fredo's broke-ass grin had elevated to a smirk. He knew Ridley was right too and that he was the only salvation of the Waves, if you could still call it salvation. With his face all tied up in that smirk like the top of a garbage bag, 'Fredo crossed his arms over his chest and threw his head back. He had no idea about the stakes.

It was a choice and it wasn't. The chances of 'Fredo actually protecting us were less than low. If I passed on Ridley's offer, 'Fredo'd probably do a clear out as soon as we left the room and then immediately turn the Waves into another puppet family for Ridley's bidding. No, I knew he would, no probablies about it. Clear outs are the worst nightmare of every kid at Kung Fu. If you got cleared out of your family, you were fair game: either to be picked up by a new family, or worse and much more likely, to be torn up. On the flip side of the coin, if 'Fredo was gone, the Waves couldn't survive. Our only fighter strong enough to step up and lead was Jimmy but he wouldn't.

Ridley stared at me, right in my eyes. He wanted a sign. The code dictated that I could call 'Fredo out but Ridley was offering to do it for me. It was the strangest thing, Ridley trying to give me the impression that he was playing by the rules. There really was no choice. I couldn't attack 'Fredo here. It was Ridley's show. 'Fredo had his long black comb in his hand and was running it through his hair, slicking it back so it was nice and straight. He aimed his smirk at me and it turned into a half smile. My stomach tried to eat itself. I tasted Cue's blood in my mouth, between my teeth. I nodded, smiling right back at him. It was almost comforting. I didn't need to beg for justice, didn't need to beg for something that Ridley was so willing to give. 'Fredo killed Kyuzo, 'Fredo must not live.

The comb was in the air, extended up from 'Fredo's fist as he patted his head along his scalp to find straying hairs, then decided to pull the long, black Cadillac of combs through his hair once more. His arm didn't get past halfway. Ridley stabbed 'Fredo in the throat one, two, opening a vertical gash, three, four, five, tearing out a large chunk of his voice box and flinging it across the room, six, seven, the point now reaching all the way to the back of his throat and rebounding off a vertebra and making a percussive sound like a dentist's scraper tool tapping on teeth, eight, nine times with a kinfé I didn't even see until it was done. And when it was, 'Fredo didn't have a larynx, or tonsils, just a ragged hole the size of a pool table pocket gaping from his throat. He never saw it coming. Ridley had come from behind too fast. I heard Jimmy moan behind me.

"There. Now we're even." Ridley dropped 'Fredo to the floor. The guy was spasming, trying to scream but only sounding like a wet and windy day. He puked too and it never made it to his mouth, just went out the new hole and onto the floor; everybody could tell he'd had scrambled eggs for breakfast. That kind of stuff happens sometimes when a body goes into acute shock. Systems screw up and evacuate. The acidy smell of the vomit mixed with the blood still pumping out of him in rhythm with his heart. The kinfé landed with a small splash on the floor, next to a pair of bulging eyes. 'Fredo was still clutching his comb, white-knuckled. It was probably the last thing he ever saw.

But a part of me believes that he wasn't quite dead when I rammed his own kinfé so deep into his left eye socket that part of the hilt disappeared and it didn't stop 'til it hit the back of the braincase. I'd lined it up. The eyeball made a squishing sound just before it disappeared and the four sharp edges tore through millions of my-elin sheaths, ripping axon from dendrite, cutting cord after electric impulse cord, turning off the power in that fucked-up brain. Just like he'd done to Cue.

I was slower with the next one. Held his other eyelid open with my index finger and used the heel of my palm to lean my weight into the kinfé. The stupid fuckin' worthless corneye wobbled like a cube of gelatin and then split apart, husked, gone forever. I half expected the brown iris to break like a raw yolk and contaminate the yellow-white of the eye, to mix. It didn't. Instead the whole membrane tore like the white flesh of a hard-boiled egg and some fluid drained out. Like a pierced water balloon. I caught the briefest glimpse of a thin, corded retina—still twitching—as I worked the blade into the cav-ity, cutting what I imagined as a gushing red cross into the ultrasoft tissue of that dead brain just behind. I pushed my ice into him, Cue's and mine together. But seeing 'Fredo's body torn from its life did not thaw me. Leftover crystals still stuck to my insides. They'd never melt. Took me some time to let go of the last kinfé. Couldn't really feel it in my hands.

Ridley had already stepped away from the mess and taken his glasses off. All the better to wipe the blood spatters off them.

"Never say I didn't do *you* any favors," he said as he pulled his bloody shirt off next, flexing his pale, hairless muscles covered in small ropes of cherry-colored keloid scars so thick they might as well have been woven onto his chest, stomach, shoulders, and upper arms. Circles, spiral patterns, zigging, lightningesque verticals and diagonal ones so thin they looked like they'd been drawn on. He was staring hard, but with admiration, at me. Mock handed him a brand clean polo shirt with a green, blue, and black vertical stripe pat-tern. He'd known all along what I would choose. So much so that he'd brought a clean shirt for afterward. Fuck. I could feel it in my chest: I'd made the wrong decision. I'd lost it. Cue wouldn't've made the wrong choice. I was hopeless as a leader. Look, my hands were shaking.

The worst part was, Ridley was right. It *was* a favor, in a real fucked-up way. He could've left 'Fredo alive and easily controlled the Waves through him, but he must've known that I was coming for him eventually. The whole thing was a game to Ridley. One way or another, the Waves would not survive as they once had, in opposition to Ridley. No matter what, he won. Machiavelli would've been so proud.

"Mock, call DBD please," Ridley said.

Leather-bound notebook in hand, he stepped over the growing puddle—the one that made tall islands of my boots—surrounding 'Fredo's unmoving body, but turned around in the doorway to ask me one last royal question before smoothing his collar down and disappearing into the hall, laughing.

"Got a date for the prom yet, Jen?"

MELINDA AND THE WOLVES

THERE WASN'T ENOUGH TIME TO TELL THE WAVES. SOON all the Hunters would know that 'Fredo had left the building. They'd be joining one of Ridley's gangs. The old rock and a hard place, I knew exactly how it would go down too. Ridley would tell the Hunters I killed 'Fredo in retribution. They would believe him— very persuasive, that Ridley. Not like it was a total lie anyway. I had to work fast and I couldn't handle Jimmy's questions. I had to broker a deal.

"Jesus, Jenny! Fuck! What did you just do?!" He didn't pull at my arm or grab on my shirt or anything like that but his presence was tugging hard at me.

I couldn't say anything. I had to find Melinda, fast. Just had to walk quickly and with purpose. It's always a good idea to do it whenever you're in an area you think is sketchy. *Especially* if you have no idea where you're going. Don't walk at top speed, just fast enough that you can turn real quick like you meant to. The worst thing to do is double back.

"This is crazy."

"I'll see you at lunch." It was all I could say.

I didn't look back when I rounded the corner. I couldn't. I was sick at me. My stomach was trying to eat itself, for real this time. Hands still shook, blood-covered. I hid them in my pockets. No, I didn't blame Jimmy for Cue's death. I didn't. That would've come anyway, whether by 'Fredo's hand or someone else's. So Ridley sayeth, so shall it be done.

Ridley's killing of 'Fredo was supposed to be a good thing, was supposed to make everything simple. Ridley wanted me to think it was the honorable thing, but the truth was, 'Fredo fucked up. There were witnesses. See, I'm not exactly sure what he was thinking, doing it in the open in front of me and Jimmy, but maybe he thought it'd be good as a show of power. Or maybe he just panicked. Truth be told, if Cue had just disappeared with no witnesses to verify the identity of the killer, we'd've been in a lot worse situation. There'd've been nobody to blame. Three years ago, the Muds got wiped out practically overnight. The same thing happened, their Pop caught three kinfés in soft spots but no one even saw it. Had no idea who did it. Didn't help that nobody left was good enough to step in. The other families smelled blood and circled every last vendetta 'til there was none. Whoever was left the next morning decided to take up the Runners on their offer of membership. But witnesses meant leverage. I knew who had done it and I knew who had ordered it: Ridley. Hands still shook though.

See, if Mr. Big-Time Drug Dealer had had ultimate power from the get-go, none of this would've happened. Kung Fu wouldn't've grown up like this with everyone in different families to protect each other. But as Ridley got more powerful, alliances got made and people started disappearing. That's called getting transferred. Slowly but surely, the number of families opposing Ridley has dwindled. I got to give him one thing: he's patient. It's been years and not once has there been a major bloodletting that couldn't be covered up fast. Every year he gets stronger.

The Wolves own the north side of the library. I passed by it and its awful green doors but there was no Melinda inside. It was more serious than I thought. So I had to double back because I knew that she must've been downstairs in the home ec room, next to the cafeteria. That's where they held their secret meetings. By now the senior Wolves would already be deciding our fates, probably already had the charts out and were ready to make some x's. But I still had one trick left.

The chances of me running into Cap'n Joe on his DBD detail had to be below minimal but there he was, right in front of me. I shouldn't've doubled back. Dead Body Disposal, as Ridley always called him, worked for Dermoody. He took care of anything that needed fixing, everything that could ever cast Dermoody in a bad light.

"Why aren't you in class, squaw?" Cap'n Joe called all girls squaws and all boys braves. I don't know why. He just did.

"I got a note," I said, and I knew he wouldn't ask to see it because he had a big black bag in his arms. It had a conspicuous 'Fredo shape to it.

I knew Cap'n Joe was going to let me off with a warning because he had no time to check into my fictional note. But a warning at Kung Fu was guaranteed to leave a mark. When this happens, do not dodge. Take it. Otherwise, there might be more, a lot more. So grit up, be ready for the blow and make it look more painful than it is. Sadistic bastards love that.

Cap'n Joe's boot caught me in the left knee and drove the cap in hard against the joint. I knew he was going for it so I kept my weight off that leg. A solid enough kick to a knee you got your weight on and it's torn ligament city but as it was, I just stumbled forward like it really hurt but actually, it was just a ploy to get past him. The pain brought me back to my body. Forced me to feel. Shifted some of the ice.

I didn't look back. That would've invited more, and he already had one body to take care of. Best not to make it two just because I didn't like how the game was played. He had to be the big macho man, the big in-charge guy. They all do. From Ridley to Dermoody to Cap'n Joe, it didn't matter who it was. If it was a guy, he wanted to be the baddest.

Melinda was more dangerous than any of them. The reason the Wolves were still around was almost completely due to her, because she knew how to play their game. Brush their egos the right way and make her moves behind their backs and nobody gets hurt. Well, too hurt. I grew up with Melinda. We went to elementary school together. We played kickball every day back then. We used to think we could be pilots. Technically, she was my first kiss. We were ten. "It'll be like training wheels," she had said, "you know, before riding a bike all by yourself." Her dad had taught her.

Of course, none of that mattered as I was pulling myself up the stairs by the handrail bolted into the redbrick walls. My knee burned, was probably swelling, which was bad because there were two guards at the door to the home ec room. I didn't know them from their faces but I knew they were freshmen. Probably had less than six rolls to their combined credit. They were just babies. Melinda was getting sloppy. Everyone was, with Cue gone: Ridley only keeping Mock in the room and not two or three bodyguards, 'Fredo without his armor, and this, Melinda using inexperienced children during an important family meeting never would've happened if my big brother was around. He was so good he'd kept everyone on their toes. Gone a day and everyone was slipping. Pathetic.

Took me less than ten seconds to get both guards on the floor. Here's a pointer to anyone trying to be a good guard. Never hold out your arm and say, "Stop!" or "Halt!" like they do in the movies and TV. Because that makes it easy for an experienced adversary to grab your straight arm and use it to chop your guard partner in the voice box and then partially dislocate your shoulder before kicking you to the ground. Valuable lessons just like how Cue would've taught them. It was the least I could do.

Open sesame.

"Melly!" I said it real loud in front of the whole Wolves council: Aunts, Uncles, even a few high-ranking kids gathered around two shambly tables in the room filled with sewing machines and big white stoves. I hadn't called her that since we were twelve.

"You lookin' to get transferred? Because you're in the right place then, missy." Her voice was raw when she said it. Girl had some power. Melinda put her pen down and stood up. She rolled her shoulders forward and then extended her arms straight back behind her to stretch them. Maybe she just did it to show me that her breasts were still bigger than mine. Of course, Mark and Rico stood up and grabbed her arms to help her stretch better and mostly to look more intimidating. Mark and Rico were her boys. They could roll. Mark was the Wolves' Pop but really, he was just Melinda's lapdog and everybody knew it.

I didn't say anything. It was her show.

"Don't make me get the paperwork to put you out of here, because we can put you somewhere nice and sunny, real sunny."

The Wolves laughed at Melinda's sarcasm.

"Wolves only." She was walking toward me, slow but purposeful. She put her hands in her pockets and came out with extra rings: one for every finger and thumb.

Cue used to tell me I could take her, just as long as I didn't lead in with my chin. I had to be ready for more lateral movement and less front-foot fighting. But Melinda was much, much quicker than me. My only chance would've been to go for the diaphragm with my first punch and hope I hit gold. If anything though, I'd get it bad.

If it was anybody else, I would have. Melinda, though, she knew about appearances and she knew about alliances. I just had to ham it up a little more.

"The Waves are gone," I said.

She needed us. We needed her. She wasn't going to let ego get in the way, but she was going to save face for me disrupting the meeting, even if I did have valuable information.

"I didn't have to hear it from you to know that," Melinda said.

"We wish to strengthen the Wolves, we will not retain our name." I said what was traditionally said in blending situations, when one family joined another. Cue taught me the right words just in case I'd ever have to say them. He didn't tell me they'd burn a little when they came out.

"Last I heard you didn't have the power to do that." As the punctuation to the sentence, Melinda hit me, hard. I knew it was coming but I didn't really spot it. She was standing right in front of me and I didn't even see it. Tough to say she hadn't gotten even quicker. I didn't flinch though. I didn't duck. It crashed me right in the jaw, underneath the joint. I felt my skin tear but still I made it look good because the Wolves laughed and did their stupid howl.

"I do now. Alfredo got a flyer." I said it looking down at the carpet. Between the sentences, I spat blood. My back tooth was loose but not too bad. My right ear was ringing, but only my right. I didn't get hit again.

"Leave." Melinda wasn't talking to me, she was talking to the Wolves. They didn't argue. Every single one of them knew she could take me.

"What happened?" Melinda asked, completely different now that we were alone.

"Ridley transferred him. Did it right in front of me and Jimmy."

"How'd he do it?"

"Throat."

"Figures." Melinda grabbed me a towel from the nearest stove door handle after she said it. I was bleeding all over the table.

"Cue was good." That was the closest Melinda got to sympathy and it was the closest she got to saying that she was the next target. She knew it, I knew it, and pretty soon, everybody at Kung Fu would know it. I understood I'd have to stand with her. Our fates were tied together like a lead balloon with two tail strings. She was probably happy I'd done what I did. The Wolves were by far the largest family now, but for how long?

Melinda opened the door with her arm around me. She was twice the leader I was and everybody there knew it.

"I will absorb the Waves." She said it more for her family than for me. "I will stand for Jimmy too."

Her eyes lit up when she said his name. Mark and Rico hunched their shoulders at the exact same time. She liked her boys, Melinda did. She kept them in line. It stung bad though, that look in her eyes. It shouldn't've. I mean, I knew he could never be mine. Cue always used to say that there was no such thing as survival without compromise. And when I walked out of there on a sore knee, with a new family name and an aching jaw, I was beginning to understand what he meant.

CHANGES

I DIDN'T SEE JIMMY AT LUNCH. I ASKED A COUPLE PEOPLE about him but no one had seen him. Apparently he wasn't in his geometry class either, that was the word. At least it made my getting punched in the face worthwhile. As a Wolf now, no one could touch him. He was safe again, at least temporarily. Some stupid Blade would probably challenge him at the first circle after classes but Melinda would stand up for him, she had to. That was the first act of any new Mom or Pop.

Overall, lunch was pretty rough. I walked in from the building entrance to the cafeteria to see that the back right corner was empty. There are three entrances, one from the outside, one from the building, and a one-way in from the swimming pool that was basically forbidden. Where you entered was real important, crossing into another family's area was strictly not done, unless you wanted to challenge. The cafeteria was the one place in the school where families tended to group up a little more than usual, not too much though, Dermoody *was* watching. Our place, Cue's and mine, was empty. One of the big fluorescent lights above the section was out too but I definitely didn't want to read anything into that. The section would stay officially off-limits for one day out of respect. After that, Melinda could move in if she wanted. It was her right now.

My books squashed my sandwitch and the plastic bag popped so I got mustard on my take-home presidents test. It was starting to look like a dirty plate. Guess I'd have to turn it in tomorrow when I had a real civics class instead of a conversation with Ridley. It figured after all that hard work I went through just to get Jimmy's blood off the paper. At least mustard was less conspicuous and my teacher wouldn't say anything about it. Or maybe she'd just give another empty speech about being conscientious citizens and taking pride in our work. Nobody ever listened to her before but she kept saying the same speeches. Must've been automatic.

While eating I didn't really taste my food, it was enough just to move my jaw up and down through the sharp soreness. Once I even had to use my hand to push my chin up and down to chew the last of it. Melinda had got me good. Cue was the only person who punched harder. Mostly I kept thinking about sitting next to four Wolves, two who used to be Waves, and not Cue.

He had the most annoying habit of shaking whatever leg was next to mine, bouncing it up and down and bumping me while I was trying to eat. He said it was because he had a high metabolism but I think it used to be a joke that became a habit after years of doing it. Whatever it really was, my leg missed it when sitting at a new table where all I could feel was the cold steel of the table leg through my nonbloodied khaks. The coldness did make my swollen knee feel slightly better though.

Compared to the stress of the morning, the rest of the day was clear sailing. I made sure to explain to every Wave I came across what happened in the least words possible. Nobody liked it but what were they going to do, argue with me? They could tell I'd taken a shot for them, for all of us really. Nobody said anything about Cue, not in words. But I got a lot of looks that told me they were sorry about what happened. The only blip of discomfort that hovered on my radar screen prior to the end of the day was when Ridley surprised me after my chemistry class.

"Well, Miss Jen, you *are* good. I'm impressed how you took care of big brother's business." Ridley got close enough to touch me.

He smelled like expensive cologne. It went straight to the front of my brain and gave me a headache on the right side of my head, behind the ear. So he'd already heard. That wás quick. I'd probably done exactly what he'd wanted me to do, consolidated the last of his two enemies into one slightly more predictable, and manageable, body. Roll over it. Dress it up. Put a flag in it. Us against them. Only two sides now.

I couldn't be sure but he must've been waiting for me to say something and when I didn't, he traced the rough shape of a corsage—or maybe a heart—on my flannel, from my shoulder to my collarbone to just above my left breast. I could only look over at his little brother when he did it. Fred smiled that super-innocent smile of his and then looked away, all shy. That was when I realized that maybe one of the reasons why Ridley kept him around all the time was that they balanced each other out so well. Somehow Fred had a way of bringing out the best in people.

"Just think about it. That's all I ask. I know you thought I was joking just to be cruel but I really was serious about the prom."

And then he was gone, with his whole posse in tow. Even though he hadn't looked me in the eyes and basically talked to my chest, I could see actual loneliness there in his movements. We can smell our own. But who really cared if an extremely dangerous sociopathic drug kingpin was lonely? I didn't. He'd have to find someone more afraid of him than me if he wanted to bully someone into a date or a fuck. I knew he was playing some kind of angle. I just couldn't figure out what that was just yet.

Really, I don't know what boys see in me. My nose is too big and it's crooked. My face is too round and I have a hard jawline just like my dad's. Puffy is the best way to describe my lips and my cheeks sort of hang down low because I don't seem to have cheekbones, not like the kinds the magazine girls have. So no, I'm not classically beautiful and I'm not even beautiful. And that's before you factor in my scars. Only one is from when I was a kid. I fell over on a potted plant and got a big one (for a kid) across my forehead, eight stitches, or was it seven? I really can't remember, that was so long ago. I got that one scar beneath my lips where a girl put her fingernail through that thin skin and tore. It's kind of a half moon but ragged on the inside. Cue called that raggedness my crater, said I was the woman in the moon, Artemis, with a wicked left hook. My best scar is on my left eyebrow ridge though: it's two inches long and extends down vertical onto my cheek like someone drew a straight line past my eye, but really it was the chipped metal edge of a table I got slammed into, opened my face up like a book. I never wear makeup because that stuff stings when it gets into a cut or my eyes: poison, all of it. I never do anything with my hair beyond tying it back. There are lots of girls more attractive, lots.

Jimmy wasn't at the circle after school, so he missed the big announcement before anyone got called out. I probably should've been worried, but I wasn't. I carried my pack in front of me as I crowded in behind Mark and Rico. Melinda was in the middle and she walked toward me.

"The Waves are Wolves now." She surprised me after she said it though by taking my hand, making me in charge of the changeover in a real public way. Whispers sprang up but it was nothing much. I followed Mark's and Rico's glares across the circle.

"But the Hunters are Blades," came the call from Merrick, keen old 'Fredo's next in line. If they had any more than forty, they probably would've tried to start a new family all by themselves. That's how stupid they were. They'd fit right in with the Blades. Second bananas in the best family to second bananas in the worst family. A step down and they didn't even know it.

"So be it, but anyone who wants to roll a Wave has to roll me today." Melinda just smiled.

This was tradition as well. If a new family stepped in, the Mom or Pop had to take care of business and settle some scores. Anyone challenged could still accept of course, but the Mom or Pop could still step in if a point needed to be proven.

I knew I was a target, especially with Jimmy gone. The look on Merrick's face pretty much blamed me for 'Fredo and there were plenty of Blades that wanted to have a run at me for what Cue did to Karl. Those two were natural allies, enemy of my enemy and all that. If the Hunters were somewhat dangerous, Melinda would've challenged Merrick and beat him down, but they weren't big enough to be worth her time. To her, they were just sore losers who got outmaneuvered for control of the Waves.

Neither was brave enough to call me out when there was a very real chance of fighting Melinda instead. So the scores stayed unsettled and then there were five: Blades, Whips, Fists, Runners, and Wolves. It was probably no coincidence that the new numbers of all four of Ridley's families and the Wolves were less than even. Ridley had us outnumbered by four hundred kids. Only a matter of time really.

HOME

JIMMY WASN'T THERE WHEN I GOT HOME SO RATHER THAN sit around and be worried about him, I took care of Dad.

"I want to go before you go, Jennifer," Dad said. "I want to go before you go," and he just kept repeating it. He'd been crying all day. I could tell by his voice before I could get close enough to see his red, old, streaky-cheeked face. The same face he used to have when he drank too much but more wrinkled now and less mad than sad.

His room was a wreck. The TV tray had been tipped over and the glass cracked on the floor but not all over the place, just a chunk of the lip. The meds had sucked up what water they could, turning into puffy, deformed-looking worm shapes and leaving brownish orange stains on the carpet. Somehow he managed to use the bed as a toilet too. At least it was just piss and nothing else. Always my least favorite thing to do, but it needed to be cleaned and no one else was going to take care of it.

So I got him up, undressed him, got him into the shower, and perched him on his little bench that Cue had installed the summer before and I was a good girl. When the memory came to me, of my helping him bolt the plastic horizontal to the tile without breaking it into chunky debris, I stayed quiet. Dad didn't need to know. Instead, I took the sheets out to the washer in the garage and started a load, grabbed a sponge, and wiped down the rubber undersheet that protected the mattress, got back to the shower to make sure he hadn't fallen, and soaped/rinsed him with that two-in-one soap and shampoo stuff that Remo said was so easy on the skin. Would've shaved him but he was fidgeting. Got him out of the shower with difficulty, dried him, and pushed him through the arm, leg, and head holes of clean clothes, sat him down in the chair next to the bed and put new sheets on it. When I got him back in bed he said the same thing but he looked me in the eyes instead of staring off into space this time. "I want to go before you go." I seriously had no idea what to say so I just left the room. That was becoming par for the course.

The bathroom door flopped closed behind me and I ran some hot water in the sink before dipping the washcloth into it and raking it across the torn skin on my jaw. The wound wasn't so bad but it was swollen. I'd gone over it earlier in the school bathroom before lunch but nothing much, just soaped it, rinsed it, dried it. I certainly wasn't stupid enough to put a Band-Aid on it. Band-Aids, bandages, any of that stuff was a sign of weakness at Kung Fu.

You got to just act like it's not there, like it didn't affect you, like you didn't even know it was there even though every time you breathed through your mouth you could feel the air rush through the partially open bone cavity in the back. The tooth was loose enough to move with my tongue and I could feel the weird glutinous consistency of coagulated blood in the socket around the tooth. There was another good thing to come from it though: as I wiggled the tooth, I actually found it comforting to taste my own blood in my mouth instead of Cue's. A coppery warm distraction, but only on the surface: it was a reminder of the real and nothing else. Shit, but it still hurt. I popped a painkiller without bothering to read the bottle and left the bathroom.

But I swear something held my feet from underneath the hallway carpet, hauled me step by step to Cue's closed door, leaned me forward, put my hands on the wood in a groan, and tried but couldn't quite summon the pressure behind those fingers and palms to push it open. I wanted to believe in ghosts right then. That Cue was there and trying to tell me something, that he was moving my limbs, and it wasn't just me, losing control. Jesus, I knew I couldn't even look inside or it'd be over, swimming-in-saltwater over. Still, I had to believe that something under the awful carpet pushed and pushed what it thought was a solid object, but it was only me, sad little hollow Jen, a child weighing approximately as much as skin and hair combined and nothing else, no backbone, no brain, no fuckin' soul.

All day Jimmy and everybody else had seen Cold Fish Jen. What they thought was Warrior Jen, Strong Jen talking with my mouth, moving my arms. The Normal Jen that nothing touched and she was so stupid she didn't even know any better so she kept playing the game without understanding all the rules, kept losing it at the wrong times, kept being a piece for someone else to move, kept being when she shouldn't. Because how much better off would everyone've been if it was Jenny *en la calle* instead? In Cue's place! Jenny as bloody human pizza, all cheap crust and freezing? Papa's *angelita* in a box? Serious.

Just as long as I didn't open the door, that baldheaded brother of mine was alive. Sure. He had to be behind me, finally returning home. He wanted to go practice. I swear he *was* behind me, just out of the kitchen, smelling like a shake, smiling but see-through. Like a real fuckin' ghost. Trying to bear-hug me out onto the back patio but failing miserably because we were different things now, different elements totally. Him, all wind and invisibles. Me, all water and solid at the same time.

There was a knocking at the front door, carried down the hall to me. I figured it was Jimmy, which I shouldn't've because he had a key and really had no need to knock. Took me almost five minutes to undo the grip beneath the carpet, to improvise bones and move, only to see that it was Remo waiting outside and not Jimmy at all.

"Damn, I was gonna ask if you were alright but your *cara* already answered that question for me. I guess I'm just glad you're here." When he said "here" he meant "alive." Remo never went to Kung Fu. He just moved in with his mom when she got sick, but after almost three years, he knew how it operated.

"Looks like you did a good job with those cuts though, just like I taught ya," he said.

"I do need your help. See that tooth?" Normal Jen opened her mouth and pointed at the general area of the pain, barely forming the sounds needed for the words, just flapping her tongue around vacant noises.

"Damn, girl, yeah, I see it." He leaned in close and tipped my head back to the light to get a better look. "I ain't no dentist though."

"Don't worry, my PK kicked in. Just pull it."

I kept my head tilted back and looked up at our brittle skylight that was basically a hole Dad cut in the roof and put glass over. I heard Remo open up his toolbox (of course he brought it) and I heard metal clink against metal. I sat down in the chair but kept looking up at the skylight that held no clouds, birds, or tree branches, just icy sky. When Remo got near to me, he held down my left hand and stepped on my feet and I couldn't help laughing. Normal Jen with her simultaneous mood swing/guilt trip. Cue was still dead. Not allowed to smile or laugh.

But it was a joke even if it was also for Remo's protection. When he pulled a kinfé out of my side once, I kicked him in the *huevos* involuntarily. Not funny at the time but funny ever after. I felt something cold press against my tongue and hold it down, then Remo released my left hand, so I grabbed the table edge and I felt the tooth wrench right out of my head with a tearing sound that my ear heard from the inside out.

"Fuck! Did you pull out a nerve too?" Blood dripped down my chin as I said the words. I felt it, missed a bit from my slurping so some droplets hit the tile floor.

Remo didn't answer me. He was dumping table salt in a glass and running the hottest tap water into it.

"Spit. Rinse. Spit. Rinse," he said, pointing from the sink, to the glass, to the sink, to the glass. I did as I was told. He wiped my blood from the floor. It bled good for about five minutes, then it settled down but I kept rinsing. I grabbed another glass to spit into. I had Remo save the tooth for a keepsake. Now that it was out I could see the crack that ran from the back enamel all the way around the side. Only a matter of time before it shifted and split really.

"Yeah, that's definitely best that we pulled that out, better than it sitting and getting infected," Remo said as he held the washed tooth up for me to see. It would not be put under my pillow for the tooth fairy. It was for Melinda.

"I brought some tuna salad for you so you didn't have to cook for a few days, I need the bowl back when you're done though." Remo ducked outside and came back in with a huge plastic yellow bowl—the same bowl he soaked my hands in—of tuna salad. He always made it funny though. He put in mayo *and* mustard as well as pickles. I didn't complain though, I nodded and kept rinsing, spitting.

After cleaning his tools, Remo made seven sandwitches with the tuna salad and some of the thin white slices of generic bread that he found in the breadbox. He put one on a plate in front of me even though he knew I wouldn't be eating any time soon. It was just his way of telling me to eat when I could. The other six sandwitches were placed in two bowls that got squeezed into the refrigerator because there were no clean plates left. Then Remo did the dishes and put them on the dish dryer.

"I gotta take off, Mamá needs her dinner. I'll be back to check on that mouth of yours later," he said, and he closed the door behind himself on the way out.

The sadness had already set in before he left though. Without knowing it, I had sat down in Cue's chair at the table for my tooth surgery. Remo had noticed because he was perceptive like that. I'd gone silent so he went quiet too, out of respect. Didn't even attempt more conversation, just made an excuse and left me to myself. I got up and moved to my chair after the door shut hard but somehow that made it worse because it was empty with no Cue there, so I sat in my brother's chair again, and kept rinsing and spitting. Rinsing clear from the full glass and spitting reddish into the empty one so I didn't have to leave the table, or the warmed seat of his chair.

STUFF SINKS IN

JIMMY SHOWED UP ABOUT AN HOUR AFTER REMO TOOK off. Though it was better than before, his face still looked bad. The once-open wounds were scabbed up like little congealing bodies of insects, unmoving brown ants trying to pick at a hardened puddle of honey, but the bruises were starting to spread.

"Have you eaten?" I didn't know about him but I was damn

hungry. I was finally ready to have a go at the tuna sandwitch. I'd just have to rinse my mouth out when I was done.

"No," he said.

"Well, when you get hungry, there are some sandwitches in the fridge." I said it around a bite. I was extra careful at chewing everything on the left side of my mouth. My own blood had only been a temporary pardon for my tongue as I was back to tasting Cue's blood, slightly metallic, instead of canned tuna. It didn't matter. I ignored it, ate anyway. Asking where Jimmy had been wasn't exactly an option.

"Is it over now?" He sat down at the table in my mom's old chair.

"This isn't the end of anything, Jimmy." I took my plate and moved over to the couch. "This is the beginning of something. Do the math. With Cue gone we were going to get slaughtered and we still might. There's only one family left that's against Ridley now and we're part of it."

I could only see Jimmy's face, not his body, with the little wall between us. He was still sitting at the table.

"Look, I'm not going to ask you to fight. But I don't have a choice now."

"Let's just go, the both of us. Let's go to my mother's." He forced a smile when he said it. Like he was trying to convince me that I was being hardheaded in vain or something. Like he was trying to forget what he saw me do to 'Fredo's corneyes.

"I can't move away. I can't drop out of school. I can't do anything but stay right here."

"What're you going to do after Kung Fu? You can't just go to college and forget it ever happened." His comments surprised me.

The answer was: I had no idea. The future didn't exist at Kung Fu. Especially with no Cue, my world was microscopic. There wasn't even a tomorrow. There was only my next breath. Because the truth is, there were no outs, not college, not community college, not even trade school. Maybe there was the military. But only because those bastards would take anyone. Fuck that.

"This is so much more complicated than you think it is," I said.

"Explain it to me."

"I can't leave Dad."

"Take him with us."

"He wouldn't leave. And even if he would, it would never happen with Dad not being able to work. I can't believe I'm even thinking about this! It goes deeper, Jimmy, much deeper. If I leave, Ridley goes after Melinda and the Wolves faster than if I was here. And she just saved our lives by taking us in, so I owe her." As disgusting as it was, Ridley liked me, if he did and it wasn't an act or some other game, and that could be played to our benefit.

I sat back into the couch and put the sandwitch to my mouth but before I could take another agonizing bite, Jimmy said: "How's that?"

"Look, you just got here. You can't understand this. But it's my life. And the Waves existed for a reason. We protected each other or Ridley would crush us. So he's finally done it. And he's about to do it again to the Wolves too."

"So what? You're going to get sucked into this revenge bullshit on account of Cue? Alfredo is already dead!" He said it in a kind of harsh whisper. Like everything was even somehow.

"Dammit, Jimmy, it's about more than revenge, it's about survival, *our* survival. So, no, I'm not going to run away. Not with Cue due to fill up a box in the churchyard, taking up my dad's plot next to my mom. And it's more than just me on the line here. Don't you understand that?"

"I just don't see how you can be loyal to these people. They aren't your *real* family!"

I stood up.

"If I leave, Mrs. Rodriguez will end up raped in the gutter! Remo will show up in the emergency room with no hands or feet! Everyone that ever fuckin' knew me will be in danger! Not just from the Hunters or Blades—from fuckin' Ridley!" I didn't care if Dad heard me. "Don't give me that look! Why do *you* think Ridley killed 'Fredo right in front of us? Because now we're witnesses! Now he's got a reason to do us in."

"So that's why we run."

"Didn't you hear what I just said? He's got an excuse to chase us, Jimmy! He's playing a game. We can't leave. Dad will die. Your mom will die. I'll die. The only one to survive will probably be badass you if you stopped being such a bitch and actually hit somebody."

Jimmy's gaze dropped right off my face and fell hard to the carpet. Like a little suicide, something hadn't survived that drop. I guess it finally sunk in that I didn't regard him as some kind of saint for giving up fighting. At least, not when it put me and others in danger trying to protect him when he was by far the one who should be defending us. That was the raw truth.

Still too upset to apologize, I said it as flat as I could: "The only thing to do now is keep playing the game. Ridley's playing to win. But we're playing not to lose."

That, somehow, Jimmy understood. No more questions got asked. The conversation over, he left the room.

ON THE NEWS that night they called Cue a gang leader and they made it sound like he got what he deserved. They said he was notorious. They made it out like the city was a better place with him gone. How wrong they were. Serious though, how do you know who the good guy is when everybody's bad? The news anchor flipped her blond hair over her shoulder and they went on to the next story, one about sudden infant death syndrome.

During the rest of the news, into the weather and into another ballgame, I put the new bed together. But it wasn't for Jimmy anymore.

He could have Cue's room. The bed was for Dad. His old one was falling apart. Besides, it was Cue's last project. I could still see where his fingers had sanded the wood soft. I didn't want to leave it unfinished even though the temptation was there to let it sit forever. Like he'd be right back to build it, just after he got home with his protein shake powder. I finished the frame at about eleven o'clock but I'd put the rest together tomorrow, that was what I told myself.

When I got out of the shower, the lights were off so I got ready for bed, assuming that Jimmy had gone to sleep. I was surprised to see him working out in the backyard. I tweaked the curtains so I could see out and just sat on the edge of the couch and watched him: out there in the chill, with no shirt or shoes on, pounding the hard dirt that had a glaze of frost over the top of it. The oven was pumping out the same old cooked-casserole kind of smell that was filling up the house and I was glad to be inside, wrapping my feet in a blanket. Mom had always cooked chicken divan casserole: cream sauce, broccoli, chicken, spices, and melted cheese on top. We loved that dish. She'd cooked it so often in that oven that it permanently smelled of divan with a slight whiff of burning. For me, it was a welcome side effect of the gas being off. If I pretended, Mom was still alive and asleep in the next room. Not mad, not arguing, just quiet and dreaming.

I squinted, even leaned forward on the couch. But I still couldn't see the details of Jimmy's forms outside. They were way too fast. I mean, I could identify something that had to be a punch or a kick but the way they flowed into other attacks or defensive postures was smoother than smooth, it felt like watching something sped up. He did forms like the best chef you've ever seen chops with his knife. Blinding fast, and I had no doubt they were flawless. It bothered me though. The combined forms weren't like any specific style I'd ever seen, certainly not any of the ones he was supposedly a near-master of. It was almost like he had no style.

118

But then he did something weird. He slowed down, way down. He started doing his forms in slow motion. It was mesmerizing to watch him do a sideways full-circular kick with a straight leg that extended up to forty-five degrees and then to ninety directly above his head and then to one-thirty-five as he turned just slightly on his standing leg before sinking through the dark to one-eighty and back to standing. I'd never seen anything like it.

I pretended I was asleep when he came back in and hit the shower. I couldn't help it though. I sat back up just to see the marks in the dirt that his movements had made. They were the only things of interest in the empty backyard that held no grass, just a cracking concrete patio that stopped about two feet away from the house foundation and a disused shed in the back corner, all surrounded by a peeling fence about five feet high.

The lamp flicked on behind me, the bent gold one next to the couch. If you weren't careful sitting down, you'd hit your head on it. I tried to turn around but he put his hands on my shoulders. I wasn't wearing a bra. So I held down the front of my T-shirt as the back lifted up and gathered in a clump at the base of my neck. The air still lacked heat, but the fingers that traced the waves of my tattoo were very warm.

Some of those waves, the ink laid in right above bone, never really sat down after I had it done. The skin stayed raised, giving them a ridged texture. Sometimes I run my fingers over the space on the back of my right hip when I'm alone and thinking. It was a completely different sensation when Jimmy's fingers hovered just barely over the skin of my back.

I probably sounded like a stupid little kid but I said it anyway, "Today was the longest day of my life."

He just sniffed and I felt a burst of his breath hit my back: the wind over the waves, almost pushing the boat between my shoulder blades as I got goose bumps and all the little hairs stood up along my spine.

THE FIRST REAL KISS

I WAS ALMOST TWELVE YEARS OLD WHEN WE FIRST VISITED Jimmy in the country. My mom and Jimmy's mom were sisters. Mine was older. She drove us out to the farm. It was five hours away, on the plains, but it felt like more when I was actually in the car. It was a real hot summer, a no-cloud-in-the-sky kind of summer, and, of course, the air-conditioning broke halfway there so we had to roll down the windows. The back ones only rolled down partway and the re-echoed air that bounced around the car and off my ears was just about deafening at eighty miles an hour. So even with no way to listen to her audio book about two lawyers falling in love, Mom kept going. She was the type not to stop once she had her mind set on something. Cue always accused me of being the same way.

I guess I was just a normal suburban kid back then. This was years before Mom died and we had to move to a smaller place closer to the "heart of the city." That's what Dad called it, but then he had his accident and ever since he's just called it a shithole. Both were probably right in retrospect. Either way, I had no interest in leaving the house for a trip to some farm in the middle of nowhere during my summer vacation.

Of course, I had no choice. Dad was working and Cue was old enough to decide for himself all of a sudden, "and really, Jen," he said it stern, "Mom needs someone to go with her." It was bullying and it wasn't fair. No matter how hard Mom tried to convince me that the trip would be a great chance for a girls' vacation, you know, a bonding experience, I still wasn't happy about it. She was always positive. Wish she gave that to me too, but she didn't.

So after driving a few hundred miles of yellowed, dried-up-crop flatness, we left the highway, drove through the crappy-looking town of Barguss and its silly-looking blimp floating in the air and made our way to back road X and then back road Y, smelling manure the whole way because the fields had been fertilized. When Mom pulled up in front of the Chang Family Farm, she nearly knocked over the mailbox, with its smaller accompanying blue sidecar of a box for the newspaper. Of course, they all came out from behind their quaint screen door and hugged us welcome, Aunt Marin, Uncle Chun Mao, and Cousin Jimmy. Too picture-perfect.

You could tell from the start that Jimmy didn't really get any visitors because he was real excited to show me all around. He was an only child anyway so he didn't know what it was like to fight for the last spoonful of food or be pushed into the community swimming pool and look like an idiot during adult swim. I saw all there was to see on the farm in the space of five minutes: the chicken coops, the empty cornfields that had already been harvested and reseeded, the corn left to die in other fields because of government grants, his favorite tree, and the main house. If they hadn't had satellite TV I would've made my mom drive us back right then, with or without air-conditioning.

Ultimately, it was fine. I can't even remember everything we did that week, apart from Jimmy teaching me some moves. See, he'd been training for years by that point and already had some national championships under his belt. That was a cool moment though, seeing the living room and all the trophies that were taller than me. They were so huge and fake golden, the biggest ones had several levels that were held up by carved wooden pillars. He showed me all of them and then he just showed me pictures and pictures of him shaking hands with people with medals around his neck. And you know, he never really looked like anything scary or special. Only about five foot four and not stocky in the least, he looked like a regular kid who played sports, not the world champion he was to become.

Jimmy's dad had converted the hayloft of the barn to a training gym. There were bars he did pull-ups on, various tilted benches for sit-ups and push-ups, and there was this mannequin-looking thing that Jimmy did pressure-point strikes on. Each one was marked with a red dot in his mom's red lipstick. His dad had rigged it up to a pulley system that could shift it any direction in a seven-foot radius and even make it jump. Jimmy's dad was a genius. Well, there was also one of those kung fu block/strike training tools that looked like a big coatrack that had sawed-off coffee-table legs sticking out of it. Even at thirteen, Jimmy could play that thing like a drum set with his block-and-strike combinations.

I watched him a lot. That was basically what I did for a week, just climbed up the ladder and sat watching while he did morning, afternoon, and night training. We talked a lot too. He wanted to know everything about the city. What it looked like where we lived, what it smelled like. Stuff I'd never even thought about before until he asked me really. I think that was the first thing that got me liking Jimmy as more than a cousin. He made me feel important with all those questions. Out of nowhere, I was an authority on something.

Back home I was nothing. I was Cue's punching bag. I was always supposed to shut my mouth because I didn't know anything, that's what my big brother told me. The summer before, Cue accidentally broke my leg by jumping off the bed and trying to scare me but he slipped as he was jumping and fell on me funny, on my left tibia bone. It broke through the skin and bled a lot. Mom freaked out and screamed at Cue that he was trying to kill me.

"Girls are gentle! Girls are different from brute boys!" She screamed those a couple times each. Women were soft and kind and worthy of respect. She screamed that too. Something like it anyway. Cue was a perfect gentleman until it fully healed.

Well, my mom and Jimmy's parents thought it was great that we had become such close friends. They actually encouraged us to spend all of our time together. So it was okay for me to watch him train as long as I didn't disturb him, Mom said. That was where it happened, in the hayloft.

It was a typical late summer afternoon on the plains, hot and dry. Jimmy confirmed it. Felt like the hay up in the loft was going to spark up around me it was so warm with the heat rising up from the ground and getting trapped in the upside-down "V" angle of the wooden ceiling so close above us. Jimmy was working out as usual. A few solid forms and he was sweating, bare-chested, having discarded his shirt. He'd put his towel next to me so really he was leaning over for it and I thought I'd be helpful by picking it up and handing it to him but he wasn't looking at me. He was just leaning over, setting his water bottle down, leaning toward me, and no, it wasn't one of those things where we didn't mean it to happen, nothing that lame. I knew exactly what I was doing when I grabbed him and kissed him. Right like Melinda showed me. I pulled the back of his head hard toward me and I sucked on his lower lip before putting my whole mouth over his, but never with tongue.

Coming in to tell us about lunch, my mom stopped dead just inside the entrance. I'll never forget the look on her face when she saw us from down below. I saw her. Jimmy didn't, he was facing away, toward the barn wall. But he noticed when I stopped kissing him, kept my lips on his, just stopped completely. It was like she pitied me, like there was something wrong with me and I just couldn't help myself from ruining the golden boy. Obviously, it was all my fault. It was my compulsive nature, my lust, and my internal corruption. It was the same look she gave mice that were foolish enough to get stuck in one of the traps Dad would lay in the old garage.

We left the next day. That was the last time I saw Jimmy before he just waltzed into the house that night. It'd been almost four years since we kissed that I saw him and I could still feel my mother's look in the lining of my stomach like an animated wrestling ring that collapsed inward to take revenge on the bad, bad wrestlers trying to pin each other.

Mom died two months after that. I used to wonder if I killed her by doing that, made her unstable somehow, made her head break. I used to think about it a lot. I used to feel guilty.

MY BACK

"HOW'D YOU DO IT, JIMMY?" I ASKED AS THE MUSCLES IN my lower back tightened at his touching. That must be low tide.

"Do what?"

"Disappear," I said, "against The Bulgarian."

"I didn't."

"Yeah, you did."

"When did you get this tattoo?" he asked in a whisper. His fingers kept gliding over my ink in circles, real persuasive in changing the subject. Like he was creating twin whirlpools on either side of my spine: each going in opposite directions. The right went left. The left went right and he shifted to the palms of his hands, to rubbing.

"I got it last summer, it's still kind of new," I said.

I was glad that I wasn't facing him because I was flushed and getting worse, I could feel it more than I could see it in the darkness of the living room. "Took like sixteen or seventeen hours total, had four different visits, one for each shoulder and then one above each hip but he did the boat and the fisherman all at once at the end."

"Did it hurt?"

That was by far the most common question of all. I knew it was coming eventually. The good news was I didn't have to answer it all that often. Nobody really knew I had a tattoo because it always stayed covered. Then again, most of the people I hung out with didn't really think to ask if it hurt or not. They just knew it did. Seems to me that tattoos are entrancing like scars are entrancing, being real visible reminders of pain. Certainly Jimmy was mesmerized.

"About as much as getting stitched, but by a sewing machine and not by hand."

Since Jimmy didn't say anything, just kept rubbing, I kept talking, blabbing, I guess. Like we used to do in the barn: him asking questions and me answering.

"It hurt worse when I didn't look though. When I put my head down on the table, it was just an anonymous pain, something I was going through that didn't seem to have any purpose, so I just looked into this double mirror that was set up for me to look into, one that reflected another one that I could see my back in. Cue was there the whole time. He always adjusted the second mirror so that I could see the needle going into my skin, sewing that ink in, you know, see the purpose of it." I stopped talking because Jimmy was poking me like his fingers were needles and he was making the lines that were already there. I tried to imagine where he was touching me: the crest of a wave rising above my kidney and guiding the other waves to the boat. But I couldn't be sure. When I couldn't see the art, like a map in the mirror, it just felt like skin.

"Over the spine though, that hurt. It rattled the bone underneath and all the other bones near it. It feels a little like getting shocked but not too bad. A little bit of breath control and endurance and it's no big deal, blood and needles never bothered me though."

I kind of trailed off when the thought occurred to me that I'd have to check Dad for bedsores in the morning. He'd been in bed for almost two days by then. And it was getting colder too. I'd have to get the gas back up and running, call the company, arrange a payment. Still, it could take a week or more. I was hoping the weather would get warmer or the oven wouldn't give out when Jimmy spoke into the air that still smelled like casserole.

"I like changing the shape of the waves, distorting 'em and then watching 'em go right back to where they were before."

"Why's that?"

"I don't know. I guess because it's comforting," he said, and he hadn't stopped rubbing. It was a full massage now and my neck was getting the treatment from his warm, strong hands.

"Comforting because there's a pattern to it? Just sitting there underneath what you can touch, keeping things in order on the surface," I said, and I knew as soon as it left my mouth that Cue would've laughed at me, but Jimmy didn't.

"Yeah, like fate or karma or whatever, just pulling things back to where they need to be."

"And the skin can die and flake off but the pattern stays there as a map, right?"

"Yeah," he said, working his knuckles into my lower back but with his other arm around me, in front of me, wrapped around my collarbone and in front of my neck and over to my other shoulder that he held in his palm. He was holding me up. It felt natural.

"Don't laugh," I said, but even before saying it I knew he wouldn't. That he wouldn't even reassure me, he'd just sit there and listen, waiting for me to say whatever I was going to say. "I used to think that everything was destined but then I thought that we all had free will but then I thought that something big and god-ish had to account for all possibilities, ya know? So I guess I just figured that there was such a thing as fate with a little *f*, and Fate with a big *F*, a capital letter."

I hoped he was following me, because I just kept going. "So there's fate with a little *f* that we can change, right, like free will, right? But then Fate with a bigger *F* actually takes that into account, because it's so huge that every single decision you could ever, ever make with the little f fits into the big *F*. All possibilities are accounted for. And because of that, big *F* was still in control over the little *f*, like it was a big abacus in the sky that never had to adjust because it knew of, and kept track of, every single choice from the beginning, like even before you were born. Even decisions that led to my parents getting together and having me."

I was seriously full of shit. I couldn't help it. It was dark and safe to talk and my brother was gone and I was trying to understand something, anything, so long as it was giant.

"The truth is I don't know how I did it, Jenny."

"What? How you did what?"

He stopped rubbing.

"I don't know how I disappeared, I just did." He was talking real slow. "Really, I didn't believe it, I thought I just moved around him, I mean, I focused on where I wanted to be and then I moved my body and I was just there behind him."

He got quiet. I could hear the cranking of the rusty oven fan in the kitchen. One of its propellers was probably crooked. I tried to focus on that sound, instead of how near Jimmy's skin was to mine.

"I talked to everyone who was at the match after, the judges and masters from the other schools, and I saw the television footage and I didn't even know I'd done it. It freaked me out bad. Real bad. For a little while I believed what those priests said about me. That I was a reincarnated evil spirit, the devil, all that stuff."

I listened, feeling his every little shift in the lumpy busted couch.

"I don't know. It's like everybody makes such a big deal out of the promise, that it's all legendary now, me giving up on fighting, like I'm some great guy who saw the light. But really, I'm just scared. I don't know how I did it, vanished." The way he said the v-word put a new flock of goose bumps on my neck. "I just did. I guess I was happy to promise my mom that I wouldn't fight anymore. What if I disappeared for good next time?"

The logical, realistic, Mom part of me wanted to reassure him that it would never happen, that it wasn't possible. But the guy had already disappeared once. There was photographic evidence. What could I say to that?

"You know my mom made me promise not to get *involved* with you? That was a condition of my coming." Jimmy changed gears and I was fine with that.

"Serious?" I thought it was kind of funny, really. Then again, I was pretty surprised to see him when he showed up. No one in my family ever talked about it. I never told Cue but he knew somehow. They all kind of looked at me strange after that, especially Mom. Like I had something following me, or hanging above my head. I was forever trying to make up for it, 'til Mom was gone anyway.

"Yeah. I guess she figured she was on a roll with the promises thing." He leaned close to me but the hands I expected never came. Instead, I felt the tip of his nose track up the base of my neck as he breathed out, up to my hairline before brushing east/west across it like the skin beneath my hair was a mountain path that needed exploring. He smelled me, bumping his forehead into the base of my skull like a playful dog.

"So you promised." I hoped he didn't hear me breathing any heavier.

"Yeah."

"That's good, because this isn't right anyway, right?" I had the heels of my hands on my hips and I was just pushing down, reminding myself of my body boundaries. I let go of my shirt to do it.

"Right," he said, and he moved his nose, replaced it with his lips, softer than I remembered.

"So why's it not right again?" I was afraid my voice was cracking.

"Because it's taboo." He stopped kissing my shoulder clouds to say it.

"Oh, right, yeah. Taboo." I had to close my eyes. "Because why?"

"Because we're related and people who're related aren't meant to be together, you know, for the gene pool." He pulled away for just a moment and when he pushed back against me his chest was bare and I could feel his heart beat against my back.

"Right. Inbreeding bad," I said. And it was, very bad. Webbed toes and pale skin, weak constitutions, Poe stuff.

"So what's left for us then?" It was his turn to ask a question.

"I don't know," I said, and I really, honestly, 100 percent didn't.

NO

TWO MINUTES LATER I HAD A PRETTY GOOD IDEA THOUGH,
and that's why I slept on the couch alone even when it was uncom-
fortable and a little cold without him. It wasn't because I didn't want
to, because I did, but also, I didn't. Confusing, all of it. It was easier
that he was behind me when I told him because if I'd seen his light
brown eyes right then, flamed up in a sliver of back porch light, it

might've been a different morning. Jimmy was good about making it sound like it was our decision, the two of us, not to go through with it. But it was my decision and I think he took it kind of hard. The kid was in love with me. Said it himself last night: "Jenny, I love you, I've been waiting for this moment for so long . . ."

And the scary thing was that it wasn't bullshit. If it was, I think it would've been easier for me to laugh off. Somehow in those words I knew that he'd probably never kissed another girl or if he did, it was only in China, across an ocean and a long time ago. That he really did love me and that he really had been waiting since that last kiss in the hayloft gym freaked me out.

So of course the thing that did it, convinced me it was a terrible idea, was Keenan Helford. I saw her small-chinned face in my mind right when Jimmy said he loved me. Keenan was a skinny little girl with huge energy that could punch for an hour straight without stopping. Big blue eyes fixed just under short poky hair that stuck out in all different directions, she looked like a girl from a Japanese video game. I don't think she showered much but all the guys liked her anyway. Like guys love dangerous dogs and raise them up to be mean, to bite. That was Keenan.

Well, after Mom died, Cue took up with this Keenan girl. She was one of the youngest Waves because she had skipped a year in school, but she was real tough. She almost beat me up once when she was over at our house and she would've too, if Cue hadn't been there and looked scary angry. Of course their relationship got real weird, real fast. Cue soon found out that Keenan had daddy issues, among other problems, but he still kept saying he loved her and wanted to marry her and she ate it up. Kid was fifteen when he was saying these things. Well, it eventually occurred to my big brother, after tons of talks with Dad, that this Keenan *chica* just wasn't right in the head so he had to end it quick. Took him two weeks to actually do it though.

By then she was showing up at the house randomly. She'd call at five thirty in the morning or follow him home from Kung Fu so he'd have to run in the house and lock the door behind him. She'd write long letters and accuse him of stealing her diary and all of her socks. She said she had three miscarriages and their children were now spirit guides in heaven. She said she was going to kill herself if he didn't get back together with her. That it would be all his fault if she died. As if these kinds of things would make Cue want to get back together with her.

It was a sight though, watching Cue transition from the boy who cared too much to the warrior man he was. He was like that his freshman year at Kung Fu. Started out soft. He'd come home and cry a lot before and after Mom died, and even after he dumped Keenan, but only in his room and with the door closed. If I went in to see what was wrong I got a smack. So I left him alone. That continued for about three months, then he just stopped. No more crying, ever. He said he cried himself out. Nothing touched him after that. Like he just decided one day that it wasn't his fault anymore and that he was going to live his life how he wanted.

In the end, Keenan didn't kill herself, just got sent to live with her grandparents in the mountains of North Carolina. But maybe that's the same fuckin' thing. Later, after all that mess was over and Cue had some time to think, he told me that he shouldn't've jumped into a relationship so fast after Mom died because he didn't even know what he was doing and he was just trying to fill a hole that couldn't, and shouldn't, be filled by someone else. I only understood about half of what he said, but I did understand that relationships were bad.

It was so easy to get sucked into that around Kung Fu though, the sex and the relationships: a drop of comfort in a coffee cup of living that always gave you sugar in lumps. Girls were always dropping out of Kung Fu because they got pregnant. You make it to graduation alive, relatively intact, and without having gotten someone pregnant or becoming pregnant yourself, you're in a tiny minority.

So I thought of Keenan when Jimmy said it, and how that sounded a step away from craziness to my ears. More than anything, I didn't want that to be me, or worse and more probably, Jimmy. So I said no and he respected it, even if he made a show of it. But it was nice for a moment there when I couldn't see his face or hear his voice. When it was just strong hands on my back and me talking and I guess I let it get further than it should've because it was just nice to be touched in a way that didn't involve fists, boots, or elbows.

After Jimmy had gone to sleep in my bed one more night, I thought of Mom. Brain cancer is about as bad as it gets. Out of nowhere, Mom started puking a lot, like *Exorcist* a lot. So I thought it was me. I thought I made her sick with what me and Jimmy did. Every time it came to mind, I apologized, and every time Mom tried to make me understand it wasn't me and that everything was going to be okay. But everything wasn't okay, and the fact that it wasn't my fault didn't sink in 'til I went to Kung Fu and had my own breakdown, my own baptism, just like Cue.

But that didn't change what happened. Dad always had two buckets by the bed and he was emptying them, cleaning them out, like a one-man fire brigade for Mom's puke. "I'm just the Nancy Fire Brigade," he would say, and laugh like it was funny. Nancy was my mom's name. At first, they thought it was really, really bad stomach flu that she got from some beef she ate at a restaurant and so they let it go two days before the headaches started. But we had insurance then so Mom got checked into the hospital so we didn't have to deal with her illness, with her dying. We were shielded from most of it. I guess after having been through so much stuff with Dad, taking care of him and all, I just look back and wish that Mom had died at home. So we could've had more time together, so I could've taken care of her, as naive as that is. Hollow Jen strikes again.

Instead, we'd just go to the hospital in the morning before school and come back for dinnertime. Her hair turned white in one big patch. Like Antarctica. Some days, she couldn't see at all and she'd wake up from a nap screaming that she'd gone blind. Other days she couldn't even speak, or if she could, she'd start talking about some guy named Ted. Dad had been with Mom since they were in high school and he didn't know any Ted. The doctor told us that the brain cancer was ruining her memories, altering them, changing them around in her head. It was Cue who eventually realized she was talking about the actor Ted Danson from that TV show *Cheers*. The brain cancer made her think they were friends in real life. That was sad.

Near the end, she just lay there in the hospital bed, lost thirty-five pounds, and died without eating, speaking a word, or even moving her eyes while she was awake for two weeks. From the day she was diagnosed to then, it was one month, three weeks, and five days. She was forty-one, I was almost thirteen, Cue was fifteen, and Dad was two days short of his fortieth birthday. To celebrate, we had a funeral and he buried his wife. I wore a black dress with gray stripes that Mom had bought me and I cried the whole time, getting mucus and tears all over the frill around my collar like an idiot. Cue wore one of Dad's navy blue suits that didn't really fit him in the shoulders and Dad wore a black suit with his NASA black tie that had silver stars with little red and green stripes and the space shuttle on it, angled, with its landing gear out.

MORNING AFTER

I CHECKED ON DAD AS SOON AS I WAS DRESSED AND READY for school, which was about six thirty. He was still asleep and faced away from the door. He'd rolled his self into a little ball at the top of the bed where his pillows were all scrunched up. I opened the window a crack.

"Dad, wake up." I said it right into his ear.

"I'm already awake," he said.

"Good, because I need to check your back, so roll over."

I was glad to see that he did as he was told. I didn't really have the energy to argue with him if he had decided that it was a bad day.

"You got to get up today, okay? I can't monitor your eating but you need to eat better. There're tuna sandwitches in the fridge." At that point I almost added something about the protein content of tuna but stopped. It was something Cue would do. Besides, I had already added a vitamin A, C, and E tablet to his meds. Remo gave it to me.

"Also, you got to get up and moving today, I know you don't feel like it but, seriously, use anything as an excuse, the ball game, the sports report, anything, just get out of bed and move around." I was looking at his back. He was starting to get red marks on his butt and elbows that didn't turn white when I pushed them. His right hip was worse than the left and all the red spots felt warm.

"When you sit or lie down make sure you shift and use pillows, don't let the pressure sink in, right? Shift every couple of hours and use your pillows."

I didn't mean to say it twice, but sometimes he needed to hear it both times. I used the saline and absorbent pads that Remo gave me. He said they were better than soap when Dad was on his back so much. No rubbing or scrubbing, he said. So I didn't.

"C'mon, Dad, you know all this." I really was Nurse Jen and I sounded exactly like Doctor Remo. Like his words were coming out of my mouth.

"Jen, I want to die. Use one of those death machines." Dad said it as I was dabbing at his back with one of the pads. I'd finished with the saline and I was actually dabbing just above my own father's naked ass with a pad when he decided to tell me about his death plans. Perfect.

"Why's that, Dad?"

"Because I'm a burden to you. What's left to live for?"

Mercifully, Dad cut the little woe-is-me dialogue short. He didn't go on and on about Mom being dead or his firstborn son being gone, which, incidentally, meant that our family name was going to go with him. I never play his little game anymore. I used to get all upset and scream about all the reasons to live, you know, all the great things in the world. But that was only after Mom died. I've stopped now. I mean, you're here for as long as you're here for. That's how I see it. That's it.

"You can tell the settlement company that it was complications from my injury, get Remo to vouch for you, and then they'll have to pay more, you can live on that for a while."

"Yeah, thanks for thinking of that."

It's 6:48 a.m. and I'm in my dad's stale-smelling room that the cracked window isn't helping and not only is he talking suicide but insurance scams.

"... at least six thousand. That's what you could get if I died, Jen. Six thousand dollars."

I only caught the last bit of what he said.

"Maybe with that I could put the gas back on, huh?" Something else I needed to take care of. Couldn't forget that.

"Yeah, I guess so, but really," he went on. He'd thought way too much about this.

"When I get home you better be watching that ball game and eating something." I closed the door behind me after I said it.

Making my way to the kitchen, it occurred to me that I didn't need the movies. I didn't need anything like *Big*. I didn't need to make a wish with some busted arcade fortune-teller to be older and wake up the next day and bam. Because the reverse had already happened. There was an old woman inside my body taking care of my broken dad and worrying about his pills and bills and heat and putting food on the table and I hadn't even graduated from Kung Fu High School yet, if I ever would.

Jimmy was washing his empty cereal bowl in the sink and he smiled a strained mouth-curve at me when I cruised in.

"You okay?" Jimmy was finishing up the last of the orange juice too.

"Your uncle wants to kill himself."

"What?" He overreacted and had to spit his orange juice back into the glass.

"Yup, you ready?"

"I guess," Jimmy said. He was wearing some of Cue's old clothes. They didn't fit him, but I was at least pleased to see that he was taking his safety a little more seriously. His purple bruises were going brownish yellow over his nose and eyes.

We had to be at school at 7:30 for first period and it probably wasn't the smartest move just to walk out the door like it was safe but really, I didn't care. If I had to roll in the front yard, I'd roll in the front yard. With Melinda to watch mine and Jimmy's backs now and the drive for survival waning, I felt less like doing anything.

Well, someone was there, standing in my front yard like they owned the place. It was a pack of Wolves.

"Time to roll with the new, kids." Melinda was standing outside the door like she had posed herself on the broken part of our fence for a fashion spread, sticking her legs out. I think she was even wearing makeup, out of nowhere. Flanking her were Mark and Rico, standing on the sidewalk though. It was a cloudy day but they were both wearing sunglasses. Chumps.

The walk was actually good for my knee. It'd gotten stiff overnight. But there was still a cold front combing through the air, for at least another week, the weatherman had said. I could still see my breath and had to pick my way along the street to avoid any black ice.

"Go to your classes and sit in the same seats, spread that around so everyone gets it. We don't want Dermoody or anyone thinking anything is going to crumble because of Alfredo. Seems simple, but I just wanted to be clear." Melinda was good at ordering people around.

"That it?"

"I also need your help tonight."

"For what?" I didn't like the sound of it.

"We're going in for a little reconnaissance." Melinda said it real sassy. "Something big is definitely going down. Moves about to be made."

She didn't just mean dropping in on one of the other families, she meant scouting Ridley. Probably his operation in the cafeteria, or I should say, his rumored operation in the cafeteria because no one we knew ever saw it. Of course Melinda would give us something dangerous to do right off the bat, just because she could.

"Jimmy, when you get home call Remo and ask if he can take care of Dad, ayight?"

"I'm going with you." He was walking behind me but it sounded like his voice was right in my ear. I really hoped he didn't think he was my protector all of a sudden.

"Wait, what?" I didn't stop walking but I wanted to. I mean, what the hell was he thinking? Melinda was looking at us with some serious interest. I knew I had to diffuse the situation as quickly as possible.

"Suit yourself, but if I have to roll, you roll too." I said it not knowing how he'd respond and he didn't. He was just quiet.

It was Melinda that made the first noise, something girly, something not like her at all. If you glanced at this solid woman, with her perfect scars that looked like they'd been painted on because they made her look better, not worse, the way they somehow matched with her calloused hands, you'd definitely have thought the sound came from somewhere else, like from me. Even Mark and Rico exchanged an uneasy glance through their smoked lenses, but it was definitely Melinda and I could best describe it as a squeal of anticipation.

140

CHECKING IT OUT

FIVE THIRTY P.M.: THERE IS ONLY ONE ENTRANCE TO THE cafeteria kitchen through the building and it's through a single sliver of a door right next to the vacant salad bar. There is another entrance but it's through the truck-loading bay, where they park the big semis that shuttle Ridley's product to the airport and points continental. And I guaranteed Jimmy that we weren't going in that way because chances were a shipment would be in the middle of getting loaded up and unless I wanted to fight through ten to fifteen Runners by myself while he watched, we'd be better off trying the building way.

Melinda had gotten the information from Janitor Will, or JW as he was known, about when to go in. JW always emptied the trash cans in the kitchen at 5:35 p.m. Melinda worked it so that he'd leave his main collecting bin, the one that had wheels on the bottom, in the door if the coast wasn't clear. If it was clear, he'd unlock the door, go in, and put the deadbolt out so that it wouldn't close all the way.

Which was exactly what happened. Jimmy and I timed our move and we swept right in after JW and undid the bolt and shut the door. JW acted like we weren't there for the most part, just emptied the trash, but he did nod toward the walk-in pantry as a good place to hide. Jimmy went first and I followed, we got squeezed in tight together next to a box of dehydrated potato flakes that was almost bigger than me. I left the pantry door slightly cracked open.

Two big metal tables dominated the main kitchen space. Behind them were four large ovens: two on one side of a corner, two on the other side. In the back, down a hall, were the floor-to-ceiling walk-in freezers. Just about all the food that came in was frozen, even the bread got iced at some point. That was also where the bulk of Ridley's store was hidden—at least, Melinda thought so. Lemon cleaning liquid, that's what the whole place smelled like.

"Mistah JW!"

"Hey, how you doing, Mr. Ridley," JW said. I couldn't see him but I knew he was nearby.

"Did you get Sally that Ride-'Em Jeep she wanted for her birthday?"

"I sure did, Mr. Ridley, thanks to you."

"It was my pleasure, you just let me know if she needs anything else, okay?"

"I'll do that, Mr. Ridley."

It sounded like we lucked out. Ridley didn't spend a lot of time overseeing the cafeteria operation: red fuckin' flag. JW shuffled out the door and didn't even look at the pantry on the way out. Good man.

"I want this out by six-o-five, Mock"—Ridley's voice again—"so send the Whips to the mall to start bashing up the food court at ten to the hour, then have the Runners take the back way to the interstate."

"Done and done," Mock said.

"This is our biggest shipment to the Conquistadores yet and they're only going to get bigger once we wipe out those big bad Wolves so let's do this first one right." Ridley always sounded confident.

"Hey, boss, did you ever wonder with Cue dead, if Jimmy was gonna start fightin'? That could be a problem, right?"

I flinched against Jimmy then. He didn't move.

"I did wonder that. Although it is amusing that he hasn't fought since, so for the moment, I think we can count on him not to. And even if he did"—I saw Ridley's arm put his notebook on the table—"haven't you ever seen *Raiders of the Lost Ark*?" Ridley mimed out the famous scene where Indy comes face-to-face with the swordsman and Indy/Ridley just shoots him. Ridley blew on his finger like it was the smoking barrel of a gun, and then said, "Oops."

Mock laughed the laugh of all cronies, half-entertained, half-afraid, and a little too loud.

"But really, Mock, it doesn't matter. We'll have all of this business wrapped up before the Grand Championships."

"Really? But that's only a week and a half away."

"That's exactly correct. You see, there isn't going to be one this year. Come the final rehearsal for the play, we will finally rule the school." Ridley chewed in the silence after his words. Like some steak dinner.

The final rehearsal of the winter play was always the night before the Grand Championships and students got free seats. They always opened on the same day. It was the only traditional event we had at Kung Fu. It was the only day of peace.

"Which reminds me, I need to go. Freddy has play practice and I told him I'd be there. You think you can take care of this?"

"Yeah," Mock said.

"Good, don't fuck up. Look at me. Look me in my eyes. Don't fuck up. This is your show now." After a sound like a slap, Ridley moved into my field of vision. He pulled the door to the cafeteria open.

"Hey, boss, who's Fred playin' this year?" Mock's voice sounded exactly like Joe Pesci's except he was six foot six and made XXL shirts look like they were for toddlers.

"Horatio. He's amazing too, his eyes get real big when he says, 'It harrows me with fear and wonder.' He loves those lines. We were up until almost midnight last night reading back and forth. Come by when you're done here, they're rehearsing Act I tonight, you'll see how good he is." Ridley grabbed his coat off the counter and headed out the door. Sometimes it boggled my mind that this guy who so lovingly talked about his brother being a good actor was the same one who murdered 'Fredo right in front of me. I couldn't put them together.

"Will do," Mock said.

The door closed behind Ridley and Mock bolted it. Jimmy and I waited for Mock to move away from our exit but he kept writing in his notebook. By the time he checked his watch and walked to the back of the kitchen with footsteps fading, I was about to have a heart attack. I didn't need to be crammed into some pantry eavesdropping for information we just could've beaten out of someone. That we just happened to stumble upon a real convenient conversation made me suspicious as hell. It was then that it occurred to me that we couldn't completely trust Melinda. Truth was, I had no idea what her angle was and that deserved more thought at a later date. What I did know was that she hadn't bargained on Jimmy volunteering to come along. Of course, Jimmy tried to stop me but I just walked right out of the pantry into the kitchen and I knew someone was looking at me.

"Come get your fucking, *puta*." It was Papa Whip his own self, Bruiser Calderón. What a sweet mouth he had. Tattooed and with curly black hair, he looked like he was wasted. Which basically meant he looked twenty times tougher than usual: slower, maybe, but definitely more powerful. He didn't feel pain when he was amped up like that.

Jimmy stayed hidden. If, in some ploy to get rid of me, Melinda had slipped the information to Bruiser earlier, he probably wouldn't know Jimmy was there too. I hoped so anyway.

There really aren't any advisable ways to start a roll with Bruiser. So I charged him, surprised him with a feinted right hook that turned into a frontal punch, as halfway through my motion I swiveled my arm at the elbow and brought the back of my fist down hard on the bridge of his nose. Broke it too.

"Lucky shot," Bruiser said as he spit a gob of blood and mucus onto the floor. There might've been some cartilage in it too but I didn't have time to inspect it. I was kind of busy.

He always was an arrogant fighter. I ducked his huge right cross counterattack and twisted underneath him. He'd overcommitted for an early knockout so I body blowed him just below his ribs and his abs thumped like a hollow wooden barrel against my fist. That just made him laugh. I backed up. He kicked low, high, low, and then brought in a roundhouse. I blocked with my shin, my forearm, my other shin and saw the sole of his shoe whiz past my face by less than an inch as I leaned away from the roundhouse. In all likelihood, he'd stepped in shit at some point that day.

I was starting to feel it. He didn't get called Bruiser for nothing. Even blocking hurt and I knew he was just playing with me, wearing me down, bleeding everywhere and just laughing. I went for his neck but couldn't get close. He kept backing me up with his wild swings that weren't even worth blocking anymore. He got some good shots in along my thighs though. I couldn't get too close or he'd throw me. So I'd jab and move. Jab and move, as I looked for my opening. But it was pretty much impossible. Bruiser was a compact fighter for a big guy. He had such a low center of gravity that even his wild punches didn't put him in a terrible position. He could always counter my counter. I dodged and went for an armlock like an idiot. He swiveled and smashed me with a heavy forearm shiver.

The first one sent me to my knees, the second one sent me across the room, sliding over a long metal table and I don't know what I smashed my hip against on the way to my hitting the oven but it was bad. Puncture-wound bad. Hopefully it wasn't too deep but I could feel it going numb beneath me when I rolled out of the way of Bruiser's knee smashing into the door of the nearest oven, cracking the glass in a neat little ring just like a baseball bat does when it's brought down on a windshield.

"You'll get it just like your brother." He had a blood mustache.

I was trapped near the entrance door, between the wall and what would've been a waist-high cupboard had I been standing up. My leg below my left hip was going slowly dead from one of the kicks I caught in the thigh. This was my fight. And I'd lost it. As Bruiser leaned back to strike me with what would probably be a low kick to my face or a preacher punch with both fists to the top of my skull, I resigned myself to some monumental pain and possibly never being able to breathe correctly again, if I breathed at all. I gritted my teeth and kept my hands up. But the blow never came.

It was then that I saw Jimmy, crouched down and looking at me through Bruiser's unmoving legs. Then he smiled, stood up, and side-stepped Bruiser like he was inspecting a statue at an art museum, once around.

146

"Damn, girl, you took some shots." He was grinning like he was proud of me. It was a Cue-type smile.

"What the hell did you do?" My second question was why didn't you do it sooner? But I didn't ask that one. I tried to push myself to my feet but I failed.

"I just hit the right spots. He'll be alright in a few hours."

"How come he can't talk?"

He could move his eyes though. And they were frantic. Moving back and forth like his face was just a Halloween mask that he had put on and could only just see through the eyeholes. I've never seen Bruiser look so scared.

"I hit that spot too."

I can't lie. There is absolutely nothing sexier than a man who can paralyze someone who is about to dislodge your jaw from your head. Seeing Jimmy in action turned me on. Well, I didn't exactly see him but I saw the results. It was a shame I didn't have any time to dwell on it as he lifted me to my feet and put my arm over his shoulder. Test passed, we had to tell Melinda that her time was running out even faster than I thought. If she didn't know that already.

GETTING BACK

BUT RIGHT BEFORE THE TWO OF US WERE GOING TO WALK out the building exit of the cafeteria kitchen, I stopped. Something was wrong.

"Jimmy, we can't go out this way." I said it as quietly as I could.

As good as Bruiser was, there was no way he was the only one.

I saw a shadow move under the door, a foot. This was pretty close to the sloppiest ambush I'd ever seen.

"Yeah, I know," Jimmy said. "So what now?"

"We got to go out the back, once we get past the trucks, we cut left, take the alley, and you know the way home from there."

More than likely we were surrounded, but if that was the case, whoever it was would bank on us leaving the way we came and not by the trucks because, supposedly, there were a lot of guys out there and none out the front. Fuck them. Trucks it was. Jimmy led and I followed as we ducked down the hall that connected the kitchen to the rear room and its giant pale green refrigerators. Over Jimmy's shoulder, I could see light coming from the outside and the open exit door. But I could also see two Runners, dropping their boxes and coming at us. Jimmy pushed me backward into the hall and I nearly fell over. I hadn't expected it.

You know, it's just never like the movies. All that back and forth and pretty blocking and kicking and drama, you can forget about that shit. When someone as skilled as Jimmy fights an amateur, or worse, a beginner, it's over before a punch is even thrown. Not that they know it. See, by the time I regained my balance and hauled myself up on a wooden cabinet, I caught sight of Jimmy flitting out the exit. I just heard the sound of Cue's old flannel ripple behind him and then he was gone.

Both Runners were paralyzed in his wake: the first one, leaning back like he was going to throw a punch, the second one, actually tipped over on his side, sprawled rigid across the floor as he'd been caught trying to kick. Jimmy must've taken pity on him and set him on his side rather than allowing him to fall. He never would've stayed balanced on one leg like that. Both Runners had the same look on their faces that Bruiser had. They looked like little boys faced with the terrifying experience of black magic for the first time.

I seriously had to get Jimmy to teach me that. I couldn't think of anything more powerful than hitting the right pressure points and getting someone to stop dead but keep breathing. And the fact that he could do the same on different people, of different heights, and that he could do it every time without fail and without killing them boggled my mind.

Couldn't stay boggled for long though because a Runner came out of one of the walk-in freezers with a box. She dropped it and it made a sound like something broke inside. Like THUD-TINKLE. The funny thing was she had a look on her face that basically said, "Oh no! I shouldn't've broken that!" just before she came at me. It was over before it began.

Must've been a new Runner because she led with an awkward left jab and didn't even sell it as her feint at all. I knew she was coming with a leg sweep before she even turned around and bent down, so apart from my hip making it difficult to jump, I cleared her leg and brought my boot down on the side of her head, it ricocheted off the wall, putting her out flat before she even finished turning around. Sad. She hadn't even learned her playbook yet. And here she was expected to defend a huge drug convoy. Poor kid. I just did her and her folks a favor.

"Come on!" Jimmy poked his head back through the exit and the light silhouetted him it was so bright.

I followed the sound of his voice outside but had to stop the moment I got out the door. One, because my eyes needed to adjust to the harsh glow of reflected cloud light, and two, because I couldn't believe what I thought I was seeing. So I propped myself up against the big black cab of the rumbling semi parked in the loading dock as my eyes adjusted, and when they finally did, it took everything in me to stop from pulling a 'Fredo and gloating in the stunned faces surrounding me.

To my immediate left, petrified midkick, was Donnie K., Pop of all Runners. His legs must've been at a seventy-five-degree angle and he was actually propped up against the side of the building by his outstretched leg, like he was a mannequin or something that was just being put off to the side to fill a display at a later time. It was seriously a freeze-frame pose out of a dojo ad that gets turned into a logo. No joke. Behind him were a half dozen other Runners caught in various forms of paralysis: one trying to block, another with her front foot forward leaning back, one down on the ground and stuck in a half kick, two or three others caught in various punching forms that never made it to full extension. But there was one I really felt bad for. He was fixed in a position where it was obvious he was turning away with a scared look on his face. He wasn't trying to defend or attack, just trying to run away when he got gripped. The Runners would do a whole lot worse to him than we ever would once they saw the stance he was frozen in.

"Let's go!" Jimmy said, but I didn't want to. I'd never seen anything like it. So many living, breathing people unable to move even though they so desperately wanted to. It was mesmerizing.

Of course, around the back of the truck were even more frozen people, six or seven more easily: some lying down on their sides in the half snow on the ground. There was even a kid inside the truck, holding one of the back doors open and trying to punch with the other fist.

By the time Jimmy grabbed me and walked us out of there, I was completely lost in awe and half-frozen myself. All I could do was look behind me at all the figures, twisted and stuck into the weird cold shapes of fighting, like action figures on a kid's playroom carpet, lying around a truck that still had its engine running: expelling enough exhaust into the narrow, high-walled loading bay to create an eerie gray smoke around the bodies.

We just did myths in my English class. That feeling I had must've been close to what that one hero felt in Medusa's lair. Everything just being stone, and having a terrible feeling, and I didn't know what was worse: the fact that Jimmy could do something that mind-blowing, that he had that much power, or that I had no idea what Ridley was going to do when he found out. I had the distinct feeling that the Gorgon was lurking somewhere and I knew I wasn't going to be the one to cut off its head.

BACK AT HOME, I could hear the ball game on in the living room before I even unlocked the front door. It was a good sign. Once inside, I made sure to shut the door quickly to keep the heat in, and spun around to find Remo watching the ball game with Dad. No Melinda, thank god. I had an ill feeling she might've been at the house waiting for us, shrugged it off.

"Yo!" I screamed it more than I said it, because I still couldn't believe it. I was so excited. "You should've seen this kid fight!"

Both Remo and Dad looked real interested all of a sudden. It was nice and warm inside so I knew Remo must've turned on the oven a while ago.

"I didn't fight," Jimmy said. That was his story and he was sticking to it.

"What?" I didn't even turn away from my audience. "Hey, he temporarily paralyzed the shit out of at least twenty dudes!"

"Only fourteen," Jimmy said.

"Yeah, outside, plus three inside, that's seventeen. I have no idea how he did it so fast!"

I must've stumbled a little on my own because Remo got up real quick and sat me down on the couch.

"Where'd you get hit?" he asked.

I pointed to my leg and also to my lower back, right on my hip. Dad looked back to the television. It was nothing he hadn't seen before. There'd been much worse. Some bloodstains we couldn't ever get out of the carpet.

"Well, no puncture wound and I can't see anything yet but my guess is you got a nasty bone bruise on that hip. How'd you say you did it?" Remo tugged my shirt back down to its original position after testing the skin underneath a crashing tattooed wave.

"Got flung over a big-ass metal table."

"Yeah, well, you probably hit the corner of it. Ice, ice, ice," he said as he got up and took the trays out of the freezer, grabbed a small plastic bag from underneath the sink, and filled it up with the hard cold stuff, then handed it to me.

"Why do I need that when I can just sit outside?" I asked.

Remo handed the ice bag to me, then pried my mouth open to look at the hole where my tooth had been. Out of the corner of my eye, I saw Jimmy slip into the kitchen and fill the empty trays with water then put them in the freezer. He must've been hungry because he opened the fridge door next. Seeing the light on his face (not too different from the cloudy white day outside, the fluorescence on his nose and forehead, his dry hair), I realized something that caught my breath up in my throat.

He hadn't even broken a sweat the whole time.

WEDNES-DAY MORNING

I'D FALLEN ASLEEP IN FRONT OF THE TV THE NIGHT BEFORE and my ice melted and leaked all over the couch. Woke up around three and tried to avoid the wetness by moving to my bed, but Jimmy was there. I didn't blame him. He still wasn't ready for Cue's room. I wasn't either. So I went back to the couch and tried to soak the water up with a dish towel but basically, it didn't work and I had to sleep with my knees in a wet spot. I tried a bunch of different positions but the couch was too thin and the wetness was unavoidable.

I got up early and took a shower before anyone else in the house woke. Steam took over the mirror and the frosted window before I turned the fan on. It was the only way to heat up the room. Every irrational cell in me wanted to ambush Melinda with a shovel when she showed up at the house in a few hours. But we had to play along like we didn't know the scene in the cafeteria kitchen was an ambush.

Now it was everyone's problem because Jimmy was back. Whether he'd acknowledge it to himself or not, he fought. Would it take much more to bring out the dragon? I straddled the lip of the tub and stepped into the shower. Maybe Melinda was just trying to get rid of me, but why? She'd need me around to survive Ridley's onslaught. Hot water made my hip feel worse. My knee was still pretty stiff too. Thankfully my face was getting better, but I still had trouble chewing thanks to the hole in my gums and my jaw made a new weird popping sound when I moved it up and down. I been hit there a ton of times and it never made that sound before. Great.

After I was dressed, I took Dad his meds and I was real surprised to see him awake, sitting up in bed, and reading a magazine.

"Um, what's up, Dad?" I asked, real calm.

Actually, it kind of freaked me out. I mean, I'd read somewhere that once someone decides to die, they get all peaceful and act different and then the next day, or whenever they decide to do it, they're gone. No hesitation.

"I talked to Remo," he said.

Dad pushed himself toward me and stuck his hand out for the meds. Yeah, maybe he was a bit of an addict, but it was better than him being in withdrawal over the last day or so.

"Yeah? So he just came by out of nowhere?" I asked. I had to give it to Remo. The guy was pretty much the best friend I had in the world right then, helping to take some of the weight off.

"Yeah, he just came by. We talked. I don't know. Figured I was being more of a burden as I was, with the crying and everything. It'll still be tough but I still got some gas left in the tank."

"What'd you talk about?" I was genuinely interested. There was absolutely nothing I could think of that would cause such a change, apart from the suicide thing.

"His mother, but mostly he listened while I talked," Dad said.

Well, maybe Remo talked about what it was like to be a prisoner in your own head. How his mom started over from almost zero every five to eight minutes. Maybe Dad realized he didn't quite have it so bad. He could still think. He was still pretty much himself. And though I thought all those things while I checked his back for evidence of his bedsores getting worse, "Oh," was all I said.

"Yup, I'm going to start painting again, *mi angelita*. Remo's coming by today with some new oils for me and he said he might even be able to snag some canvases too."

I WAS STILL in a state of semi-shock when I walked out the front door with Jimmy, hearing Dad's words echoing inside my head. He hadn't done any painting since Mom died and that was over three years ago.

"Jen!" It was Melinda, but her voice sounded far away. "Jen!"

"What?" I asked, and probably at exactly the right time too, because she looked like she was about to start shaking me. Or worse. And if she'd done that then I wouldn't've been responsible for what I did to her. The hand on my shoulder was Jimmy's and he looked a little concerned.

"What the fuck happened yesterday? There're stories going around already." Melinda was pissed off.

I nodded to Mark and Rico at their usual places behind her, but that just made Melinda worse. Her whole face and neck were going red, and maybe she would've hit me if the cops hadn't driven by right then. Real slow, measuring us up. Of course, they had to know something was going down soon.

When they'd left, Melinda said, "I'm only going to ask you one more time—"

I interrupted her, "I don't know what Ridley's planning but we're in trouble. He sent a huge shipment yesterday, just a little later than he thought he would. I guess he was trying to avoid paying the cops their share. Maybe that's why they're on patrol today. Sending a message."

Melinda nodded a "get on with it" type of nod. She was still red and not wearing a hat either. Steam was coming off the top of her head and pushing up into the air. It was freezing out. She probably ran all the way to my front yard.

"I heard him say that there wouldn't be any Grand Championships, that they were going to take care of us before then."

Melinda's face changed when I said it. Couldn't've been a full second, but she was more than surprised. See, the thing that tipped me off was she didn't ask why not. She didn't make me talk more about it. She just turned inward for a second like she was checking it against something she already knew. I'd known her long enough to know that it wasn't her usual run-of-the-mill surprised reaction.

"What else happened?" She was seriously wigging out.

"We got spotted. We had to fight our way out." I said it flat, didn't even look at her when the words came out, just started walking. Everyone kept up.

"So I heard. Supposedly it was a fucking wax museum in there." Melinda looked at Jimmy but something wasn't right with her.

"He didn't fight," I said. I knew Jimmy was going to say it anyway. Denial, justification, whatever. At that point, I really didn't care what he told himself. We made it out of there without a trip to the hospital.

"Well, *you* didn't do it." She was still breathing hard as she walked. I'd be real tempted to say that she had run all the way to my house after all.

"Anything else?"

"That's it," I said.

When he got to school the aura around Jimmy had been magnified by a factor of a thousand. Everyone got out of our way. Some even half ran. I heard later that there were disturbances in his classes because plenty of kids refused to sit next to him. Hadn't they heard? He was *el Diablo*. It was official. Jimmy Chang = Satan.

Of course, I didn't make it to my first class of the day. Mock was standing outside the door to civics.

"Let's go," was all he said.

"Is Ridley gonna rig up my civics grade too? Can't get a good one if I never get to class." Sometimes I just can't help myself. Bad hip or no bad hip, I could take Mock. He was tall but he was weak. I was taken to Ridley's office. That's right. He actually had an office: an old portable classroom, basically an RV with no wheels dropped out in the parking lot between the tennis courts and the gym. The school stopped using them a few years ago when the student population took a dive, so Ridley moved in. No one complained.

"Melinda sold you out, Miss Jen. She didn't even think twice about it. She agreed to join me if I fulfilled a few requests of hers." Ridley was sitting down at his desk when I entered. The floor sounded hollow under my footsteps as I moved to the chair opposite him. The whole place had the odor of wet cardboard.

"How was my acting though, pretty good? I've been practicing with Freddy. But you knew that. I told you while you were hiding in the pantry." He looked at me and I was sure that he had no soul in there. The eyes were just foam-filled holes painted like pupils.

"You know what the problem is?" he asked.

"Not exactly." I shifted in the small seat so that I could put my leg out and take some pressure off my hip.

"The problem isn't that Freddy is a bad actor, because he's a great actor. See, the problem isn't with him, it's with us, or, at least, people like us. Normal kinds of people. We only see him as 'retarded,' and as nothing else. Did you know he's written fourteen plays?"

I wasn't really supposed to respond to that.

"Well, he has. We'll be staging one next summer with a mixed company. It's going to be great. It's a murder mystery called *The*—"

"I'm not getting this," I said.

Ridley inhaled, manipulating the silence. Outside, a gust of wind skirted the building and rattled the thin walls.

"See, Jen, I don't think anyone sees your potential. You're female. You come from a bad background. You're a half-breed. You're poor. You live in a shitbox and make ends meet with a little over nothing. You take care of your dad and your cousin, not to mention yourself. I know your circumstances and I admire that you pull through so commendably.

"But you haven't been given any chances to succeed because people aren't seeing you. They don't see you for the same reasons that they don't see Freddy as a person. They only see his condition. My point is this: Don't you think it's time you got a chance like real people get, like all the rich kids on the north side get? A good education? Training in the arts and sports? An opportunity to travel and see the world? I could make it happen for you, Jen. You're not just a fighter. You're so much more than that."

My face was rock. Strike one for him on the "you're female" bit. A seething strike two for calling me a "half-breed," followed by a quick strike three for calling our home a "shitbox." Yeah, it needed the gas back on but it wasn't that bad. As for his supposed act of charity, it didn't matter. He was already out.

"When you first got here you were ranked two up from the bottom, did you know that? If it wasn't for your brother you would've been gone in the first couple of weeks. Part of the yearly flies," Ridley said, leaning back 'til his chair squeaked.

Kung Fu had the highest dropout rate in the state, about 20 percent, maybe higher. Those are the flies. Every year it happens at the same time pretty much, just after the freshman kick-in. Usually a few mothers squawk to the administration, to the cops, anyone really, about the beating their kids took but nobody ever listens. The cops write stuff down. They say they'll pass it on to their superiors, but they don't. That's just a show. The community is pretty much used to it. The silent acceptance took over long ago. That was just how it was.

"I thought for sure you'd be gone after that first real beating you took. Slipping away from the first one, only to get much worse the second time, huh, Jen? You were the damn skinniest girl that whole year, the skinniest girl I'd seen in a year or two, but you came back. You took a few more beatings and you kept coming back.

"Damn. You're in the top twenty-five now, you know that? All in a little over a year. I've never seen anything like it. Guess I shouldn't have been surprised though. Cue probably beat you harder than anybody here, just so you'd make it." He looked at me right then, to see if it was true. I didn't move, didn't blink when he leaned forward and put both hands flat on the desk, oozing out two sweaty prints of palm skin onto the coffee-colored wood.

He'd never know and I'd never tell him. He'd only ever have a real good idea, but yes, it was true. Aside from the broken leg, I got all the highlights to prove it: over eighty stitches total, torn muscles, plenty of fractures, shoulders that had tasted a dislocation each, ball-and-socket joints like cracked-tooth mouths with the tongue pulled out and put back in all nice, and a back-alley corneal surgery on my left eye. Got an infection from it too, but I was real lucky. No long-term damage. That was how we met Remo. He fixed it as best he could and we went back to him ever since.

"You're the toughest fighter here. I don't know, I guess it reminds me of me. *You* remind me of me. It wasn't easy getting started. I had to keep coming back too. Even after I got run over. Even after I got stabbed. Yep, shot too." As he rubbed his shoulder, he spoke with all the pride of the survivor of an airplane crash that killed everyone else. "There's a rumor going around that you have a tattoo, a big one, on your back. I want to see it. I want to see your scars too, Jen. Something tells me they're a lot like mine."

He had this look on his face that gave me the oil-slick feeling again. Like an ooze of petroleum got poured down the back of my shirt while he was sizing me up with a look that said he'd most likely put scars on my insides if I ever let him that close. Well, I knew rumors too. The one about how he liked scars way too much, a fetish or something. Or the one about how he cut himself, ritually. Even cut up his girlfriends, not to hurt supposedly, just to bleed. It's called blood play or something. Yeah right, "play." Probably he drank some too. And who'd ever know if he got too carried away? No one'd ever find a body. Plenty of girls had disappeared before. Remembering what his chunky naked skin looked like underneath those polo shirts, I knew in my twisted-over gut that they weren't just rumors. It was all true.

I was seriously going to lose it if he kept looking at me that way. Like his eyes were a little too big for the sockets. Like there wasn't enough pain and shit in the world, like there weren't enough people looking to cut him, that he had to cut himself too. Not me. I was just trying to stay *intacto*. My stomach was moving up now, wrestling with my lungs. Sick bastard, he sure knew how to make a girl feel special. Across the desk from me, the intake of breath was audible, just below a whine as Ridley pushed his glasses up and spun his loose platinum watch toward me on his wrist, out of habit.

"So how did her face look when you told her there weren't going to be any Grand Championships?" Ridley got up from his chair and walked to the window. He probably saw it in a movie. Nobody really did that crap. But he was a damn good manipulator. I had to give it to him. I never knew where he was going next. I thought I did, then he was off in another direction.

"Come on, I know you noticed. You're too smart not to. Your mind started asking questions the second you saw her veneer drop. The second you repeated my words to her. And as smart as Melinda is, that passion for winning is a serious weakness. It blinds her. It was so easy for me to promise that she'd win the GCs in a weak field. No Karl, no Jimmy. She'd waltz it. Right?"

Damn, a sham win in the Grand Championships was enough to sell us down the river? For less than one second, I wished that Cue was still around.

"See, Cue isn't around to win them anymore."

Jesus, was he reading my mind?

"There aren't going to be any more GCs. There will never be another tournament again. They've served their purpose and now it's time for the families to pack in, get a little smaller. Besides, it's my gift to you, to Cue's memory, that he be the last ever Grand Champion."

Patronizing fuck.

"It's inevitable, Jen. I will win. Join me and I'll take care of Melinda and let Jimmy leave to wherever Jimmy wants to leave to, but he can't stay here, and you know that." Ridley seemed to be implying that he would take care of me in Jimmy's absence. "Think about it, get back to me."

Of course, the bastard thought it was a business deal. He was still trying to push me into corners. Flattering me about rankings. Giving me choices and taking them away. He knew I couldn't take that deal. Not with Jimmy gone. Besides, the second I let my guard down, Ridley'd pull the strings and send Jimmy to the morgue. But you know what the worst part in the whole thing was? I actually thought about his offer. I actually thought about going to Europe, about leaving Kung Fu for good on Ridley's dime. Going somewhere I'd have to learn a new language just to get by. Even if it was as a project, a pet. I hated myself for even thinking it.

Mock pushed me down the steps and went back in, locking the door behind him. And in a day that could only get worse, there was a note on my locker when I got back to the main building. It said to report to Dermoody's office as soon as possible. I should've given it to Melinda to deal with, seeing as she was my family Mom now and it was her job to handle that stuff, but I decided not to; whether Ridley was right or not, I still wasn't 100 percent sure I could trust her.

Besides, something was odd about the note. It looked different from any note I'd ever gotten before. It was yellow, not pink, and the handwriting was all different, in blue ink, not black. I wondered, did Dermoody actually write it his own self? And if so, why? Curiosity may have killed that cat, but I had to go. As I saw it, the chances of me getting in a worse squeeze than I was already in were pretty damn low. I mean, I might as well include all the major players while I was at it. Maybe it'd give me something to work with: play them against each other. Keep 'em honest. So that was how I broke the biggest unwritten rule around when I took the long walk to the principal's office at the end of the main hall. It wasn't nicknamed "The Pit" for nothing.

DERMOODY BLUES

DENIZEN OF "THE PIT." DECORATED VETERAN. THE WHOLE of Kung Fu knew about Lt. Col. (Ret.) Clarence W. Dermoody. He'd styled himself as the model of the rough-and-tumble high school principal, righting the sinking ship of a troubled learning institution. Two tours in Vietnam. Everyone knew that Dermoody saved Cap'n Joe's life when they were both serving there. Saved him from some kind of ambush in the jungle. Supposedly it was an amazing story, but I wouldn't know. I never really listened when people told it. I was always more interested in the present. In the last year or so, Dermoody had been on the cover of plenty of magazines preaching his own specific brand of "tough-love education." He even trade-marked that term and sold a kit with a videotape in it of him just going off about how educators should handle themselves in tough environments. The man was vain.

His office got called "The Pit" because there was an exit door in his second-floor office that opened into an inaccessible hallway that led to the parking lot. So it was possible to enter from his secretary's office and not leave via the same door. You know, like you just fell in a pit. That was the primary reason no one ever answered notes from Dermoody, not voluntarily anyway. Everything went through the heads of the families. But I had a feeling that Dermoody was just sending out notes, then marking down who showed up to take care of it, slowly compiling lists just to see who was in whose family. It was only a matter of time before he used that information to his own advantage.

He couldn't turn us all in though. He needed us, well, certainly needed those families loyal to Ridley to keep pushing the product. He needed his 15 percent cut of the operation to finance his sizable gambling habit. Just seeing his face when the secretary opened the door let me know that he was ready for more than 15 percent. A lot more.

"How good of you to join us. I was sure you wouldn't come. In fact, I was just telling Joe that, wasn't I, Joe?" Dermoody was red. Bright red from a nasty sunburn, which meant that he was probably off in Barbados again, banking offshore money. His big plum of a nose was peeling too.

As a rule, it's best not to look at Dermoody, but to kind of bow your head instead. He loves that crap.

"Yessir." Cap'n Joe stood at attention on the back wall, right next to the American flag in its little brass holder.

"Don't sit, stand," Dermoody said.

I stopped midsit and stood up to the left of the chair. I was a puppet, being walked from one office to another while fixing to snip these strings. That was the game though and, for now, I had to keep playing. Two picture frames full of medals were hung on the wall about the same height as my eye level. It was obvious why he didn't want me to sit. Because this way, I was forced to see the "mystique" of the man. Face-to-face with the reflected light from the medals that made me squint. I was pretty sure one of Dermoody's desk lamps had been purposely angled to create that effect.

Next to the shiny brass lapel pins and pretty ribbons were pictures. Black-and-white mostly, there was one of Dermoody and Cap'n Joe together, both holding big guns and smiling like hunters, like kids. Even if it was from years and years ago, it was weird seeing them smile. I guess the photo was taken in Vietnam. In it, a pack of cigarettes was tucked underneath Dermoody's helmet, covering his left ear, but he wasn't smoking in the picture. He had a real deep voice, Dermoody did. It brought me back to the situation at hand.

"Ridley's gone soft," Dermoody said, and then exhaled like it was some huge revelation. "You know he just doesn't listen to me anymore, doesn't listen to good sound advice."

Joe put a hand on my shoulder. When I say put, it was more like slammed. I slipped to my knees on the floor. Of course, I hammed it up a little. Made it look like it hurt worse than it did. Still though, it was bad.

"Joe here tells me that you were a witness to a certain sack of Alfredo potatoes that needed to be buried in the garden. Now, how could that be? Ridley made sure to tell me that there was only one witness, this new friend of yours. What was his name, Joe?"

"Chang, sir."

Jimmy.

"Ah yes, Chang."

Why would Ridley protect me? Maybe he really did like me and it wasn't some kind of angle? Maybe he was running something on Dermoody as well? He had to be. Everything was an angle.

"You know the score, young lady. Technically, you shouldn't be here and neither should your friend. This is the time of year when we need more fertilizer than ever for our greenhouse."

Greenhouse? Fertilizer? He was just trying to scare me. The only good news was that if he meant to transfer me, he would've already done it. He wanted something or I wouldn't still be alive.

"Now the way I see it, he's scared, Ridley is. I mean, it used to be minimal and manageable with his affection for you but now, with that little stunt your friend pulled yesterday, well, I'd say he's real scared and prone to doing something rash any day now. See, it doesn't help that this stunt is damn near causing hysteria around here.

"Do you know that I've already had fifteen teachers telling me they had trouble keeping order because of it? And we both know that little Jimmy isn't even in fifteen classes. Such is the spillover effect. It's chaos, and I'll tell you what, we don't need chaos at King High School. We need order. We need rigidity for our wayward young minds."

Ridley didn't seem scared to me, but I wouldn't blame him if he was. Jimmy was the X factor, the only thing in all of Kung Fu that could keep it from spinning out of control or tear it all apart before anyone was ready to make a move.

"Yes sir, that sure was a real neat trick though. For my part, I can't understand how he did it, but more than that, I don't care. What I see is potential, and potential is such an important thing, young lady."

Uh-oh. Here it comes.

"But see, we can be friends here. Ridley's getting much too big for his britches and he's slipping. Everyone here at King would be so much better off if he wasn't running those despicable drugs through here." Dermoody took a sip from his big gray mug that said "Principal of the Year" on it. "Ah, that's good coffee, Joe."

I had a pretty good idea what he meant by that. Goodbye days of the 15 percent cut, hello everything.

"If Ridley had an accident and you and your friend didn't, well, I think neither one of you would need to go to class anymore. I could arrange a pass on your high school equivalency tests and you'd never have to fight for your survival again. No more circles, no more 'rolling' as you kids call it. Sound pretty tempting? You could just disappear into the hills and never come back." He licked his lips. "You could be free."

With that, Cap'n Joe let go of my shoulder and opened the door behind me. The door to the secretary's office, thank god. I got up, dusted myself off, and walked out. Probably the only thing that made the ordeal worthwhile was the look of surprise on the secretary's face as I walked out that way. Apparently she hadn't figured me for using her door twice. I moved past her, swung the outer office door open so hard it banged against the wall, and ducked out.

Everybody was still in class, so I walked the vacant halls solo. Needed to think. Dermoody wanted me to look at the carrot on the stick and not the person holding the pole that dangled the damn thing in front of me. Even if Jimmy and I survived a showdown with Ridley, Dermoody would transfer us permanently. He'd do what any good prince would do. Take power and clear out everyone who had anything to do with the taking of it. We'd seen Ridley kill 'Fredo and I'd seen Cap'n Joe doing his DBD thing for Dermoody. So even if Ridley didn't care, I was still a witness, and still too dangerous to keep around. The Ridleys and Dermoodys of Kung Fu certainly didn't get to where they were by leaving people behind to rat on them.

Maybe everyone was right, or at least half-right. Ridley wanted Jimmy dead, Melinda out of the way, and me for himself. Melinda wanted survival, Jimmy for herself, and me out of the way? Hard to tell. Then again, Ridley would never let that happen because Jimmy was too much of a threat; that still wouldn't've stopped him from agreeing to it. And yet that meant Dermoody was probably right too, Ridley was slipping in even wanting to keep me alive, and they were both scared by the threat that Jimmy posed, especially now. Slipping or not, the scariest thing about Ridley was that he was invisible. That he could still do anything without needing to make a big show of it. He was as dangerous as ever, maybe even more so. And yeah, Dermoody was still scared of him. Otherwise he wouldn't hide in his office all day.

It was enough to give me a headache. I slowed my steps, checked the hall clock. Second period wasn't over for another three minutes yet. So it was just little old me in the hallway in front of my locker, bending down, checking to make sure the scuff marks on my boots hadn't gotten any bigger. Kung Fu wasn't such a bad place when it was empty. I twisted the lock set into the flimsy metal, put in the combination, and pulled the handle when it clicked. I opened it damn sure the only thing I could count on was that the showdown was coming and whether it really was the Friday after next, or sooner, it was unavoidable.

WEDNES-DAY AFTER-NOON

TO TOP OFF YET ANOTHER GREAT DAY, I GOT CALLED OUT on the afternoon circle. I was the first one. It was Merrick again, still a Hunter, now a new Blade. He was ready to make his name and get his revenge, not just for 'Fredo but for Karl. So I was an easy enough target.

"You gonna do this?" It was Jimmy. Everywhere else in the quad was absolutely packed with people, but there was a six-foot radius of emptiness around him. Kids just backed up when he got near.

"Got to," I said.

My hip was better but still numb, then again, maybe that was to my advantage. Knee stiff enough that my left leg kicks wouldn't have much power. What was really bothering me was the hole I had in my jaw where my tooth used to be. I should've rinsed more. Ah well, I'd do it when I got home. I tucked my flannel in, tied my hair back even tighter, and wrapped my wrists and hands. One of the freshman Wolves was my cornerman and he helped with everything. Double-checked that my laces were tied and tucked in. That was always a sucker's way to go out, tripping over your own laces. I stretched real quick and did two simple breathing exercises to get the blood up. Merrick was already waiting.

When I took my first step in, it started. Of course, it took Merrick all of two seconds to break the rules. He pulled two fleshhook kinfés on me when he spun out of the corner. Everyone in the quad went: "Kooori, kooori," real loud, all at the same time. Typical shout. Birdcalls meant danger, as if I hadn't seen them. Probably the tradition was stolen from some movie about gangs or something. Roll over it. Dress it up. Put a flag in it.

See, the whole crowd knew weapons were illegal in a normal roll but at Kung Fu, we didn't have referees, so the fight went on but the stakes got higher. If he won, he'd be punished; if I won and chose not to end him, he was in trouble with his own family. I switched my forward-facing stance to lateral and winked at Jimmy. Just so he knew I had this taken care of and didn't need him to come rushing in and paralyzing this guy before I could finish him.

"You're gonna bleed, bitch," Merrick said, then spat on the ground in the grand tradition of 'Fredo. The crowd hissed. I let them. I had no words for him. I told myself that this guy, this boy, right here in front of me took my brother away. I saw red then, but a controlled red. A background-type of red that only fueled the right strikes and didn't push me into unnecessary action. I'd like to say I was going to take it easy on him until that came out of his mouth, but I wasn't. He was going to get his anyway for taking my big brother from me. For being party to it. I tasted Cue's blood on my tongue sharper than it'd ever been, more bitter.

See, Merrick had one weakness, and it was a really big one. His first attack with a kinfé was always a lunge. Just looking at his stance and the semi-wild look in his eyes, I could tell it was coming. That was a downfall of fighting someone who used to be in your family. He moved toward me, real slow, then two quick steps, quick, quick, then slow. We were dancing as the circle screamed for us to come together, to draw blood. The wind blew his flannel open. He really should've taken it off or tied it down. It also threw his hair into his face so he had to push it back and I feinted like I was going to take advantage of his stupidity in not being ready and he backed up and looked clumsy. That got some laughs.

After that, I couldn't hear the crowd anymore, couldn't smell the factories. Only tasted Cue's blood in my mouth. Like it was fresh and still liquid. Merrick circled. I kicked out at him with my left foot to keep him on his toes. And he looked perplexed but not for long, see, once he'd gauged me, gauged the distance between us and where he thought I'd block to, he faked like he was going to rear back and instead, just shot his right hand in, blade aiming for my belly button. A toothy grimace played on his face as he lunged. He didn't even know what was coming.

I turned my body sideways, one foot directly behind the other, to get as skinny as I could as the kinfé slid right past me like I was a matador. The kinfé cut a rough arc right through the plaid of my billowing flannel. Merrick ducked his head as I grabbed his right wrist and jammed my thumb into the topside of it, right on the joint, bringing all four fingers in on the underside, and bending his hand backward on itself as I used his own momentum to guide the kinfé and the hand attached to it away from me. I stepped to the side so I could bring it up hard behind his back.

Of course, as he was being turned he attempted an awkward stab across his body, at my ribs with his other hand, but I caught that one too and bent that wrist inward so that his arm stayed bent at the elbow and pulled tight across his body, while the wrist plus kinfé got stuck in his other armpit and cut the backside of his arm, right on the triceps. Flinching, he bit down hard in pain. But I was nowhere near done. I kicked in the backs of his knees, both at the same time, with my left foot just hard enough to get him to the pavement and then I switched my stance to my stronger right leg and kicked him in the jaw: once, twice, three times a lady, knocked him out then, felt his spine sag but I went through with a fourth on the bridge of his nose and a fifth that he caught with his eye orbit. When he slumped fully and awkwardly onto the concrete, it was done. There would be no more talk of retribution for Karl or 'Fredo. I took Merrick's flesh-hooks but not before wiping his blood off one of them on his shirt. They were mine then: spoils of victory and all that.

It was Melinda who looked the most impressed on our side of the circle and she even stopped talking to Jimmy about Hong Kong to offer her congratulations. Jesus, had everyone heard about HK but me?

"Well done, Tigress," she said. "Couldn't've done it better myself. Almost looked like he told you what he was going to do."

"Thanks," I said. Even though I didn't feel like saying anything to Melinda, I knew pretenses had to be upheld until I could figure out exactly what to do. "He did."

Melinda just laughed. Jimmy gave me another look. The kind that was disapproving and approving at the same time. Out of anyone, I wouldn't have to explain to Jimmy how someone could dictate their movements before doing them.

I dropped Merrick's kinfés in my backpack and threw my jacket on even though I was real warm already, but with the wind as it was, I knew I wouldn't stay that way for long. Caught sight of Bruiser Calderón and his purple-black raccoon eyes across the circle and he just nodded to me so I nodded back. Not a downward head tilt, an upward one.

"You coming?" I asked Jimmy. Melinda had her legs around him and she was making she-bear noises. To her, it must've looked playful. To everyone else, desperate. She was a good actress, pretending like she didn't know what I told her in the morning. Like she was care-free as usual, sitting there on one of those square concrete blocks.

"Yes," Jimmy said, and he attempted to step away from Melinda but she wouldn't let him go.

"Just try me and see," she said.

Well, Jimmy said, "Please."

But of course, Melinda said, "No, you have to free yourself."

So he did. Jimmy put his hands on her legs real gently then must've put his thumbs in the right spots because her legs opened right up like a clamshell and she got a look on her face like it hurt but she liked his show of force at the same time.

"See you tomorrow, Mister Man," was all she said. I didn't need to look in the direction of Mark's and Rico's sunglasses-covered eyes to know how they felt about the whole thing. Same as me probably.

The crowd backed up as Jimmy and I walked out; I can't say it was a bad feeling, that residual power rubbing off on me when I was near him, within his circumference. I looked up at the second-floor window. Ridley wasn't at his usual spot. Something was stirring. I didn't think about it too long though. I had to go ice my hip and find out if my dad was hanging from our living room ceiling.

FIXING THE BEDS

JIMMY AND I WERE ALMOST HOME, JUST CROSSING THE last street before mine, when a big chunk of sadness landed on my skull and soaked in. Like it dropped down out of the sky, a snowflake the size of Remo's car. I could see the house. I could see the street as I walked, lugging the thing inside me. Melting down to gelatin at the base of my skull and thickening, a memory tumor capable of affecting my breathing and heartbeat, shutting down systems on my brain stem with the spun-out truth I was intent on not thinking about: my brother was gone forever.

There were no cars. No kids out. I didn't see a single bird. Even though Jimmy was just behind me, crunching in the gritty, freezing slush still left on the side of the sanded road—the stuff pushed all the way to the rain gutters by passing car tires that hardened when it got to twilight—I wasn't all there. Still, I stepped and he stepped too. When boots landed in the grubby snow mush, they crunched. Water not yet frozen pushed away from our soles in thin, chocolate milk swirls. Shards of ice, with trapped pebbles and sand grains inside, broke and settled in the empty space of the uneven boot prints we left behind. The dirt would just have to wait for the melt before it was free. For those moments of walking in unison, it kind of felt like Jimmy was tagging along on this journey, like we were kids again, but then we were there too quickly, thirty feet from where it happened, moving closer in a gray daylight so different from that night, and I wasn't much more than a ghost skirting the ground beside him, carrying nothing.

It was the first time I'd actually looked at my neighborhood in I don't even know how long. Before, it was just something to pass through as quickly as possible: walking fast, always on high alert, watching my back and everyone else's, not concerned with the squat houses in seventeen different shades of brown, not a single one over a story tall. Most had cracked driveways. None had front porches. All had tin screen doors. All had chimneys but none worked. Only two trees grew, each in ill-defined yards for a whole block to share. No fences in those front yards. No grass. It used to be just those things—wood, brick, concrete—but now it was marked by something invisible. A place I had to pay respects. Soiled ground. Every house looked to me like it had moved a few inches closer to the edge of the cul-de-sac and huddled, or maybe each one had imploded a fraction of an inch, had constricted to its foundation a little, all with windows as eyes, sagged and sad. I was losing it. It was all in my head. Had to be.

Halting at where I thought the edge started, where asphalt met the slope of the curb, I was almost floating in the spot. The big spot. I purposely didn't look in its direction the last few days. Maybe that way, it wouldn't be any realer than it was. You know? If I didn't look, it wouldn't be there. Wouldn't be the rough size and shape of a kiddie pool and the color of squashed plum skin. The opposite of an ostrich, I'd kept my eyes buried up, on everything eye level and higher, away from the street. Maybe that's not such an opposite. The tumor was becoming a headache.

A late snowfall on Tuesday night had taken most of the big bloodstain with it. The last of Cue, for real. At that moment, I was kind of glad that the lazy cops hadn't bothered to clean it up. It'll snow, they must've told each other over one last cigarette before going home to their wives and lives. Only a vague circle remained visible on the blacktop, underneath the milky-clear slush layer. To someone else looking, it could've been anything. Old oil, maybe grease, an exploded carton of grape juice that fell from a ripped grocery bag. Somehow, it was comforting to see. Like he wasn't quite gone yet. Part of Cue was still there, preserved and frozen, under the tooth-width of ice.

Low and stupid and sentimental, gaining form, Ghost Jen evaporated and left me there to deal with what was left. I turned, feeling my soreness, the weight of my backpack, and fatigue. I'd gotten sloppy with the last kick to Merrick's face and I was pretty sure I jammed my right big toe. I always did that. It's never been the same since I broke it a year ago. Checked the mailbox even though I knew we didn't have any, but we did: a small manila envelope for Jimmy, from his mother. Weird that she'd write and not call. I handed him the letter and he put it in his pocket without opening it. My hand shook while unlocking the door.

First thing I noticed when it opened: the heat was on, and not from the oven because I couldn't smell casserole. Dad was in the living room, sitting down and leaning over an old easel on the portable table. With his back the way it was, he couldn't paint at an angle. It needed to be flat. He looked up and smiled at us, just a little one but I could see the vein in his neck move. It was the best sight I'd seen in a long time.

"Why's the heat on?" I put my bag down and moved in behind him to see what he was painting.

"Remo got it turned on. Said we were ruining the oven," Dad said.

He was laying down a real thin white line over a darker brown background: for my shirt. He was painting from a picture, an old family portrait that we had taken in some crappy studio at least five years ago. My hair was all frizzy and Cue's ears were too big because he hadn't grown into them yet. Mom wore her hair up and had taken her glasses off for the picture. You could see the double pressure marks from them on the sides of her nose. Dad was wearing a shirt that was too tight and he had huge sideburns but he looked strong, real strong. I hadn't seen the picture in years.

"Heat is heat, but he's right," I said. "Is that where you got the paints too?"

I couldn't believe Remo did it. If he got the gas on so fast, it meant he used a credit card or something.

"Yup, he was here on his lunch break." Dad put his tongue back in his mouth to say it, then stuck it out again, and leaned close to the canvas, putting the first brushstroke in on my nose.

"Make it good and crooked," I said.

There was a real big difference between my nose and Jen-the-ten-year-old's nose but sometimes when I look in the mirror, I can't remember what the old one looked like. It takes pictures to recall, but why bother? Paint that kid how I am now. I didn't tell Dad that, just left him to his painting, his re-remembering. Can't say I completely approved of the subject matter. Maybe a landscape would've been more relaxing or productive but I wasn't going to tell him what to paint. I wish I knew what Remo had said to him.

Unlaced my boot and slid it off to check my toe. It was definitely jammed so I clutched it between thumb and forefinger and corkscrewed it into the joint until it popped. Took me almost three minutes. The more times I hurt it, the longer it takes to get it back to working condition. Great. I'd probably get arthritis in that joint because of it. I checked my face in the mirror, washed, and got some bacitracin zinc on over the scabbing spots. Then I made sure to rinse my mouth with saltwater real well. At least the gums were trying to close the gap on the hole. That had to be good.

Just before Dad went to bed, and before I started icing my knee and hip, I had Jimmy help me move the new bedframe into Dad's room, the one Cue and I made, and removed the old one. It fell apart in our hands, which made it easier to carry out in pieces. I asked Jimmy if he was okay about moving into Cue's room and he said he was, which was great because I needed to sleep in my own bed again. The couch was messing up my back. Already I had a baseball-size knot where my neck met my shoulders. The tumor-headache was overwhelming that though.

Taking the last of Dad's bed outside and putting it with the other scrap wood, Jimmy opened his mouth.

"So what happens now?"

"We wait for everyone else to make their moves, and then we react," I said, dropping the last armful of wood onto the concrete edge of the back porch.

Jimmy just nodded, looking all kinds of serious. It was a relief that he didn't say that he wouldn't fight right then.

Needing that ice bad, I went back inside and closed the rolling patio door behind us. By the time I had a cold pack wrapped on my leg and one stuffed in the back of my waistband, I changed the subject. For some reason that look on his face made me think of the looks in the eyes of all those kids at school that made sure they were at least six feet away from him at all times. Some of them even ran when he was near.

"What's it like having people fuckin' terrified of you?"

"How do I feel about it? I don't."

Jimmy moved toward the hallway but stopped after he'd passed the couch.

"It used to worry me, in Hong Kong mostly. People would light incense and say prayers and stuff when I walked by so my 'evil spirit' wouldn't infect them or take their luck away. It was pretty crazy. I should've never gone back after that last World Championship. But what could I do? All my stuff was there." And he half laughed after he said it. That was the first time he'd laughed since Cue died. It made me feel a little better for having heard it, even if it was a kind of sad sound. Like giving up, or maybe surrendering to Fate. He disappeared into the bathroom and the door made a hollow bang against the frame behind him, not quite closing all the way.

I took the second shower of the night right after Jimmy, waded through his leftover steam to do it. I had homework to do but I didn't really feel like doing it anymore. What was the point? I just wanted to sleep in my bed. The headache was a fist just then. The tumor was a hard hand and closed fingers smashed into the disk-space between my neck and cranium. I couldn't deal with the pain anymore. I took one and a half pills of Vicodin and crashed in my own sheets, finally.

KNOCKING

THURSDAY WAS BAD. SEE, WHEN I WENT TO BED ON WEDnesday night, I had a lot of things in my head to discuss with Melinda. I just had no idea how to bring them up, where to lie, how to find out more than she wanted to give up. Yeah, she most likely sold us out. She definitely told Bruiser that somebody would be there like some twelve-year-old playing spy games in the front yard. And if Jimmy hadn't been there, I'd probably be done.

There was a part of me that still wanted to believe that we were on the same side as Melinda. But then I took that Vicodin and conked out, and in the morning, I took one more. A full pill, not just for my back and hip but for the tumor, for everything. That was what messed the whole day up. Messed me up anyway. One, I don't handle that stuff real well and two, fading out was definitely the worst thing I could've done when a giant hostile takeover of Kung Fu could happen at any moment.

In my gut, I didn't believe that Ridley would wait until the Friday after. He said it himself that he knew I was listening and that bastard was guaranteed to use the art of surprise. It was just his style. Shit, it wasn't like he didn't know where I lived. Anything could happen at any time, anywhere. That was his power and he exploited it. And I'd gone and taken too many painkillers and put myself in a real bad position. Stupid.

All I remember from the school day was the feeling of the hallways rushing past me like moving things, like twin subway trains passing a platform with velocity, in opposite directions. That and I was walking real slowly up the hall. Such an odd contrast, the train/walls flying past me so fast that I could feel the air on my face, while walking beyond slow in what felt like mud. It was possible that I'd been lost in the hallway all day, walking back and forth, I don't know. Somehow I made it back home, thanks to Jimmy. At least, that was the only way I could think of. I ended up in bed for a nap and didn't wake up until about ten at night when someone was banging on the front door.

"Is anyone else gonna get that?" I called out to a dark house but I got no answer. Dad was sleeping of course, but where was Jimmy?

I got up. Flicked on the light. I was still pretty much dressed so that was a relief.

BANG. BANG. BANG.

Well, anyone come to transfer me would at least've been more subtle. I actually thought that as I shuffled into the hall, straightened the leftover half of the busted woodcarving, the bridge and river, the sugar-cane-white/yellow core of the wood hiding underneath the stain, and unlocked the door without asking who it was. I swung it open and walked into the kitchen. Really, I needed a glass of water. Vikes gave me cottonmouth, bad. I just assumed it was Remo. It wasn't.

"Just what in the fuck was wrong with you today?" It was Melinda.

"Here to see Jimmy?"

For some reason, alarm bells weren't going off in my head that she'd paid me a visit so late at night.

"No, I came to see you." Melinda was confrontational and she had blood on her shirt. Great. Exactly what I needed with my head and half my body feeling like it'd been dipped in glaze and left to dry. If she wanted a fight, it'd be pretty one-sided.

"I took too much Viking," I said. "Want a glass of water?"

"No."

"So," I said after a long glug from a smudged glass, "if you're not here to see Jimmy what are you here for?"

"Rico's gone."

"Well, you ought to treat your dogs better then, feed them puppy chow instead of that store-brand shit."

She pushed a palm into her fist and cracked some knuckles.

"See, I asked some real hard questions around about why you guys had to fight your way out of that cafeteria kitchen. At first, I just assumed you messed up, got unlucky, I don't know, something, but then with the way Ridley's been acting, not even looking in on the rolls yesterday, I knew something was wrong."

The silence in the house was different now that the oven was off.

"You knew the whole time, didn't you? You knew someone set

you up and you just figured it was me, huh?" Melinda was pointing her finger at me. On any other day I probably would've broken it.

"Yeah, I figured it was you." No use lying to her now, although it probably wasn't the best time to cop to my meeting with Ridley, and what he'd said about her. That'd just bring up too many questions that didn't need to be answered with half a working brain. Besides, I knew she wasn't acting. Maybe it wasn't her that set us up.

She got close to my face. So close her hair brushed my droopy eyelid and made me blink her back.

"Fuck, Jen! How could you think I'd sell out like that? To Ridley? Jesus, what about Connie?"

"Who?" I asked, still not 100 percent awake or alert.

"Connie! My fucking sister, Jen! Or did you forget what Ridley did to her?"

Oh god. That one made me lose eye contact. I couldn't believe I'd forgotten that. Connie was Melinda's older sister and used to be an Aunt in the Wolves. She got a little too fond of Ridley's prime product. There were rumors. Like Connie sold her soul for that shit but Ridley only ever wanted her body. Like Connie was the first person he ever cut, how she gave him a taste for it, fostered him along, said she loved him, maybe she even liked it. Yeah, there were rumors, but the bottom line is still this: she took too much junk into her veins and she died. That was before Cue even went to Kung Fu. Blame it on the stress. Blame it on my jealousy of her and Jimmy. Blame it on a missing Cue. Blame it on my crazy dad. Blame it on anything. Still should've remembered. I couldn't even look at Melinda, hearing her breathing all heavy in front of me but still feeling so numb that her breath didn't register on my cheek nerves. I could smell blood though. I didn't want to know how it got in her mouth. I fully expected her to hit me.

"Good news for you, I did find out who it was, who sold you out, and you know, I had every intention of keeping it low profile, changing this person's mind, and using their information to our advantage against Ridley, but"—she opened the door and went outside, when she came back five seconds later, she was dragging a very bloody Rico onto the tiles of my hallway and closed the door on his foot—"I got a little carried away."

"Fuck! Is he did?"

"No, he's still breathing."

"Are you gonna transfer him? Here?"

"Nope." She kicked him. "We're going to clean him up and drop him on his mama's doorstep and ring the bell."

"*We?* Aw hell no! *You* need to be doing it, you started it!"

Really, I was sorry and all but she was asking for too much.

"And you're gonna help for not trusting me!"

Shit. It'd been a long time since I'd seen someone so thoroughly beaten, just picked apart. Ten times worse than what Karl did to Jimmy. I leaned in close to Rico. Even his ears were torn up. Eyes swollen to the size of small planets in orbit, the left was caved in at the browridge. His left nostril had been carved open, probably not intentionally, just with one of Melinda's rings. He was missing two teeth and he'd bitten part of his tongue off, the tip. Which probably meant he hadn't expected Melinda to hit him and his mouth was open so he bit down by reflex. There was a real bad cut on his scalp. He was breathing like he had more than one broken rib: short little wheezy gasps. I didn't want to look under his shirt to see more damage.

"I wouldn't know where to start on this kid," I said.

"Call your doctor friend up then, he can help."

But there was no need, because Remo and Jimmy walked in right then. Perfect timing. I found out later that Jimmy'd gotten Remo to come over and make sure I wasn't sick and after he figured I just needed some sleep, Remo invited Jimmy to his mom's for dinner because he had to cook for her anyway. Turned out I missed out on his only decent dish, *frijoles negros*. Damn.

"Oh, what the fuck is this? Now I gotta make house calls for randoms too? Sheyit." Remo dropped to his knees and checked Rico's pulse. "Help me get him into the bathroom!"

"Is this Rico?" Jimmy craned his neck sideways to get a better look before picking up the right leg. That's how torn up he was, the kid genuinely needed confirmation. I got his left leg. Remo had his left arm and Melinda grabbed his right.

"Yup, that's the motherfucker that sold you out to Ridley, right there. We in this together now."

Rico got put in the bathtub, mostly because it was the easiest thing to clean in the whole house. Jimmy swabbed the tile and the front step. Melinda and I helped Remo as best we could with his requests for gauze, disinfectant, soap, needles, surgical thread, benzo. Good news was we had a lot of that stuff in the house. I had to dip into Cue's old stash for some of it. Still though, it was a weird situation. A love-hate thing watching Melinda freak out about Rico's health after doing all the damage herself.

"TOMORROW," MELINDA SAID, "after school, we're taking it to Ridley before he has a chance to take it to us. I'll be here early. Be ready."

And with that, she dragged the stitched-up Rico out the door and pushed him into the flat bed of her dad's pickup truck. I had no doubts that the kid's mother was about to get the shock of her life.

It was probably the right idea. Attacking first before they could attack us. Ridley would probably be halfway ready for us though. I mean, he'd be bound to notice that something had happened to Rico. Guess I really didn't have time to think about why Rico sold us out when he was sitting there bleeding, but the more I thought about it through my mild haze, it made sense. Jealous of Jimmy for one, and for two, maybe he thought Melinda had gone soft. I don't know.

Maybe if I was in his position I would've done it too. The Wolves were going down sometime. And at the end, it was all about survival.

Jimmy wanted to talk but I told him to get some sleep instead. Remo had an early morning, so he took off without really saying goodbye. Dad must've taken his meds because he hadn't woken up through the whole thing. I was up for another hour after everyone left and Jimmy had a shower and turned in. Stretching, mostly. That, and trying to get the numbness out of me. Taking my own time in the cold of the backyard to loosen up my joints around the floating lack of feeling. Work a few combos anyway. Practice the Sand Witch and imagine Cue there to laugh at me. See him leaning up against the side of the house like he used to, always there to correct my posture, my form.

"Look here now," he would say, always sounding funny, the funny teacher. "You need to coil your leg sooner, start at the toes, then the ankle and flex all the way up your leg," and he would point with his fingers, "your calf, your knee, your quad, your ass." Then he'd poke me in my splenectomy scar, habit, and we'd both laugh, habit too.

"Now," he'd say, "try it again, and when you start that leg whip, really feel it. Feel the ground through your foot as you wind up, don't start by just flexing the quad and kicking, you'll hurt yourself. Keep your whole leg tight for the strike."

And you know, he was right.

STILL NUMBED UP

I COULDN'T TAKE A SHOWER. FOR SOME REASON, I JUST felt heavier when I got back in the house and brought the thick glass deck door to a shut kind of rest before popping the safety pole down to keep it closed. The heat leaned on me, a wounded family member, and I alone was carrying it. As a general rule, I never take drugs because they stay in my system so much longer than a normal person. Remo tried to explain it to me once but I wasn't listening. Something about metabolism, which was weird because mine's pretty high. I always figured if I had a high one it'd get the stuff out of me right away but that's just not the case apparently. Probably should have paid better attention.

It was all quiet inside. So much so I couldn't hear Dad snoring. I chalked it up to that same heat. Heat makes everything shush. That, or it was the Vicodin. The pills were still a massive coat over my entire body, pulled up over my head and zipped to the collar, the lining stuffed into my ears, mouth, and nostrils. No lights on at all. Dark in all corners, the living room no longer smelled of casserole. I wished the gas wasn't on so that I still had to run the oven 'til it croaked and stopped giving me warmth, the sound of a warped fan, and old smells that put my mom back in the present long enough for me to miss her and hate her all over again. She was gone and definitely not sleeping in the next room. Felt that.

So of course I bumped into the wall as I turned down the hallway. Didn't even feel it, just threw me off balance a little which produced a big lean into the last family portrait Dad ever painted. I was losing it. Needed to feel something, probably more psychological than anything. The wall held me up and the carpet made sure I didn't pitch over. Peeled my sweatshirt off once I got to the threshold of my room and bumped the door open with my nonhurt hip. Sheets pulled tight over my ribs and cocooning my chest, that was what I needed to feel.

But there was a person sitting on my bed, blocking me off from that cotton chrysalis I just had to have. It was Jimmy. I knew it. Didn't need to see him but the outline of his posture against the white wall told me that this was an Armageddon-type thing, a last-night-on-earth thing. A what-would-you-do-if-you-had-thirty-minutes-before-the-nuclear-bomb-got-plunked-down-on-your-head kind of thing and even given the scenario in fourth grade, not even knowing what it really was, everyone in my class agreed it was sex.

A whole mob of ten-year-olds had said the word like it had two *x*'s, then giggled excitedly. It was a word our parents would never let us say but we watched television. We knew the rule. If everything was going to blow up and be gone, you had to have sex with your last moments on the planet. You know, if you were going to die. So no, Jennifer, eating your favorite food was the wrong answer. It was the worst answer. The answer was sex. Everyone knew that! How could I not? What was I, retarded or something? A big fat moron? Because somehow I should've known that you had to have "it" to be human and no one wanted to miss out. If I didn't know that instantly then I was stupid. That was what my classmates said to me.

So my big fat moronic mouth wanted to say: Leave, Jimmy. Leave, flesh of my flesh, blood of my blood, skeleton in the marrow closet of my bone. Leave, you son of my blond mother's blond sister. Leave, my link of denied whiteness, because see, we're not white together. We're not cream together. We never shared that skin. So different, me, the half Latina and you, my cousin, all half Taiwanese. Like we each got ahold of the albatross and we're tugging the body but not rocking no boat, trying hard to break the wishbone inside by new rules: nobody wants more, we each want less. We each want the little part. We each want the smallest broken bit of forked connective tissue. So shatter that hollow density. Tear that too-white bird. Unfuse those clavicles, I say, pull. You can have your wish.

But it can't be like this Jimmy no middle name Chang. You know it and we've discussed it already, because what would my "no" mean if I went back on it? So get your near-to-naked ass out of my bed and stop looking so fine. Stop tempting me. You scare me good, and you probably know I got this strange thing inside of me, the not wanting to, but wanting something, but not being able to feel it, and I mostly don't know, just like always, so give me an excuse to kick you right out of here with my toothpick arms that feel like stripped timber logs piled up in a quickly clearing forest.

Instead, I just asked, "So, boy, what was Hong Kong like?"

And I went and sat down hard on the homemade bed right next to him, my knee pressing against his. The carpet had thrown me, the bed had caught me, held my weight up, and my skin felt nothing. The boards underneath the mattress didn't make a sound. They wouldn't tell.

"It wasn't really Hong Kong, that was just the nearest big city," he corrected me. "I just tell people that so they don't ask too many questions."

"Right, yeah, okay." My words were slowing down.

"It was exactly like home except bigger and with no . . ."

I could feel pressure as I let go of my lean and crumpled against him, my arms going tight to my body as he caught me, like a chicken's wings once it realizes it can't ever really take off and stay up in the air. That it's just fooling itself with all the flapping. If they ever do, realize that, I mean. Jesus, the Vicodin was still crawling around in my head too, all up in my brain. I wondered if the water I drank made the effects worse. Like if it got digested first or something but then I could only smell Jimmy's soap-clean skin on me. Mostly it was the scent of the generic crescent spring stuff that sat in the back corner of the shower that we all used and it just made me sad. It was too familiar. It was still the brand left over that Cue used to buy, what he used to smell like. Jimmy wasn't talking anymore though. He was lowering me, flat-backed, onto the mattress.

I didn't want to sniff soap anyway, never Cue soap then. I didn't mind the not talking but I wanted to smell the licorice I smelled before when Jimmy raised his body up from sleeping in my bed and I tended his wounds, his first real wounds, his broken cherry blood. That was us, together, that scent. I needed it again, to light my brain up somehow, to wake up my legs and spine gone heavy, to lift up my head gone soft to pillow, to turn the warning lights on inside as he leaned over me and rubbed my stomach in little too-close circles like I was some damn car and he was waxing me, grazing my pubic hair through my thin shirt on the rotating downward turn of each circle and then back up, onto my belly. He bent down to kiss me and got turned-cheek instead of mouth. That was for you, Mom.

"Is this okay?" Jimmy's words sounded far away.

I could feel the pressure of his weight pushing my intestines against my backbone, at least that was how I visualized it, already full inside. And I tried hard to imagine how it would feel, him touching me with vertical strokes better than his massage, his confident working of my tattoo. I'd seen his hands, those skinny fingers that looked like a secretary's—too damn soft—where even the calluses seemed like they'd been filed down and I wanted to remember how they felt. Not like a fighter at all, but like someone who types too much. Someone who'd never had a broken hand start to look like rotting fruit even when healed but nonetheless purplish on the edge of what was still considered the flat of the hand even if it was now normal for it to be more bent than a pot rim.

I felt his breath on my neck. He brought that small mouth of his to my ear.

"Is this okay, Jen?" He asked twice more. Didn't say my name the second time.

Maybe I just nodded.

Don't hurt me, Jimmy. Don't hurt me too bad. I've never been punched on the inside before and I need to walk tomorrow. I need to run. Those words didn't get to my mouth. They left my tongue well alone and just rebounded off the walls of my skull.

But none of it mattered because I would die tomorrow. Nobody would ever find out. I would die and I wouldn't tell. See, breathing was ease in his arms. Not easy, not easier. Just ease. No other word for it. My fingers twitched less, even when he pulled me over onto my side. His hands snuck behind me, spread over my tattoo, gripping at it and maybe even pinching but being frantic like someone so new and inept at putting a body together with another and I guess I felt a thin pity then, a see-through veil over my brain that covered my eyes from the inside, as he rolled me again to my back. I felt bad for him. How he was untouchable. How he'd never learned. How most women must've been afraid of him. Like maybe he would break them, even in his temple suburb of Hong Kong, I just knew he was the loneliest boy.

So would I actually be able to feel him inside or would it just be pressure? Would it feel like my fingers felt or just more strain, rounder, larger? And would he taste me? Maybe I wouldn't mind if he kissed me just afterward so I could taste too. How I tasted on him. Not like licorice at all. Probably like sweaty hidden skin I mostly wished wasn't there and clean teeth and tired tongue and of course it was pointless. I was numb inside too. I didn't bother moaning, didn't fake pleasure or pain I couldn't feel, didn't touch him more than to hold on, but that was all I needed then, to clutch our heat between us and grab him tight as I possibly could while knowing—just a deep-down, silent kind of knowing—that he'd never ask me to let go or loosen my grasp, wouldn't even twitch if it was too hard because there was no such thing. Jimmy could take my strongest grip and never, ever complain or wish it gone. He was a rock.

My view of the ceiling was part-covered by limp cords of damp-ish hair connected to the face in the dark, pressed firm to the crook of my neck. That was when I knew we were the two notorious puzzle pieces in the box that my mom always complained about. She had sworn always that in every puzzle there were two mismatched pieces that fit perfectly together even when they didn't make the bigger picture. They never made up a part of the mountains or the old, old train engine or whatever it was supposed to be, and that was confusing in the solving rhythm, made it slower, but the hooked peninsula of what looked like a turned-over leaf really did fit the receding grotto-shaped cutout of half a coal furnace and the spotty cardboard locked together even though the top pattern was all wrong and I felt so light-headed, so finally awake in a deadened body that I fully expected the walls of my room to take off on their subway rounds again, like they had at school, in streaking redbricked horizontal lines of very real velocity, leaving me here with him, to be slow. Too slow. One dragging foot in front of the other, going nowhere, for just one night.

THE FRIDAY OF ALL FRIDAYS

GETTING READY LIKE IT WAS MY LAST DAY ON EARTH: NO
Vicodin ever again, no real breakfast, just a protein shake, an old tuna sandwitch, crusty on its edges, and an extra long shower where I took about all the hot water. I wanted to wash everything twice. So I did. In between my toes, the back of my knees, I rubbed the skin raw with a balding washcloth and then worked in all the parts I

usually miss or just gloss over with a fluff of soap bubbles. I even cleaned behind my ears and inside them. I washed my hair three times but didn't bother with conditioner because it was just going to get frizzy anyway. Shaved my legs and armpits, didn't sweat my bikini line. Couldn't even look down there. Lower back and my shoulder blades and the arch of my neck too, they all got scoured, as best I could with my reach anyway. I popped a few pimples, one on my shoulder, two on my right cheek, but for the most part, took it real easy on my face and the wound on my jaw. Rinsed my mouth with saltwater real good three times.

I dried off every bit of me with a clean towel, a blue one that used to be Cue's and happened to be within reaching distance as I balanced on one leg on the bath mat. Almost scraped my wrist on the counter when I lost my balance but caught myself. Yeah, I was nervous. I had no idea what to expect. From school or from Jimmy. So I did my best to concentrate on the simple, small tasks at hand. Dried my face, chest, toes, legs, belly, arms, and ruffled up my hair helmet. Then I wrapped a towel around me and another around my hair and jumped the hallway carpet into my room and shut the door.

Waited fifteen minutes until the majority of skin was good and dry and then I put on lotion, with vitamins. I didn't do it enough. That was why my skin was so raw all the time. And also because I wore so many layers and never worried about sweating so long as I was protected. So this time I felt kind of greasy as I slipped my padded chonies plus specially made cup on. I didn't mess with T-shirts and went straight for the long-sleeved turtleneck with Kev protection all the way down the arms, front and back organ protection, and most important, plastic-molded throat protection. Leggings went on. I put a plastic kinfé in the sheath. I needed the lightest, most protective stuff I had. I grabbed all of it and even lined my khaks out with hard plastic shunts: over my kidneys, thighs, and calves then clipped the insides of my khaks to my leggings so that the weight of the shunts wouldn't get wild and bunch the fabric in the wrong places when I needed to kick. Two pairs of socks, then the boots. At about that point, I felt like I needed to throw up. Just nervousness really, about what was to come, not the previous night.

Flushed the toilet and part of my protein shake down with it, then proceeded to not put any books in my backpack. Not a single piece of paper or a pen either. The first thing that went in was a full water bottle. If I was going to have to roll anywhere near as much as I thought I would, I'd need that. Of course, when shit went down, I had no idea when I'd have a chance to drink it, but at least I had it. Next in was a pair of chuks wrapped up in a sweatshirt. Chuks = Nunchaku: two rounded pieces of wood about a foot long and connected with a thin rope. I didn't know them too well, but it extended my reach and that'd be huge when forced to fight in groups. In went a pared-down first-aid kit, stuffed to the zipper with extra gauze and duct tape. I zipped two plastic kinfés into the bottom pocket. In the same pocket, there was just enough room for a pair of hard industrial plastic knuckles, like brass knuckles but without the metal. They're just as hard and cause just as much damage, trust me. Left at the top was enough room for my lunch and a padded hat.

It crossed my mind that there could be a double funeral at my house soon. Cue was still in with the coroner for an autopsy, at least that's what the cops said. Fact was, they hadn't released his body to us yet. They were still looking for clues supposedly. They knew they'd never find the killer. Not even his body. By the time Cue's remains would be released to Dad, it was a distinct possibility that I might've already joined him. I dismissed that line of thinking though. It was just too damn depressing. To make it easier, I had to see Dad in our living room inside my head, leaning over his new painting and sticking his tongue out as he worked on Cue's shaved bald head with a light beige and highlights of white-wine white.

My stomach was going crazy when I walked out of my room but

I was ready as I ever could be. Looking into Cue's room, I saw Jimmy's naked back: shirtless, little curves of muscles curled underneath that skin. I don't remember what time he left my room, but there he was, kneeling on the matted carpet and meditating calmly like he'd had a full night's sleep. My first instinct was to turn away. Somehow that posture was barer than anything I'd seen the night before. But I wasn't thinking about it, purposely pushing it away, thinking of anything else really. Like, did I have everything? So I double-checked my pack again. If I could do it, meditate, I would've right then. Serious.

I poked my head into Dad's room, real glad to find him still sleeping. By the time I put his meds and glass of water next to his bed, my hair was dry enough to tie down. So I braided the bushy stuff hand over hand until it hung down the back of my neck in what must've looked like a tiny little rattail. I used a rubber band to finish it. I had thought about shaving it all but that would have given the game away. Everyone would've known today was the day.

"Remember that letter I got from my mom?" Jimmy was in the living room, putting his books in his bag. When you're that good then maybe it's worth it carrying books. I had totally forgotten about that letter. No change in his voice though. No fawning over me. No glance or two at my body. For a second, I wondered if it even happened, or maybe if I was that bad the night before, that hazy, that he just wanted to forget the whole thing?

"What about it?" It didn't feel like there was any blood in my face. I mean, rolling was one thing, but this was pretty much suicide. The only good thing about it was that it was on our own terms.

"Yeah, well, it was pretty emotional. She's all lonely and she freaked out when I told her about Cue. She wants me to come home."

His words made me even queasier than before. "So what happens now?"

"I'm not leaving you, Jenny."

Whew. I didn't want to care about Jimmy's misplaced ideas

about chivalry or even love at that point; I'd say I gave him a hug but I'm sure I just kind of fell on him. Where there was Jimmy, there was a chance.

"She said something else though, she said if it ever got down to it, that I should protect myself. She doesn't want her baby dead."

I could understand that. He smelled good through Cue's sweatshirt that was too big for him. And there was just something about his face that calmed me down. The look really. Like the fact that he couldn't lose was just big enough for me too.

BANG. BANG. BANG.

I pulled away from him and moved to open the front door.

"How many ex-Waves can we count on?" Melinda blurted as soon as I let her in. She hadn't calmed down from the moment she left eight hours before, I swear.

"How many Wolves can we count on?" I asked in return.

"No idea, rumors already going round that we're finished, that Rico turned maybe three or four hundred before I knew about it." She put her fists on her hips. "Jesus, it's good to see you, Jimmy. You may be our only hope."

The Jimmy I knew would've ducked his head at that and looked sheepish, like he wasn't comfortable with all that pressure, but he just nodded.

Our walk to school was the fastest of my life. I was on automatic pilot. Just following Jimmy and Melinda.

"Well, get the word around. Make sure that whoever's loyal is on the north side of the quad before circles," Melinda said. "I got to go find Mark. He'd better have good news."

All three of us broke in separate directions after the metal check and no one gave us a second look.

First period: I put the feelers out about what needed to be done after last bell then just tapped my foot too much the rest of the class. No Ridley of course. By second period everyone should've heard the message. If they were down, they'd be there. I spent most of the day staring at the clock and sizing people up. Seeing my exits and wondering what I would do if the fighting broke out at any moment.

Lunch was tense. Sure, people talked but there was some serious waiting hanging in the air. You could probably've grabbed it and pulled it down it was so thick. Fourth period, I just stared at the clock and let myself think about Jimmy, just for a second. I can't believe how stupid I was to let my guard slip like that and since I was on drugs was that like rape? It was really messing with my head and my stomach. Got called on twice and had to say, "I don't know," and get a disappointed look from the teacher. And somehow, I got out of there when the bell rang and kept my back to the wall as I made it to my next class. I didn't know how much longer I would last through the waiting. It was starting to hurt.

Well, when the bell came to start fifth period, I didn't need to wait anymore. I stood up from my desk because the bell was different. The teacher hadn't even showed up. Except for two Wolves and an ex-Wave, my entire class was Runners or Fists, fifteen on my initial count, and one kid got up and locked the door. The funny thing was, I just felt relief as I bent down to push the nails forward out of the soles of my boots and made sure to shrug my flannel to the ground while I was down there. Nice and slow. Then I reached for my bag.

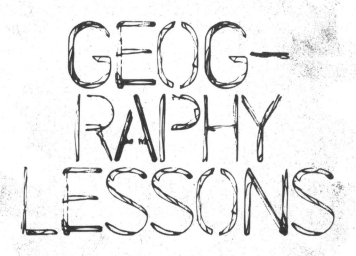

GEOG- RAPHY LESSONS

THE CLASSROOM I HAD FIFTH PERIOD GEOGRAPHY IN WAS no different from most at Kung Fu, except for one thing, it was a corner/end room. That meant it was obviously two things: on the end of the square building and in a corner, which also meant it was less accessible than most rooms, and harder to get out of. Two of the four walls were solid redbrick and one of 'em had a skinny window. Even though it was on the first floor, the main building was scrunched up against an excavated hill, so it was really a two-story drop to the ground below, but that assumed you could get out the window that was made of crisscrossing, steel-tinsel-reinforced glass in the first place. The other two walls were standard penny-pinching drywall and thin as saltine crackers.

In this particular classroom, the chalkboard was on the redbrick south wall. A corner triangle of it had been hacked off with a machete once, then stuck right back on with a couple of brackets. There were world maps attached to the top of the board and the room was the shape of a rectangle, about fifteen big paces from the north wall to the chalkboard and twenty-five paces from the whitewashed drywall to the west brick wall. Technically, not a whole lot of room to work in when there are twenty color-coded chairs with a right-handed arm desk attached. The biggest desk in the room was for the teacher, wooden and bolted to the floor right in front of the chalkboard and facing the students' desks.

I sat in the middle, just my luck. Worse luck for my Wolf friends, who were scrunched in the back corner, but probably even worse for the ex-Wave-now-Wolf who was near the door, and because of that, nearer to every single adversary. Perhaps the only good news for me was that the two Wolves in the corner were twin brothers and they were pretty good. Much better at fighting as a duo, but I had no idea how they were going to hold up against this many.

"Don't kill her!" the turncoat ex-Wave screamed. "She's Ridley's."

Great. Now I was property. A frigging Helen with no Troy, no walls either. And worse than that, the odds took a dive: 3 on 16.

In movie brawls, kind little bad guys wait their turn and come one by one, to get their asses kicked by the "overmatched" but noble and triumphant male hero. Fuck that. It sure as hell doesn't work that way at Kung Fu. Once the first move is made, kids organize themselves into small groups of three or four and surround on all sides if they have a clear path, kind of like animals that hunt in packs. Two sit back, kick you in vulnerable places when you're engaged in combat with one or two of the others, and if you slow down enough, you get jumped on: law of the jungle. Sloppy and frantic, hard breathing and ruthless, in close quarters the only rule of thumb was to never stop moving.

I weighed my options as they formed a quick perimeter and slowly closed in. One, escaping via the back window was out. Too thin to squeeze through, it would take way too long to break it out and then they'd be on me. Two, taking a hostage was definitely out, because no one would care if I shanked someone. There was not a single person in the room important enough to take because we were all sophomores, plus one or two freshmen. Three, I could reach the light switch and hope for confusion, but that wasn't a possibility because it was next to the door, the only exit, anchored firmly in the east drywall. Besides, the darkness would've been negligible, not even worth it. Four, clear a space and get busy, when I'd drawn enough to me, track back, and hit that door fast. It looked like it was option four. Always remember: in group fighting situations, you must stay at least five moves ahead, that's critical. Use combos. Know what moves flow to what. Kick to throw, use your opponents' bodies and superior numbers against them. If you can't stay five moves ahead, I'm sorry, but consider yourself swarmed. Like hyenas on an antelope.

The twin Wolves glanced at me, sharing the same look in their green eyes, and we knew we were on the same page. I'd take the lead and they'd bring up the rear, taking people off my backside as quickly as possible. If they could.

The Fists grouped left and started clearing desks off to the side, stacking them, being slow, you know, letting the tension build. To the right were Runners. They were the first surge as they moved two at a time down the aisle to my left and straight down my aisle after sweeping past the teacher's desk. They had already divided me from the twins. I couldn't wait any longer.

While facing forward, I claimed the first move by kicking a desk into the waist of the advancing Runner to my left and he must not've expected it because he fell over it awkwardly and smacked himself bad on the tile and started bleeding. Lucky shot. No time to dwell though, another Runner took his place. I stomped on her toes as she scrambled over her bleeding family member and then brought my plastic-knuckled fist right through her glass jaw. She wasn't out, but she was malleable enough for me to snag by the collar and waist with both hands and hip-toss her toward the advancing Runners straight ahead of me. Her flying body took one out and impeded another, which bought me enough time to duck the fist coming at my head from behind. Go for the body, son, the head is too small a target sometimes. Staying low, I finished with a hard elbow to the unprotected urethral area right above the cup of my unlucky adversary and he dropped all his water right there and went down in a lump with possible internal bleeding. Three for me.

The twins' score: one. They'd gotten a Runner in a double headlock and somehow had cleared enough room to spin him and sling him at the oncoming others. Not the prettiest, but effective. They were getting closer to me, which was good and bad. The good: they could protect my back. The bad: I was running out of space and the Runners were creeping in along the north drywall, coming at me from three sides now.

One smarty kid tried to jump on a rickety desk and right before he settled his weight on it, I kicked it out from underneath him and as he fell in front of me, I smashed his skull with my plastic knuckles on the way down. He made a quick red spot on the floor. At that point, I kicked another desk toward the group coming toward me from the teacher's desk and I blocked a high kick from an overzealous Runner and absolutely smashed her in the solar plexus, so hard that she lost her breath as her lungs turned into a vacuum. I didn't even have to finish her off, just had to jump out of the way as her buddy smacked her in the throat while trying to hit me high.

What little air was left escaped from her like a punctured balloon. Like cutting the string with scissors but accidentally getting the tied-off rubber part too: she just crumbled. Her stunned buddy, on the other hand, caught the heel of my boot in his nose and I heard it burst, like a snapped carrot, as I was using my momentum to swing down low into a leg sweep and take out the guy behind me. Once he was on the ground, I punished him with a swift neck chop. I shouldn't've done it though because I was in a bad position. I was too low and the others were coming.

I looked up to see a knee coming down at face level. I put my arms up to block and started to get my momentum going forward to roll but it was the quick thinking of one of the twins to smack my attacker with a tipped-over desk right before he hit me. As it was, he just fell on me and I threw a quick triangle choke around his neck to put him out. At that point, I was hauled up to my feet by both twins to see the second wave coming at me, straight on. After five or six kids, I should've been dead tired. But adrenaline makes you do funny things, I could feel every muscle fiber in my body. So far so good though. Us: nine. Them: zero. Odds: 3 against 7. It was becoming doable.

THE SAND WITCH

THAT WAS PROBABLY THE WORST PART, I NOTICED THE ODDS shift and I got overconfident. So instead of sprinting up to the teacher's desk, which I had brief access to, I decided to cut behind the twins and take two quick leaps on the chair portions of the student desks but it didn't work out so good and I slipped right off the second one and fell hard on my elbow. Cue would've laughed at me, even harder at the fact that I would've broken the damn bone if it wasn't for the elbow cup in my turtleneck. But as it was, I was only in minor trouble when I went crashing to the floor and slid to the back wall, hitting the brick right next to the window. Again, thanks to my padding, the wall didn't take off a few layers of skin but a pushed-out, uneven brick caught me in the shoulder pretty good.

With a tomahawk kick coming straight down on me, I did all I could. I put up both forearms to block and thanked god for those shunts when it hurt minimally. I gave a solid kick to the standing leg of the tomahawk kicker and I felt his knee buckle so I slid forward to my left, bent my knee, and brought my right heel backward in a devastating crab kick that wiped out Señor Tomahawk. He hit his head hard on the brick wall behind me while falling forward. I had just enough time to pop up and jump over a desk to get more to the middle of the room but I caught a nasty kick in the ribs as I did it. It threw me off balance but I landed well.

The twins, however, were down and bloody. That meant it was just me left. Facing the door, I had two Fists coming from behind me and the other three coming straight at me. So I went sideways and hopped up on the teacher's desk. Another smart guy decided to push the desk as hard as he could and ram it against the wall, knocking me off. Which, in theory, would've been a great idea were the desk not bolted to the floor. He should've known that. Every bathroom in the school had no mirrors, no doors on the stalls, and when you went to use them, you had to bring your own toilet paper because the rolls always disappeared. Quite simply, everything truly worth taking was bolted to the floor at Kung Fu, even the bookcases, filing cabinets, and certain chairs.

Because of that little oversight, he merely smacked hard against it and caught my boot toe and all three nails in his mouth as a reward. His jaw collapsed like an empty tissue box and at least one of the nails drove into his tongue and under it, cutting into the sluglike soft tissue and lodging there. Fuck. It took a reflex effort from both of us to rip my boot free of his mouth and as he screamed bloody murder on his way to passing out, multiple fragments of mandible bone and shattered teeth fell clean out of his face and scattered across the floor. Following soon out of the newly vacated hole was a wad of greenish chewing gum—spearmint probably—riding a wave of clumpy blood, a barrel going over a waterfall. I jumped down from the desk, grabbed the rusted-but-still-rolling teacher's chair from underneath it, and slung the thing toward the exit door. It aced a big Fist right in the knees. I dodged laterally and a punch clipped the side of my head as I felt the hardness of the chalkboard rebound against my back.

And then I just reacted. Didn't even think about what I was doing, I just swept, got low, then jumped and followed through with a kick that had my whole soul behind it. And somehow, the Sand Witch connected. The kid I hit stuck flat to the floor like they were made for each other. I didn't know how it worked. I couldn't explain it and as I was trying to put it together in my mind, I shuddered hard and the room shuddered with me. Walls moved with my breathing. My ears popped. No. It couldn't be. I was good at this, shutting down, going to work, training my brain not to feel my own effort, my punches that immobilized and chipped chunks off my knuckles, split them wide open, snapped the odd carpal bone as the collision instantly transferred its force through bone, joint, muscle, and tendon, like a tornado spiraling all the way up my arm, through my shoulder only to blow itself out in my chest, the kicks that cracked bones, jammed my toes, strained tired muscles, twisted my ligaments into obscene shapes, flimsy paper things that threatened to tear at any time. I couldn't start feeling now. I wasn't at home. It wasn't dark. I wasn't safe.

Worse was I could see Cue in my mind's eye, smiling at how I did the Sand Witch, did it right and didn't fall or hurt myself too badly and then the thought slapped me: I was in the corrupted temple. I was the little girl in our made-up story. The one the Sand Witch thought was a boy but didn't eat when she found out the truth. I was the spared one.

Through the blanket-thick blur across my vision I didn't see the last few faces, only their awkward splashes of movement, like they were underwater with me. Like we all fell in a pool. So I just followed through, powered by every last decent memory I had of Cue. Powered by all my fear that I'd be left in the corrupted temple, all alone. Everyone else would either be eaten or far away. Couldn't smell or hear, could only taste Cue's old blood on the last buds on my tongue and it made me want to vomit, to get it outside of me. I could feel bile climbing up the vertical of my throat like it was a mountain slope and summitting, creeping into the back of my mouth, searching for daylight, and as repulsive as it was, that sticking stain, I didn't want it to go. I couldn't puke now. That salt-blood taste, I needed it. I hated it. It drove me. I didn't want it to leave. It was all I had left of him, the last of his life. I stood up.

Lucky for me too. Just in time to see the last Fist coming at me, I kicked her with a straight leg in the diaphragm and as she was doubling over, she caught my plastic-protected knee in her mouth. She spit chunks of teeth onto the tile and they sounded like rolling toy cars beneath her feet as she stumbled forward, looking like she was about to come up for more so I stomped on her fingers and whacked her in the side of the neck. She keeled. I wanted to kick her again but I didn't, better to save it.

I wasn't crying. Not real tears anyway. I wasn't thinking about what Jimmy and I did. No. Hard, I brushed at the water trickling down my cheeks with the coarse plastic knuckles. Dusted the shed shavings from blunt contact at the same time. Didn't mean to. But even good plastic wears like bad carpet, loses chunks along its edges with rough use, and in doing so I accidentally mixed a wet, anonymous smear of blood on my cheek like an artist's palette, like Dad's palette? I confirmed it. The tears were real, but not attached to anything. Crocodile tears, the kind the sharp-toothed reptile cries when it eats its prey, when it's swallowing. Yeah, that was it. They weren't for Cue. They weren't for Jimmy. They weren't for me. Couldn't be. Not now. The more I breathed, leaning over my knees, the more the room came into focus. Now was not the time to lose it. I had to survive.

Two opponents left, had to be, but they were nowhere to be found. The door was unlocked and open. They must've run. And that was a huge relief, because I was so sore I didn't think I could throw another decent punch for a month, my muscles were aching so bad but my adrenaline was still flowing, just had to channel it in the right direction, away from Cue, no more memories, only toward the present, to the sounds of chaos in the hall: hoarse, raging voices, metal slamming down on metal or wood or tile or wall, screaming reverberations of fighting, glass breaking, even one-note laughter. It seemed like all of Kung Fu was rolling at once, every single room in every single building. What was left of the Wolves was getting wiped out. Melinda? I had no idea where she was, in the main building somewhere. I had to get to Jimmy. Had to think. Fifth period was his gym. Shit. That meant this little girl had to use whatever was left in her, to fly.

GETTING OUT

I WASN'T STUPID. RETRIEVING MY BACKPACK, I PULLED OUT the chuks and then strapped the pack on, good and tight. Prior to my exit, I dragged one of the smaller, unconscious Runners to the door and pushed her through the open portal only to watch her get kicked by phantom legs from both sides. I'd found my last two kids, and the looks on their faces were comical as they realized they'd kicked the wrong person, one of their own. I almost felt bad bringing the swinging nunchakus down on their nearly innocent faces. No I didn't. They fell like tipped-over cardboard cutouts.

The hallway was anarchy: I ran past a Wolf smashing a guy's head with an open locker door that was nearly off its hinges. Two Whips were dragging the body of a Wolf down the hallway to the bathroom. There was a fight in every room. Some doors open, some doors not. I didn't check them all, just ran the hallway gambit smacking anyone who looked at me funny. Had to find Jimmy. Had to get to the gym. And that was all the way across the quad and the possibilities of me getting there became a lot more remote the second I turned the corner and almost crashed headlong into a mob of Blades that shouted those oh-so-clichéd-but-terribly-true words in unison: "Get her!"

I didn't even hesitate. I turned right back around and took the nearest corner staircase, leaping the stairs three at a time as I dodged two kids getting tossed down. I wasn't seeing faces so much as I was seeing mannerisms, postures that indicated fighting styles, body movements that told me who was hostile and who was a friend. These weren't really nameless, faceless bad guys. These were kids I went to junior high school with. They all had their fucked-up stories, lives, hobbies, secret dreams, and families to go home to. They all wanted to survive just as much as I did. Too bad. I got no apologies. Emotions got attached to nothing, so long as I could keep it together. Because right then, it was merely cause and effect, only action and reaction. There was simply a running commentary of moves, counters, a flat description in my head. I couldn't handle anything else. By the time I reached the top of the stairs, pulling myself up on the railing, the only thing that mattered was an exit. It was time for the unexpected.

I banked right at the top of the stairs and found myself in front of the huge reinforced hallway window, maybe five feet by eight feet, that looked down on the cafeteria roof. I could hear fighting, but no one nearby. I slung the chuks at the glass: one, two, three, but they kept rebounding, only making tiny holes in the huge pane. I needed something bigger. Twisting the chuks onto the hammer loop of my khaks, I broke the glass for the fire extinguisher behind me on the wall and hoisted the heavy thing above my head and brought it down as hard as I could on the holes I already made.

I got maybe six good shots in before the first of the mob came up the stairs and they briefly pulled left like they were all one body, one big amoeba, before they saw me at the window. The first Blade forward tried to yell something but the poor guy caught the bouncing extinguisher knee-high and toppled with a torn patella just as I backed up as far as I could for a six-step running start into a jump kick, Bruce Lee–style, straight-legged, whole body forward. I put all my one hundred and thirty-five pounds into that kick. There was no way in hell I could've broken that window if it was any other school, but the sheet of glass gave and my relief turned to immediate fear as the whole thing flopped out into the air in front of me like a hinged Japanese screen doing its best impersonation of a paper airplane. Never let anyone tell you that falling is like flying. It isn't. Falling is like fuckin' falling and the landing is the worst. I came down on the cafeteria roof relatively flat-footed and far enough from the window to be safe. I rolled well, but some cracked triangles of glass embedded themselves in my neck, scalp, and probably my back along the way.

A little dazed and reflexively picking the glass from my neck, ear, and head, I thanked the school board for cheap workmanship on the buildings. That is, until I saw the first guy from the mob jumping down onto the cafeteria roof behind me. As it was, I was about twenty-six feet off the ground and I hadn't thought much beyond taking a running leap at the flagpole about five feet into the quad from the cafeteria entrance. So that's what I did. I just jumped, again.

I missed the pole but caught the metal rope for the flag in my hands somehow and rode it all the way down to the bottom, banging my head and hips on the pole because of my momentum, cutting my hands so deeply I could see metacarpals peeking through chunks of ragged redness. Skin and fat torn up and clumped together like overdone pasta, the tiny spirally kind, lay heaped on the tendons that ran down to my fingertips. I used to have palms. That burn of lost flesh was by far the worst burn I ever experienced. The worst pain I ever experienced period, worse than getting stabbed. Only good news was the guy behind me on the roof decided it wasn't worth it to make the jump and he was trying to scramble back into the window hole as the rest of the mob took off down the stairs after me.

I had maybe thirty seconds to pull off my plastic knuckles for slightly better flex in my fingers, claw open my backpack, and wrap loose, ugly bunches of gauze around my hands, and then finish with the most inexpert duct taping ever. I couldn't tell you how I was able to tape both hands into fists in under twenty-five seconds. Everyone tells me it's impossible, and I agree with them, but that doesn't change the fact that it happened. I was in shock, dragging my backpack behind me by my elbow and running toward the gym entrance before the mob came out of the main building behind me.

By the time I pulled myself through the front entrance to the gym building, the one with eight doors that opened onto a raised floor that held the remnants of the past, the old school treasures, Jimmy was right in front of me: fighting in the entryway. He was using the stuffed cougar mascot's outstretched paw to defend himself. The trophy case had been shattered and one kid was already laid out on the ground in front of Jimmy, bloody-headed, with a guilty-looking trophy nearby, dented and red.

JIMMY, A.K.A. GYMKATA FOR REAL

WHAT I FOUND OUT LATER: THERE WAS METHOD TO RID-
ley's madness. See, we're not allowed to wear street clothes to our gym
classes. The gym building is actually connected to the main building
by the cafeteria extension, which snuggled up to the indoor swimming pool. And fifth period was Jimmy's gym class, so he went to the
locker room and put his gym clothes on. No weapons, no protection,

just Jimmy in a pair of school-issued red shorts, a yellow T-shirt that said MLKHS in red above the face of a roaring cougar, and some socks and athletic shoes, white ones. Probably not the best idea to leave his protective gear behind but he did what he was told and followed the coach and the rest of the twenty-five kids in the class up to the second-floor landing and into the gymnastics/weight room.

The coach pushed open the big wooden double doors and led everyone onto the blue gymnastics flooring as the different-sounding bell went off, and the idiot must not have known what it meant because he just kept on with class, saying something like:

"Alright, y'all got your circuit training forms, now I want those filled out before the end of the period, and Drew, Peter, and Billy, y'all better actually do the exercises this time. I'll be watching ya."

It was only Jimmy's second time in the combined gymnastics/weight-lifting room: L-shaped and large, it was yet another cost-cutting measure of the school district administration, severing what used to be a large rectangular room meant for only one thing, gymnastics, into three pieces and making it multiuse by bricking off a quarter of it for a wrestling room that was padded on every wall with the school colors and had a big red wrestling mat doubling as the floor. It had no windows. That was the county's money at work.

Right next to the wrestling room was the weight room, the skinny bottom part of the L, occupying the other quarter of the rectangle but it didn't have a wall between it and the gymnastics equipment. The uneven bars were right next to the leg press sled. The only border that separated them was the color of the carpet. Weight-lifting room: maroon pile. Nearly every piece of equipment was for free weights, bench press, leg curl, and shoulder press. Each little metal skeleton lined up along the wall except for the far one, which was full of mirrors and hand weights on metal shelves.

On the far side of the gymnastics room, in the corner, was a climbing rope only accessible by the giant pad in place for the vault and springboard. In front of that was the runway. Stretched out along the wall, next to the uneven bars, stood the balance beam. It was all too close together.

Normally, every class started with stretching. Everybody got in a circle and the coach would tell them what to do. But that didn't happen.

"Alright, y'all, circle up. Stretch it on down now," he said, and looked at his clipboard, shook each leg like he was about to start running, and then rolled his head on his neck and popped a new piece of gum in his mouth.

Jimmy was the only one who sat down. He knew that wasn't good. He didn't need to look up and survey the eyes of his class-mates. He just pulled his right shoe off, then the sock.

"What the hell? All y'all need to sit your asses down or we'll be running laps." He was starting to get mad. Coach was like, "Lots and lots of laps."

Three Whips and a Blade shut the big double doors and locked them by driving a metal rod from the shoulder press, which was conveniently lying next to the wall, down through the horizontal push bars. As it was, no one could pull them open from outside. Jimmy had his other shoe off, the sock too, and he was still sitting. The rest of the class moved behind Jimmy, blocking off the exit through the weight room.

"That's twenty laps right there, boys! Want more? Fifty! I can't wait to see ya puke. Whew, I didn't think y'all were that stupid. Be-sides, I got the keys." And the rest of his talk was really to himself as he turned his back on the doors. "Bunch of dumbasses, man, I don't know where they get this stuff . . ." The sound of a ten-pound iron weight on the back of a skull isn't the most pleasant noise in the world. When the coach hit the floor face-first and bounced one inch up off the cushioned mat before settling, it began.

Jimmy hopped to his feet as if on a wire, took one step back, and without even looking, grabbed the collar of the smallest kid in the whole class. He didn't strike the kid as the others gathered weapons: weights, bars, jump ropes. He just waited. The kid was so scared of Jimmy that he started to cry. Big, uncontrollable, where's-my-mommy tears and it wasn't long before the kid broke out in moans that came from the bottom of his lungs and sliced through the buzzing of the fluorescent lights high above them like double foghorns.

Fighting back didn't even occur to him, he was so terrified of Jimmy. He stood stock straight on his tiptoes and had his palms up in surrender. Just like a poisonous insect was on his neck, something that would sting if he moved, something he wasn't quick enough to take care of himself. This was psychological warfare. Jimmy turned three hundred and sixty degrees in a tight circle so that every class member in the room, even the stragglers trying to circle him, could see the urine soaking the smallest kid's thighs and look in his scrunched-up face as he pleaded to live. He had devolved to a six-year-old in Jimmy's grip and his noises were truly scaring everyone else, picking on the last nerve in all of them, but they had weapons. They had superior numbers. Most of them were high on at least one of Ridley's concoctions. They thought they had a chance.

It was no surprise that the biggest Runner brought his metal pole down hard on the face of the kid Jimmy had collared. Then he did it again. That shut him up. Crying wasn't aloud at Kung Fu. Never. Everyone indoctrinated into the school would've had no trouble with the punishment. If the kid wasn't helping to defeat Jimmy, he was only in the way. That was expected. What wasn't expected was Jimmy pushing the kid's body into the crowd and taking off on a diagonal across the room. He was running for the springboard before the kid's body settled on the floor next to the coach. The bright blue gymnastics flooring absorbed their blood like a hungry sponge, leaving only patches of purple-red behind.

PLAN B

THE QUICKEST KIDS TO REACT TO JIMMY'S SUDDEN SURGE
in movement were two Blades. One used his long strides to attempt
to intercept Jimmy before he hit the springboard, while the other
one brought up the rear in case Jimmy doubled back. But he didn't.
He kept on, full steam even when the long-legged Blade got to the

springboard before him and effectively blocked it with his body and swung his metal pole toward the blazing figure in front of him.

That didn't stop Jimmy though, he leaped a good four feet before the board, sprang off the wall to dodge the pole, and brought a high kick to the forehead of the long-legged Blade who tried to block it at the last second but was merely crushed by the force of Jimmy's velocity and fell backward right onto the springboard. But Jimmy didn't stop there, he cracked the Blade's head against the end of the board and kept his momentum going, jumping up over the pommel horse, into the air, and grabbing the rope. He swung into the wall, pushed off, and turned one hundred and eighty degrees to catch the other chasing Blade in the face with a heel and sent him sprawling. Landing hard, Jimmy changed direction and ran toward the uneven bars, while not a single one of the larger group realized that he was herding them.

I sometimes wondered what Jimmy was thinking then. If he was thinking of me, of anything, as he methodically disposed of the other members of his class. How much did he worry about disappearing as he balanced on the beam and used his adversaries' momentum against them, as he paralyzed Whip after Whip and Blade after Blade just before they brought a heavy metal object down on his wrist, hard against his hip or neck? I mean, it had to be there somewhere in the back of his head. Every time he pivoted too quickly, focused his mind too strongly on where he needed to be next, was he relieved when he turned and chopped someone down immediately after that, happy he was still there? Or without the benefit of something like television cameras to scrutinize and rewind his movements was he free to act as he normally would? Really, he hadn't even known that he'd disappeared before. It was only after, looking at the footage of the fight, that he got scared thinking about it, racking his brain about it, wondering how it ever happened, how it was even physically possible.

In the weight room, the two groups that had retreated from the fracas on the balance beam were emptying the weight holders and readying the circular discs to throw at Jimmy. The plan: get two people to go after Jimmy while the other six threw the weights at him and tried to slow him down. They expected him any second. But he didn't show. Any second. Still no Jimmy. It took a brave Whip to stick his head out around the corner and into the gymnastics room in the direction of the balance beam to confirm the truth: three bodies paralyzed standing up and all the rest on the ground, but the same Whip that peeked was confronted with an even worse sight—Jimmy from two feet away swinging hard and then there was blackness.

Jimmy dragged the Whip in front of him as a human shield and the unconscious body got pelted with twenty-five-pound weights as Jimmy slid under the leg press and out the other side. Springing forward from all fours, he rose high into the air and caught the chin-up bar—bolted to the wall above the bench-press benches— before shimmying across it like the nimblest of monkeys. He was headed toward the wrestling room, the unlocked door.

The weights came flying from the hands of all adversaries. Some hit high and left dents in the whitewashed brick wall, revealing the pale gray of the cinder block beneath, while others hit low and clanged off the weight-lifting machines like broken church bells. The rest, thrown like discuses, went awry and brought the huge panes of mirror crashing down on the next wall over. Not a single one hit Jimmy as he cruised through the air, landed, pivoted, and dispensed a high dragon kick to a Whip, pivoted, crushed his body low to the floor like a lizard, and swept through the doors to the weight room. Shutting them hard behind him, Jimmy could feel the clangs of weights against the doors through his arms, and the sounds of them echoed throughout the boxy wrestling room. His fingers found the latch and snapped it closed.

He'd just have to hurry out through the other double doors and into the hall, rush down the stairs, and make a beeline for the quad because maybe that was where I was. So it must've been disconcerting to turn away from the doors, just as the banging of the heaved weights was subsiding, to take a step forward and find that he was not alone in the cramped wrestling room. On the edge of the mat and its painted-on ring that separated the competition area from the out-of-bounds like a cutout piecrust, various weapon-wielding fighters stood at the ready. But now that Jimmy was standing there, feeling the warm smoothness of the plastic mat with the soles of his feet, it looked too much like an oversized target.

THE DUEL

MARIA R. WAS SITTING IN THE MIDDLE OF THE ROOM. MOM of the Fists. The most powerful fighter at Kung Fu. One well-placed shot from her could leave you needing plastic surgery. To welcome Jimmy, she stood up and unfolded her bulk from her sitting position. Not fat, strictly compact muscle built to destroy. The assortment of handpicked fighters was scattered about the room, five in all, plus

Maria, six. It was impossible to tell what families they were from. It seemed it no longer mattered. Ridley had consolidated his forces.

All the other fighters in the room must've thought the odds were fair, considering Jimmy's rep. They had tied black masks around their faces, like generic, bargain-basement ninjas. Jimmy didn't have to be told the rules. He'd fight Maria but no one would watch his back. Every single fighter had throwing weapons and he was the mark.

The room was hot. Like sweating hot. It was kept that way on purpose. Long ago, the wrestling coach had ordered no ventilation to the room so that it would encourage his athletes to perspire, making it easier for them to lose weight. For lighting, there were only three large, circular fluorescent lights above the mat. Each was covered with a metal exoskeleton to protect it from being broken by a projectile. They were probably castoffs from the gym lights though, built to withstand direct hits from basketballs and all manner of large objects.

Maria held out her palm to Jimmy, an indication to begin when he wished. With precisely the same movement that had snagged the scared kid earlier, Jimmy seized a fighter crouched four feet away from him and broke a wrist, an arm, and a shoulder for the trouble. The scream ended in the throat before it really got started but the glottal stop of a sound lingered in the padded, windowless room. The other fighters pushed their backs to the walls, rigidly shifting well out of his reach. Five Chinese throwing stars dropped to the mat from the worthless fist of the limp fighter and Jimmy grabbed two and slung them at the right and left lights, which shattered easily and went out, leaving only the single light in the middle and shrouding the outer rim of the mat, and all four walls, in complete darkness. Jimmy took one large step backward and disappeared from view.

Chinese stars and throwing kinfés flew wildly across the room, embedding themselves into the padded walls and the thin stretch of painted wall below the ceiling. One hit Maria in the arm. She shrugged it off. Something whizzed past her ear. Another hit her in the leg. She turned sideways. Something hit her stomach, probably bounced off. She didn't even think about it, nor did she look down. She was wearing armor, what was to fear? Besides, none of the thrown objects was intentional. But one by one, the limp bodies of fighters tumbled into the single light from the center as evidence: an outstretched hand, a wrapped-up head facedown, two feet, until there were none left. The only audible noises were the loose thuds of bodies collapsing upon the mat, unexpected exhales, and the occasional, harsh crack of bone.

Maria was doing her best not to look disturbed. After all, she trusted in her thick boots and armor. Jimmy was barefoot and in gym clothes. Advantage her, with all the broken bulb glass on the slippery plastic of the mat. Just as her eyes were nearly adjusted to the new low level of light, Jimmy stepped out from the darkness behind her, right in front of the exit doors. He pushed. They did not open. He pushed harder. Nothing happened.

Maria turned and smiled. She didn't need to angle her neck to the leftover light so that it would hit the key that dangled on a chain there. Like silver. Jimmy knew she had it. Removing a kinfé from his right forearm, he straightened his body, and tore one sleeve away from his T-shirt, using it to wrap over the wound, below the elbow, nice and tight. He dropped the kinfé, the one stained with his blood, onto the mat beside him, then nodded.

Maria rushed toward him, pushing the pace. She started with a jab that hit Jimmy's blocking forearm like a ton of bricks. He stumbled backward and quickly decided not to block with his hurt forearm. But Maria was on top of him, keeping her punches tight and not swinging wildly: a thundering hook to his body, a jab toward his jaw that caught his shoulder, an uppercut that caromed off his collarbone and just missed his chin. He slumped to all fours on the floor. She backed off, looking confident, not wanting to end it too early, still a bit afraid of his capabilities. Never had she thought it would be so easy.

"Get up!" she said, feeling the rush of power in beating up on an opponent that was supposedly superior.

"Get up!" She yelled it this time.

Jimmy was on his knees on the edge of the lit circle, holding himself up by his unwounded arm and crouching.

"Get up!"

Maria was becoming impatient. If he didn't get up, she'd hit him while he was down. She didn't care.

Slowly, Jimmy raised himself up to his full height. Even in the dim light, Maria could see the tremendous bloodstain spread across his chest, completely blotting out the red cougar on his yellow shirt. She hadn't hit him that hard, she thought. But Maria's pleasant feeling of surprise turned into a sinking thing, a lump in her throat dropping down to the growing burning in the lining of her stomach, for in his other hand, Jimmy dangled the key on its chain. Maria touched her neck for confirmation but she knew it was gone. She was feeling strangely light-headed. When she looked down, the sight of two kinfés sticking out of her stomach was not surprising. Though she did wonder, how did they go right through Kevlar and miss the trauma plate? Not that it mattered. In fact, it didn't even feel like her body as she fell to her knees then over onto her side, crushing her outline into the mat with a crinkly thump.

TROPHIES

LOOKING AT MARIA'S MOTIONLESS BODY, JIMMY SHOOK his head. He hadn't thrown the kinfés, but he'd pushed them in. It was his fault. She'd rushed him with those pointy things sticking out of her. All that armor must've dulled it at first. That, or made her feel impervious. He couldn't dwell on it though. He had to go or he'd be next. Unlocking the double doors, Jimmy kicked them open and threw a star above him to break the remaining light in the wrestling room.

More fighters were waiting outside when the double doors opened, but they didn't dare go into a dark room. Two got pushed forward by the others. To check it out. They caught stars in their ribs and turned screaming, showering the air with bloody droplets, just as Jimmy bounded out of the room like a free tiger. Staying low along the landing, he broke through the group and leaped off the balcony and high over the lobby. He landed atop the tallest trophy case, a huge oak thing that stood at least fifteen feet tall.

Balancing easily, he turned just in time to see one kid stupid enough to make the leap after him. Too bad the kid didn't jump far enough. Jimmy didn't even need to kick out at the poor bastard as he slid through the air and hit the hard tile with a sickening open fracture of a splat. He started moaning and Jimmy jumped down to the top of the soft-drink machine to the right of the trophy case and then shimmied over the stairway rail to the front of the gym lobby, the main entrance to the building.

Two kids coming in through the front doors took up fighting positions but that didn't distract Jimmy from the Blade behind him, jumping a high kick toward him off the top of the soft-drink machine. Poor timing really. Because Jimmy grabbed his leg in midair, ducked, and slung the Blade over his head like a bowling ball still in its handle bag right into the two kids near the door. Picked up a spare on the 3/10-pin combination.

No time to gloat though. Three Runners were almost on top of him. One kicked at Jimmy, missed, and ended up roundhousing the plate glass of the trophy case right out. The rectangular pane wobbled, then split in a huge V, the top half coming down like a guillotine, hitting the floor and spreading out in shards like a wave hitting the beach with mostly sea foam at high tide. Unbalanced by the force of the blow, the stuffed cougar mascot tumbled from its perch among the trophies and onto the floor. So Jimmy kicked it in the flank and it spun on the slick floor, sending chunks of glass skittering across the tile in the process. The still-sharp claws of the outstretched paw mauled one of the Runners in the leg. It stunned him just long enough that he wasn't able to block the trophy coming at him. He got clocked with a 1978 Division 4A Cross-Country Fields Cup trophy, at right about Lucerne in the countryside of Switzerland above his ear.

In my experience, the best way to take leg fighters is just to step up and use good old front-foot boxing on them. Get in tight, use solid body control and footwork, back off from the low kicks and push in when they kick high but watch out for the knockout blows. Of course, it helps when they're focused on Jimmy and don't see you coming so you bring down a vicious rabbit punch on two of them and they turn only to get kicked by Jimmy from behind.

See, I came from the quad side into the gym entrance. And I brought a whole army in behind me. We couldn't go back out those doors and we didn't need to speak. I led. We had to take the five stairs down and to the right, cut left around the drink machine, in front of the other huge oak trophy case and head for the indoor swimming pool because its chemical-soaked exit doors were the only things that connected the gym building to the main building. Then all we had to do was go through the cafeteria and make a decision, either back out into the quad, to the original meeting position about an hour too early, or up the stairs and into the classrooms. Either way, those were our only hopes of finding Melinda.

ANOTHER WAY

AS LUCK WOULD HAVE IT, OUR PATH TO THE SWIMMING pool side door was blocked by seven kids looting the concession stand. They'd already lifted five or six boxes of candy out from underneath the roll-down black metal security gate. Somehow, they'd managed to wedge it up and now the thinnest girl I'd ever seen was trying to push out a cylindrical container of soda, but it was stuck in the maw of that stingy gate. She must've been the only one tiny enough to squeeze through the hole and empty the concession stand from the inside. A bailing line of sorts had been formed and the kids would pass a box of candy from arm to arm like buckets of water before the last guy dumped the box into a big plastic trash can with no liner that was obviously meant to carry all the boxes together for a quick getaway.

Deer in headlights, that's how every single one of them looked when they saw me with my busted hands and Jimmy with his blood-spattered T-shirt, shorts, and bare, cut-up feet. Bound to happen, I guess. Rogues just trying to help themselves out, taking advantage of the chaos and not following the plan. Which would've been fine if not for the fact that they stopped midlooting, dropped boxes, and decided to roll on us. And with at least thirty guys immediately behind us, turning around wasn't an option. So I cut right, down the narrow hallway.

We'd get to the pool the back way, down the hall and out through the locker room. We'd have to. Contingency plans were running short and there were no more exits. I was already looking behind me when I flew around the corner, setting myself to slam the huge black door behind us so it would lock automatically and we could pick our way through the locker room carefully instead of having to sprint with more kids on our tail. Of course, I hadn't planned on catching a hard shot to the shoulder that spun me, sending me hard into the wall. I crumpled. Felt like someone had opened up my shoulder blade like a car's hood, stuffed a burning coal inside, then slammed it shut so I couldn't pull it out. It just smoldered.

It was Jimmy that shut the door instead. I heard the click as I pushed myself to my feet and saw Donnie K. standing there. Mr. Big Bad Runner flexing his shoulders, stretching his neck. Like he'd been waiting a real long time.

"Snuck up on me last time," he said, resetting his body from the vicious shot he just put on me. "Was long past time for a little JB on that ass."

Big Paybacks are called James Browns at Kung Fu, JBs for short. He must've meant to kick Jimmy, but one was just as good as the other to Donnie. Only problem was, he just made Jimmy mad. Usually, Mr. Humble Little Farm Boy respected his opponents. He honored them, did not humiliate them, never crushed them. But I could see it in his eyes when he put the soft edge of his hand on my arm and pushed me behind him: Donnie was going to get crushed. I felt a surge of cruel excitement that gave me goose bumps on the parts of my skin that weren't torn or bruised.

The banging sounds on the other side of the door had stopped and the hallway was dead quiet. That meant two things: the looters were probably back harvesting candy bars and the other thirty or so kids chasing us had split in two, fifteen to watch the door I was leaning against, while the other fifteen headed through the pool-side door and backtracked through the locker rooms to catch us in this very hallway. Whatever Jimmy was going to do, he needed to do it real fast.

"D'ya know that I couldn't even move my hands to eat until yesterday because of what ya did? I dare ya to fight me without that paralysis magic-trick shit." Donnie was wrecked out of his mind. He had to be. Nobody sane or sober would call out Jimmy Chang and expect to lead a normal life with a functioning body afterward. Donnie'd been lucky and he didn't even realize it. So Jimmy walked out to the middle of the hallway and Donnie backed off to the end, blocking our only exit: the boys' locker room.

THE JIB

THE OTHER THING THAT DONNIE DIDN'T REALIZE WAS THAT the extremely narrow hallway favored Jimmy because Donnie's leg-fighting style had much less room to maneuver. Should've picked a better venue. There'd be no roundhouses. No dragon kicks. Only straightforward stuff. But, although the hallway was narrow, it didn't feel cramped. The ceiling was real high, about twenty feet off the floor. The redbrick walls extended all the way to the top, pinching in along the white paneled ceiling.

It was Donnie that started it. Kicking furiously with high-low-high combos, he brought his kicks in faster than I've ever seen them: left, right, left, right, but every time he aimed for Jimmy and then slung a leg shot at him, Jimmy wasn't there. He'd already moved out of the way. The foot came left, Jimmy was right, the foot came right, Jimmy was left, every time. Jimmy didn't block a single kick. He didn't have to. Not a single one came close to hitting him.

Jimmy crossed his arms and leaned against the wall. Mimed a yawn. That just pissed Donnie off worse. He came even harder. He got up on his standing leg and continued with a flurry led by his right foot, as he hopped forward and unleashed a series of hard high kicks at Jimmy's head. But each time Donnie kicked, Jimmy would move his head just enough to avoid them, then he'd sneak in the quickest of movements, and pinch Donnie's calf hard. Like Mr. Miyagi catching flies with chopsticks.

I didn't even see them, just heard Donnie getting madder and more out of control, grunting and cussing, heard the strained movements of his clothing whipping about. So he kicked harder and each time he did, he got a pinch on the calf, a horse bite. He wasn't smart enough to realize that Jimmy was degrading his muscle strength, that eventually he wouldn't be able to lift his legs higher than his waist because of the bruising and blood rush. Like getting a real gradual dead leg instead of all at once.

By the time Donnie was breathing heavily, Jimmy had jumped a foot up the walls. He was spread-eagled across the narrowness of the hallway, holding himself up with an arm and leg each on the opposite walls. Donnie fell for the bait. He kicked the wall where Jimmy's right hand was, but Jimmy moved it up, so Donnie brought the same foot left but missed again, crashing his foot hard against the wall. When he saw he had no chance of catching one of Jimmy's hands,

Donnie kicked out at Jimmy's unprotected torso but Jimmy went from vertical to horizontal on the walls faster than I've ever seen a human being move, like he was defying gravity.

If I hadn't seen it with my own eyes, I would've sworn it was impossible the way he jumped and kicked his back legs out to new positions on the walls above, and his whole body was completely vertical, so that Donnie's foot flew past him by a few centimeters and I saw Jimmy's shorts ripple from the air created by the power of the kick. So stupid Donnie kept kicking. Back and forth like a pendulum at Jimmy's hands and feet, trying to bring him down, probably breaking his toes and mangling his heel but never once getting close. Jimmy just crab-walked up the walls, higher and higher until Donnie was jump kicking high above his head, missing all of Jimmy and getting slower and slower. If Jimmy was the fisherman, Donnie was the marlin and he'd fought his fight. He was done.

So, as amusing as it was to watch Jimmy utterly humiliate Donnie, I knew we didn't have much more time before fifteen guys streamed right through the locker room entrance and cluttered up all the fighting space in the hall like hair in a drain.

"Jimmy, we gots to go!" I yelled, and my words echoed off the high walls. Apparently, it was the only signal he needed.

Donnie was hunched over, hands on his knees and breathing too hard when Jimmy sucked his arms and legs in and collapsed into a freefall of easily ten feet. But just above Donnie's head, Jimmy brought his hands together and behind his own head in what we at Kung Fu would call a preacher's punch, dropped his legs to a more vertical position as he slammed both fists down onto the top of Donnie's back as one, not very hard because he was arching backward and bringing his legs back to horizontal, already a goddam one-hundred-eighty-degree turn in midair, just as Donnie felt the preacher punch and stood straight up.

Right then he caught the full force of Jimmy's uncoiling

double-legged kick right in the abdomen. The kick was straight up old-school kung fu. Aimed not at Donnie's body but three inches behind it, Jimmy finished the move clean through the ribs and then bounded off Donnie's body into a back handspring and landed easily on his feet. Donnie didn't have it so good. His broken body slid all the way down the hall, three feet, five, seven feet, nine, then slammed into the wall headfirst, cracking a bit of his skull off and leaving a nearly instant poodle-piss-size puddle of blood on the tile in front of the locker room door.

HALL BRAWL

IT WAS THE MOST BADASS MOVE I'D EVER SEEN IN MY LIFE.
I actually had to push my mouth closed with a duct-taped fist before wiping my own blood off my chin with a trailing sleeve.

"Let me see those hands," Jimmy said.

"We gots to go," I repeated.

"Not if you can't punch!"

He took my bleeding fists in his secretary hands and I couldn't look down at those trespassing fingers of his. He pulled a strand of tape up to see bone underneath and I was right back in the present.

"Agh! Don't take it off, just retape me. Harder!" I demanded.

He reached into my backpack and did them up quick, like fixing a leak on plumbing.

Perfect timing too, because a group of five Fists busted right through the locker room door, slamming it hard against the brick. The first one slipped on Donnie's blood, tripped over the prone body, and then face-planted on the wall. Hello, Mr. Concussion. The other four didn't bother picking their compatriot up. They just came toward us one at a time, making sure to hop the body and avoid the blood. There was no other way: the hall was too narrow.

Jimmy pushed my backpack up onto my back and pulled the drawstrings so that it stayed tight. Then he did the unexpected. He took one big step and jumped so high into the air that the first Fist had to look up to see the sole of Jimmy's bare foot coming down into his grill, and then Jimmy kept going, he actually "walked" on the heads of the Fists, jumping and kicking down hard on the crown of the second one, then to the third one, then to the last, before dropping down easily behind them all and blocking off an escape.

Dazed and caught in the middle of a two-pronged assault, the Fists caved: the one nearest to me was still grimacing in pain and bringing his hands to his face by reflex when I pulled his left shoulder hard toward me, bending him forward as I kneed him hard in the gut. Pulling my patella out of his midsection quickly, I extended my same leg backward in a V-shaped follow-through, just to make sure my heel smashed the space on his face that his hands had vacated when I kneed him. Then he got tossed to the side.

Jimmy had already finished off number three and number four, and number two couldn't decide whether to swing forward or backward so he displayed a little ingenuity when he kicked for me and then arched backward with a drunken-boxing-style punch toward Jimmy but there was only one problem: I caught his foot between my forearms and Jimmy caught his fist. We didn't let him squirm too long though. Jimmy did the honors with a perfectly swift elbow to the face. Goodbye, Mr. Torched Eye Socket.

I picked my way through the mess of contorted bodies like a football player running the tire drill, knees up. It was already starting to stink in that enclosed hallway, bad. Sometime between being kicked and hitting the wall, Donnie had lost all control of his bowels. He'd dropped his load right there in his pants. Either he was dead, or his body didn't know how to hang on anymore. The brain just lost contact with the large intestine, the sphincter. Sometimes systems screw up and evacuate. It happens.

I dodged Donnie and ended up stepping on Mr. Concussion on my way through the open door and into the gridded locker room. To my right was a wall with a mirror and a scale. To my left were three C-shaped banks of lockers with a bench in the middle. Beyond them and through a portico with two sinks in it was a shower room and to the right of that was the exit to the pool. I'd never been in the boys' locker room before. It was exactly the same as the girls': gray concrete walls, rusting steel lockers, and alternating blue/light blue/white/turquoise blocks of tiny tile on the floor.

"I saw your face, Jimmy." I lobbed my words over his shoulder as he ducked a nasty right hook from a female Blade that leaped out from the second bank of lockers.

Jimmy unloaded on her midsection. Five quick punches before she even knew what hit her, then he froze her. I saw the fingers of his right hand dig into her jacket above her heart and twist, almost like he was turning a doorknob while the left hand stabbed hard into a space near her stomach and did a similar movement rapid-fire to her neck. Must've been reflex. Her face even stayed the same. Just like all the others, a mixture of surprise and pain.

"What?" he asked while jumping to his right and avoiding a swinging kick from some red-haired kid. He brought his fist down hard on the outstretched leg and brought the kicker to her knees before finishing off her face with a kick of his own. I heard the kid's head make a dent in a locker and then the rattle of the reverberating latch.

"You liked it," I yelled while being pressed into my best Jackie Chan impersonation when a female Whip kicked past me and cornered me in the first locker bank. She jumped off the bench at me but I swung open the big locker and she didn't quite fall into it, more like smacked half her body on the corner of the open locker and bounced off.

Reeling, she backed up but threw a punch and I opened a locker right into her fist. DING. She kicked, but before she could extend, I opened a locker fast into her knee. PWONG. Damn, right on the grated top section. That had to hurt. I didn't wait for her to make another move. I ducked her awkward hook and drove my fist into her stomach then popped up and KO'd her on the cranium by swinging open a corner locker door right into her ear.

Nobody had locks on their lockers at Kung Fu. What was to steal? Athletic shorts masquerading as swim trunks? A moldy towel? Not even worth it. If anyone wore anything worth keeping they'd put it in a bag and set it on the wall alongside the pool to keep an eye on it during class.

"Liked what?" Jimmy asked. He was in front of me. That meant he'd cleared the room.

"Finishing Donnie," I said.

"Let's go," was his only response.

PLAYING POOL

THERE MUST'VE BEEN WATER OR SOME MIXTURE OF LEFT-over shampoo or soap on the shower room floor because it was slippery as hell. It was weird to watch Jimmy, by far the most coordinated person I knew, lose his balance while turning the corner and go into the tile face-first. He slid to the recessed drain along the shower wall before stopping.

"Fuck. Just smacked my chin." Jimmy got up all wobbly and curled his tongue over his teeth, behind his lower lip, and stuck his bleeding chin out at me. Like he had a chaw in.

His eyes were fine though. No concussion that I could tell, thank god.

"Jenny," he said. And the moment it came out of his mouth I fuckin' knew he was gonna say something stupid about last night, something gross. He felt vulnerable or open and he wasn't sure we'd both live, so he wanted to assure me that he really did love me and didn't want me to worry about him or maybe he'd go off about his dream of us going somewhere where no one knew we were cousins so we could live in happy-fun-love-land and—

"Don't," was all I could croak. Nobody needed his sentiment, me least of all.

"Thanks." That was all he said. Maybe he meant to say more, or wanted to say more, but he didn't.

So I forced my stored rebuttals to the back of my brain and I felt dumb as I kicked open the beat-up old door of the visiting coach's office. It'd been vacant for years because Kung Fu didn't exactly have a swim team. I pawed the dusty old first-aid kit off the wall shelf. Thankfully, the kit was still good. Jimmy opened it and I blotted him with an eye patch, then stuck it on good with both fists. I tried to help him duct tape it on because there was no med tape in the kit but I was worthless, my hands were still on fire and I couldn't use my fingers. So he used the office glass to see his reflection and tape lengthwise on the curve of his chin and then one from his voice box to the bottom of his mouth. They'd suck to pull off and it looked like a funny little patch of beard when he was finished.

Solid news though, there was a backboard just inside the office. A tall, flat piece of wood with ovular holes that could be used as handles or places for straps should the patient have a busted neck and need to be tied tight. Sometimes that happens in diving. You know, people smacking their heads on the board. Jimmy lifted it and I took it between my forearms and squeezed it hard, so that I had a real good grip on it.

"I've always wondered what it would feel like to hit someone as hard as I could," Jimmy said out of nowhere. "My whole life I've been holding back. I still haven't done it though. Hit someone with all of my strength."

Then what the fuck was that thing he just did to Donnie that threw him ten feet and broke his *cabeza*? Before I could even begin to fully contemplate his statement and its ill-timing, Jimmy threw open the door and pushed me hard in the back.

"Go!"

I had no choice. I was a reverse battering ram. Flexing my abs hard against the board, I powered out into the open pool area, pushing with all my Jimmy-fied feelings of confusion and hurt. The smell of chlorine took up residence in my nose right before I plowed into two waiting Runners and let go of the backboard. My momentum drove them into the pool with two wicked splashes.

I'd've laughed if I didn't have to dodge a ten-foot-long lifeguard hook getting stabbed at me. I yanked it right out of the guy's hands by wedging it underneath my arm against my body and then backhanded him with it. I spun and swept his legs before collaring him around the neck with the loop: him and the hook went right in the drink with a little push from Jimmy.

Then my forearm got grabbed and Jimmy dragged me around the far side of the pool, around the diving board, away from two Runners who slipped in the splashed water of the two I pushed in with the now-floating backboard and we took the stairs two at a time to the three sets of double doors that led to the cafeteria.

Jimmy busted through the fifth door from the right like a fuckin' locomotive and I was right behind him to slam the door shut when we were through. Now to find Melinda, I thought. But when I turned back to survey the cafeteria, I couldn't move. Jimmy was smothering me against the solid black doors with his body, holding me back with his arms and guiding me to the side. I soon saw why: Dermoody was holding a shotgun and keeping a group of six or eight Wolves at bay, including Melinda, while Cap'n Joe had Mark in a severe triangle choke near the cafeteria exit to the quad.

Melinda was screaming at Cap'n Joe not to do it, not to break Mark's neck, but it was too late as far as I could see. Cap'n Joe opened his arms and let Mark drop forward. He slid through the air like a crash-test dummy going out of a windshield in slow motion. His head was facing me and Jimmy but his body was facing Melinda. More than just about anything I've ever been sure of in this life, I was sure that Mark's open eyes didn't see us as he wrinkled up limp on the floor like a discarded T-shirt.

MELINDA, A.K.A. MISS CHEMISTRY

WHAT I LEARNED LATER: WHEN MELINDA GOT TO HER FIFTH- period science class, the Bunsen burners had already been set up but not plugged into the natural gas spigots sticking out from the huge two-inch-thick black tabletops that covered the locked beaker drawers and extended four inches up the walls. There were six big black tables in the room and four seats at every table. The countertops beneath the elevated cabinets on the walls were of the exact same material. No one knew exactly what they were made out of, just that you could do anything in the world to them and it wouldn't matter. Light some shit on fire? Sure, no difference. Wipe the ash off when you're done being a joker. Acid? Why not? Once it's neutralized with a base all that's left is a small circular stain. That's it. The stuff was basically indestructible.

Maybe they were going to make "snowflakes" that day, with alum, pipe cleaners, and string as a demonstration of crystal formation and precipitation. Mr. Wilkes loved that experiment. He called it one of his fun ones. Nearly sixty-six years young and with a big bushy gray beard, Wilkes was an institution at Kung Fu. He'd been teaching there since it was built. The guy was incorruptible too. Rumor had it that Ridley liked Wilkes so much that he tried to give him a ton of money to stop teaching so that he could go fish out the rest of his life at a stream somewhere but Wilkes said no flat-out and then tried to talk to Ridley about doing something good and decent with his life. See, Mr. Wilkes never wanted to see the bad in people, only the good. He had a way of looking at you, right down in you with his blue eyes and you'd just have to tell him the truth if he asked.

Yes, sir, that really was my blood on my homework but I did do all the calculations myself, sir. Wilkes and Dermoody were the only guys in all of Kung Fu that got called sir. Wilkes, for real, and Dermoody, because you didn't have a choice. You'd get a smack in the mouth if you weren't what he called respectful. The school board had a funny way of looking the other way. And who could blame them, really? Hard to tell what bruises were caused by Dermoody and what weren't. Not like they cared. If we hit each other then Dermoody could hit us, as long as we stayed in line enough that they didn't have to call in the National Guard.

So Wilkes was just Wilkes when he showed up for another day of doing the only job he ever loved. Scrubbed the tabletops down himself, then set out the lab notes next to the ring stands. He'd already unlocked and locked the big ingredient locker at the back of the classroom, the one that was opposite his gunmetal desk, and put out just the right amount of the stuff needed for the experiment. To the milliliter.

The kids would file in and he'd greet them all by name, ask them about their parents. Ask them about good things in their lives, then shut up and listen. Wilkes was the only one who ever listened and he'd always pull you aside at just the right time, when nobody else was around. He was like our only guidance counselor. The rest left three years ago after a big brawl in the guidance office. Supposedly they considered it an unsafe work environment and because they had a different union from the teachers, they could walk. Dermoody didn't care and neither did we. For him, it meant more budget money to switch to security. For us, it meant we didn't have to go to stupid meetings anymore.

But the kids came in and didn't want to answer questions. Ricky only mumbled when Mr. Wilkes asked about his mom being back home from the hospital. Cynthia couldn't look in Mr. Wilkes's face when he asked her about her club basketball team winning the weekend before and he heard she had six assists. Mironov pulled his hood up over his head when Mr. Wilkes asked how his driving license test went. Something was truly going down. He had felt it, but he was forced to believe it now. Wilkes recalled how he had brushed past the other teachers in the lounge before they could even tell him what was happening or that there was a signal to get out. He wouldn't do it, wouldn't get out, even if he had known. Everyone abandoned these kids. Not him.

Mr. Wilkes knew he was running out of time, never in his forty years of teaching had he felt such a chill in a room, so he started speaking before the bell rang, before all the students had come in: "I know you're all lonely, scared, hurt, and upset, but don't do this. Whatever it is, we can get through it." Mr. Wilkes's chin was wagging as he said the words and his beard shook like a snow-covered Christmas tree getting sawed down as he leaned hard on his desk with his left hand so his old army watch pushed down on his wrist. It made extra wrinkles because it was too tight.

"Don't put your rage outside you, don't hurt others because you're hurting, you'll just end up alone. Trust me. It'll just be worse. Violence is never the answer to a problem. It just prolongs it, becomes a web, involves more people and hurts them too. Even ones you love, innocents. Please don't do this." Mr. Wilkes had to take his glasses off and wipe his face, because maybe he was crying.

Nobody'd ever seen Wilkes do that before. He knew the rules at Kung Fu better than anyone. He'd seen the families grow from nothing and then start shrinking. He'd seen the culture develop. And one of the reasons he stayed around and alive was because he never spoke out against them. Just treated the kids like individuals and tried to help them that way. He was still kind of shaking when he turned his back on the partial class and took up a piece of chalk to write on the board behind his desk.

Melinda came in halfway through his little speech but she felt like Mr. Wilkes was talking right to her. And of course she felt bad, a bit of shame that Mr. Wilkes had to break protocol and say that. He must've felt that something was going to happen, something that would change Kung Fu forever, and she hoped so. It was just the alone part that must've got to her. She had to think it weird that he didn't go off on a moral rant about how violence was bad. She knew he couldn't since he'd fought in a war and all.

She thought about how violence can teach powerful lessons: a smaller pain to avoid a larger pain. Like the time her mother hit her hand real hard when she was five years old reaching for the handle of a boiling pot. Right before she almost tipped it over on herself. But then Melinda became aware of the threat in the room as she was taking off her backpack at her stool on the far side of the first table to the left. And she wanted to respond to Mr. Wilkes, start a conversation about how sometimes people more powerful than you can make the decision for you. They can take it away. Impose it on you. And then all you can do is choose survival in the only way possible: to fight. Because it's that or die and might as well go down swinging, right?

Then the bell rang and it sounded funny to her ears because it wasn't the normal one and she looked up at the chalkboard, at the sappy-ass message that Mr. Wilkes wasn't done writing in gangly capital letters on the old ashy green background: VIOLENCE SOLVES NOTHING PERMANEN

SWINGING

SEE, MELINDA KNEW IT WAS TIME. SHE HOWLED TO FIND out who was with her and it was damn depressing, only three more out of sixteen, all in the middle of the room. Well, four against thirteen it'd have to be. Like good little cronies, her opponents shut and locked the front door and the back door too, the one that went to the science offices. In the back, Mironov pushed the plastic tubing onto the spigot and started the flow to his burner, before using the sparker to light it, to get the blue flame to jump up.

Melinda didn't wait, she claimed the first strike, grabbing her burner and leaping across the tabletop to smash Cynthia in the forehead with the curved metal base. It came back with a wicked dent on it. Melinda swung it again but Cynthia got her arm up to block and instead of the base cracking her skull a second time, the newly sharp edge created by the dent tore into the radial artery just above her wrist and Cynthia toppled over awkwardly, clutching her bloody arm and wailing.

Wasting no time, Melinda hurled the base end over end at Ricky's head while she stomped on Cynthia's throat as hard as she could, crushing the wail into silence. Spinning on her back foot, Melinda unleashed a vicious roundhouse to the kid who had locked the door and as he was trying to recover, she plunged her fist deep into his solar plexus and then slammed his head, eye first, against the corner of the nearest wooden cabinet. It made a sound like an eggshell shattering. By then, Ricky was on her.

He faked a punch and as she dodged, he hooked her left arm with his right and tried to hammer throw her, tried to slam her flat-backed onto the nearest indestructible tabletop but Melinda flipped out of it, landed on her feet, and retaliated with a nasty shot to Ricky's knee that forced him to stumble. He didn't even see the chop to the back of his neck that Melinda delivered with stunning accuracy. He just hit the floor with a full-on smack.

An unseen leg kicked her in the back of the knee and then she caught a hard right hook with her ribs before recovering enough to scramble onto the tabletop. From there, she jumped the six feet across the room to the other tabletop and just by coincidence missed being hit by a flaming projectile. A Runner threw something wet on her and she didn't know what it was but that sure as hell wasn't good. Probably flammable.

She kicked the alum into the Runner's face, leg-whipped him in the neck, and jumped down, dodging another flaming projectile from the back of the room. One of her Wolves wasn't so lucky though. He was trying to get his clothes off while being kicked by three kids. His entire chest was on fire and as he spun the flames shook in the wind of movement, flags on the flagpole of his body. In a last desperate effort, the Wolf jumped on his attackers, trying to light them up too. They all hit the ground hard.

Melinda dodged another mini-fireball and absolutely crushed a kid coming right at her with a stiff clothesline when her remaining Wolves slung the kid with a throw. She had to stop Mironov from burning the place up. Fast. But before she could do that, she had to dodge a crane-style punch combo that nearly took one of her ears off. Whoever the girl attacking her was, she was good. Melinda retaliated with Iron Fist hung gar, a tremendous punch to both shoulders to slow the girl down and throw her off Melinda's true style when faced with multiple opponents: capoeira.

The little crane must've expected a less straightforward tactic, as she did not move her foot when Melinda stomped down hard on her toes. She merely grimaced but it gave Melinda enough time to dance left, bend low, and shoot her leg out in a backward kick, delivering a devastating blow to the shin of the Blade coming up behind her. He'd thought he had a clear shot at her. He didn't. Instead, what he got was Melinda rocking her body forward as if she was going into a handstand but kicked him in the nose with her back foot instead. The force of her boot crammed his nostrils back into his face as the bridge of his nose shortened by an inch and the cartilage dislodged from the nasal bone, disappearing into his sinus cavity, charging into his brain in a burst of blood that sprayed across the room like a popped-open bottle of champagne that had been shook. His whole body went limp long before hitting the floor.

Little Crane was on top of Melinda before she even maintained her balance, using long, straight arm movements, keeping Melinda far enough away that she couldn't go for a quick body blow to end it. The girl's kicks were impeccable too. Very stylish but lacking in power. Melinda had a chance to test them with her shoulders, waist, and forearms. Yes, Little Crane was impressive but Melinda was wasting far too much time when there was a roving arsonist in the room.

So she sprang forward from her back-and-forth dancing position and swung both arms toward the head of Little Crane. Melinda knew Little Crane would duck them, which allowed her some room to jump forward and spin on her hands and kick her legs out above her like helicopter blades. Little Crane blocked the first of Melinda's kicks but she caught the next one squarely in the chin, and the kick after that knocked her to the ground for good. Melinda might've taken another moment to relish the victory but when she came up from her spinning position, she was on fire.

Immediately, Melinda stopped, dropped, and rolled, like the old public service announcement always said. She wriggled out of her still-flaming vest despite solid kicks to her ribs, thighs, and shoulder. Lucky nothing else on her was on fire. Whoever her attacker was got a shot squarely to the cup, then to both knees and in his voice box as he bent over.

Melinda rolled forward, dove through the splayed legs of one of her Wolves and bounced up right in front of Mironov, who was so surprised that he dropped his burning missile by reflex when the flames singed his fingers. Not even hesitating, Melinda swung her special move at him from close quarters: her Frostbite Cross Combination left Mironov no chance. The first punch hit him in the neck while the second one went clean into his jaw, crushing it up into the socket.

Up to that point, she had blocked out the noises, the screaming, and the awful stench of burning and alum mixed together like the chem lab was some kind of death camp. She felt light-headed as she turned and darted for the front door. Her two remaining Wolves did not stare at the smoldering and screaming bodies in the middle of the floor. They followed her.

When Melinda ran across the hall to Mark's English class she was only thinking of herself, of survival, and not the bodies behind her. It would be Mr. Wilkes that would emerge from the corner behind his desk to get the fire blanket out and pat down the burning bodies that used to be whole boys and girls and see if anything could be done for them. Old Mr. Wilkes would have to tend to Ricky, Cynthia, and Mironov. He'd be the one that had to stand on a stool and unlock the high cabinet in order to get the first-aid kit down and care for all of them. Alone, Mr. Wilkes would dispense bandages, lay cool wet towels on burns, smooth on ointments, and tie tourniquets with his wrinkled, shaking, arthritic hands.

GOING DOWN

MELINDA AND HER TWO REMAINING WOLVES FOUND MARK and six others cleaning up their room, tying up the living and gathering dropped weapons like it was some kind of yard sale from an isolated incident. Like it was coincidence that their whole English class just up and turned on them.

"Don't bother!" Melinda screamed. "The whole Fu is going up! Right now!"

Mark didn't believe her. It couldn't be possible.

There was no time to explain. They had to get to the quad, to the meeting place, before anyone else did. Then they could rally. The fastest way was out the door, left down the hall, then down three flights of stairs and through the cafeteria. So all ten went together and they encountered minimal resistance because they traveled in such a large group. Isolated Blades or Whips would turn and run in the other direction when they saw them coming. Those kids would jump six steps down on the stairs and take off for the nearest open space on the next floor, just to avoid Melinda.

But when the group got to the cafeteria, they were in for a surprise. Dermoody was standing on a lunchroom table, holding a shotgun, and screaming something about martial law as he plugged one kid, a freshman Wolf, that was running away from him, right in the back.

So it was Mark that made a run right at Dermoody, completely devoid of sense, just insane-crazy; maybe he thought he was protecting Melinda, protecting his family. Dermoody saw him. Shot again but missed Mark, and the scattershot piled itself into the Wolf in front of Melinda. He collapsed in a heap, groaning. But Mark never made it as far as Dermoody because Cap'n Joe moved out from behind him and in one large step, cleared the table and crushed Mark with a tackle. The whole cafeteria echoed with the smack like a hundred pairs of hands clapping once.

Melinda lined up Cap'n Joe's skull for a lobotomy kick, effective immediately, but Dermoody had reloaded with one more shell, quick as a cat. He pointed the gun in her direction. She could only halt her movement by reflex, her leg still in the air as she watched Cap'n Joe slam Mark's head into the floor, once, twice, smashing his fragile brain against the unforgiving wall of his skull, and pick him up like a rag doll. Mark's legs twitched as he tried to find his footing but there was none to be had as Cap'n Joe lifted him off the ground with a firm chokehold.

"Why?" It didn't come out so loud at first, but Melinda tried again, "Why?"

Mark's ears were bleeding.

"Because I can," Dermoody said it loud, "because nobody's going to miss a bunch of poor gang kids that would be better off in jail or dead anyway. So go ahead and do it, Joe. I want to see this."

"No, don't do it!" Melinda shouted but didn't move. The shotgun was still pointed at her.

And with Mark's neck in his spinach-eating forearms, Cap'n Joe just twisted.

That was about where me and Jimmy came in.

DEALING WITH PRINCIPALS

"WHAT THE FUCK IS GOING ON?"

I couldn't help it. It just popped out of my mouth from sheer surprise as I stayed bunkered behind my Jimmy shield. Hearing about Dirty Dermoody and Cap'n Joe's deeds was one thing, but seeing them was another thing completely. Still though, it was Dermoody.

Of course he had a fuckin' gun. I expected that shit out of someone like him. It was par for his crooked course.

Jimmy held me hard to the brick wall next to the doors. His body between me and the gun. He was wet, and whether it was sweat or blood or falling in the showers, all of it combined, I didn't know. I didn't look down. The shoulder where Donnie kicked me was aching bad. Still that hot coal in the car hood. Like an overheated engine. I guess the good news was I couldn't even feel my hands anymore. They'd gone completely numb from almost my elbows down. All I could feel was Jimmy's pressure and it took an effort to hold back a sad laugh. Nothing ever changes. Curiously, none of the Runners had followed us into the cafeteria from the pool. Maybe they knew something we didn't.

"Why, I'm trying my utmost to discourage a riot in progress, now isn't that what I'm doing, Joe?" Dermoody cocked open his shotgun and discarded one empty red shell with a brass-colored bottom. It clinked on the tile and rolled over near Mark's body, stopping next to his outstretched hand. After moving the remaining red shell to the empty chamber, he took another shell, this one yellow, from his back pocket and put it in, clamping the gun shut and cocking the hammer for the barrel with the red shell in it. The other hammer stayed down. I don't know much about guns, but it looked old.

"Yessir," Cap'n Joe said. The guy was a fuckin' automaton.

"Joe here, he's doing the same thing," Dermoody said as he stepped down from on top of the table. "Why, that kid was coming right at me, and you know what? He could've killed me."

Without warning, Dermoody smashed the face of a she-Wolf right next to Melinda with the butt of his shotgun. The girl fell over, hitting the floor straight-backed. If the blow didn't break her beak, she was a real lucky girl. Of course, Melinda tried to kick the gun from Dermoody's hands but Cap'n Joe was too close. He grabbed her midmotion and threw her to the ground. She bounced right back up but stayed put.

"See now, I'm doing my best to protect myself and my staff from being overrun by teenage killers." He held his gun across his body, almost lazily. It was still pointed at Melinda but he was looking at me. "Now any sane person with the wherewithal and means would do the exact same thing."

As soon as the words were out of his mouth, he pulled the trigger.

Melinda hit the floor fast, hard and flat on her back. That was how much power the shotgun had. She coughed loud, then had a massive intake of air like every breath she ever took in her life needed to come back right then. I swear it looked fake. Like special fuckin' effects. Like she was on a wire or a snare that snapped her to the floor and maybe they sped up the camera speed in editing.

"Aw, don't look so sad, it's just homemade scattershot anyway. Rock salt mostly. Stings worse than a midnight smack in the face but isn't even lethal." Dermoody kicked Melinda in the head and she moaned. "Sure wakes you up though. See?"

"You can't do this," Jimmy said. Still in front of me, I felt him flex his back muscles and push off, walking a beeline toward Dermoody.

"Can't I, China Boy? Look, why don't you do us both a favor and save this righteous shit for the real bad guy, huh? The Evil Ridley's in the theater. It's Fred's drama period. I suggest you head on over there before he (a) escapes, or (b) finds out you're both still alive. It really is the only way to stop this thing. You want more people to die?"

Jimmy kept walking. Dermoody smacked another Wolf, this time in the jaw. I kept my distance, moving right, around the perimeter of the action and behind a table. I didn't believe Dermoody was gonna cap us. He needed us. Then again, I wasn't about to get shot if he changed his mind, but maybe I could flank them if I went slow enough. So Ridley wanted me transferred? I didn't know if Dirty Dermoody was lying or telling the truth. I wouldn't put it past either of them. Both were more than capable of lying convincingly to complete the angle. And yeah, I did believe that if Ridley couldn't have me he'd end me. Some fucked-up romantics are like that.

"Why don't you just go take care of Ridley for me so I don't have to handle you and him at the same time, huh? Thanks. Oh, and P.S., Ridley just sent out the biggest shipment he's ever produced. Just now, within the last twenty minutes. That fleet of trucks must've had everything on it. I'm talking tons. Everything was a ploy. Wipe out the opposition and cash in on the ensuing chaos at the same time? Why not? Greedy bastard." Dermoody turned his back on Jimmy and Cap'n Joe stepped between them.

From where I was standing, the cafeteria kitchen looked like it had been ransacked. Pots and pans were scattered across the floor in front of the door, which was nearly off its hinges. So that was what brought Dermoody and Cap'n Joe to the cafeteria, to see if it was true, to see if they'd truly been cut out of the biggest deal ever. So there they were, blowing off steam, coming down on us.

Made sense though. Ridley trying to kill two birds with one stone, except we were one of those birds. What a diversion. Hell of a game to play. The guy thought of everything, up to and including how to play me against Melinda and Dermoody. There was only one problem: he'd overextended himself. I was wondering why it'd been so simple for us to fight our way out. I mean, why he hadn't sent huge squads after each of us individually, why we weren't crushed by one, or even two, hundred kids each. That was our answer. He needed the hands to load the trucks and create the diversions elsewhere to keep those trucks moving. For real though, that sure was some bold shit. I had to give it to him.

"Look, now, I'll make it easy." He pointed the shotgun at Melinda's gasping body; she'd rolled over onto her chest with her arms out like a scarecrow that had only just been blown over in a strong wind.

"You leave, and she lives. Stay, and everyone dies." He said it slow.

I suppose that was the point it occurred to me that a red Dermoody shotgun shell was homemade, but the yellow one most likely wasn't. That it was probably something nasty. Something to suit his temperament, I don't know, flechettes or punkin balls or disintegrator slugs. The kind of crazy shit Remo heard the coroner pulled out of dead bodies from time to time. Black market, illegal stuff that outsiders tried to peddle to all the families. But I don't think Jimmy knew that because he kept walking. Dermoody placed the double barrel of the shotgun on Melinda's back, caressing the ridge of spine between her shoulder blades.

"Son, I wouldn't walk much farther, if I were you. Joe?" the principal said.

"Easy there, brave," Cap'n Joe whispered.

Probably Cap'n Joe's biggest mistake was going for Jimmy with one hand. Maybe he figured that because Jimmy was so small, he could just knock him flat with one fist. And really, the Cap'n wasn't even trying to punch Jimmy, just put a paw on his shoulder and stop him from walking forward but see, he got too close. Before that enormous hand of Cap'n Joe's clamped down on his neck, Jimmy grabbed the fingers and bent them back and the hand was next, then the wrist.

The exact moment after Cap'n Joe's wrist snapped and dangled, Dermoody pulled the trigger and Melinda's back exploded. Like a waiter carrying a huge plate of pasta marinara in a restaurant that slipped on the newly washed kitchen floor and threw the whole thing in the air and the chunky red sauce got everywhere when the big dish hit the floor. Whatever Wolves were left standing around ran for the door without ever once looking back. I didn't blame them. I felt like running too. There was just nowhere else to go.

Really, I don't even think Dermoody meant to do it. That it just kind of happened, an unintentional reflex. He was scared of Jimmy. Might sound funny to say that about a former military man who saw combat action, but Jimmy was no ordinary adversary. Shit, I would've been scared too if I was a fifty-something-year-old man staring down one of the youngest and most experienced kung fu fighters around, shotgun or no fuckin' shotgun.

Dermoody must've thought he had a better chance pointing the gun at Melinda and "convincing" us to go take care of Ridley rather than actually pointing the gun at Jimmy and making him mad, or worse, missing with a huge scattershot if the kid did his mythic disappearing thing. But there was only one problem now. He was out of shells and had no time to reload. That was when Jimmy took his gun away.

Quicker than a cat, he yanked it out of Dermoody's hands and threw the metal thing so far that it clunked on the floor and slid to a stop right in front of me, dinged against the bloodied nails protruding from my boots. It took effort to pull my eyes from it. Part of the shrapnel from the shot must've hit the floor and rebounded back and hit Dermoody too because he was holding his face and not looking quite so tough when Jimmy knocked him to the ground. In fact, he just looked like a sad old man, covered in fake-looking blood.

THE SHOWDOWN

I DON'T CARE IF IT WAS TWO AGAINST ONE ESSENTIALLY, I'd've bet on Jimmy ten times out of ten. I think it was just the look on his face as he set his body between the two men and slightly bent his knees, kept his hands up, open palmed. A look of crystal-clear determination wrinkled his chin around the duct tape and bloody chin patch that made him look tougher than I'd ever seen him. Stay out of this. That's what his eyes told me.

So I lingered where I was, behind the table that Dermoody had been on when we rushed in. Every part of me wanted to steam in on Cap'n Joe and clip him from behind before he even saw me coming. I had plenty of room to do it in. But I didn't.

Tables had been pushed away from the entrance leaving a big open area, apart from the bodies. I had a strange feeling then. That was for sure, standing in the cafeteria and seeing bodies on the floor and somehow trying to merge it with the same big room I'd spent some part of almost every day in for the last two years. They had to be fake, those bodies. Even though I'd seen it happen, they couldn't be real, could they? Melinda wasn't really dead. Right? My gut knew the truth. My brain just hadn't caught up yet. Guns didn't make any sense to me. How they could kill without effort.

I could see right out the big glass entryway, the six black-trimmed bulletproof doors, and into the quad. And there was something strange going on because there was no one in it. It was absolutely deserted. Pretty much the only sign that someone had been there was my dripped bloodstains on the concrete right by the flagpole. Probably left a good bit of skin on that metal rope too.

It gets dark real early in the winter and twilight was ending outside. What was more, it was snowing and had been doing so for about five minutes if I had to guess by the real light dusting on the big, squared-off sections of concrete. Bound to be a heavy one, most likely. At least, judging by what I could see of the fading sky. The dark gray clouds that were floating in low and bloated, like a bunch of B-52s, heavy with a cargo of moisture that would freeze as soon as it left the millions of tiny bomb bay doors and dropped to the ground to accumulate instead of explode. It'd be a hard, dry snow. Especially with the sun gone.

It occurred to me that Cap'n Joe was like most big men as he lumbered into position across from Jimmy. One little scratch and they were worthless for the rest of the fight. I mean, there he was, all of six foot eight and way over two hundred pounds, cradling his broken wrist and hand like it was a kitten that needed to be protected at all costs and not something that would heal eventually. Jimmy knew this. All it would take was a feint to get Cap'n Joe to spin away and not go through with a planned move.

If there was anyone to be worried about, it was Dermoody, big and angry, having picked himself up off the floor. His fighting style was completely unorthodox. Which is not to say that it was bad, because it wasn't. If he had anything going for him, it was unpredictability. He lined up like a boxer. His strengths were throwing and holds. Jimmy just needed to make sure he didn't get close enough to get thrown. Not a problem.

It started quickly. As far as Cap'n Joe was concerned, Jimmy was merciful. He faked like he was going after Dermoody and then spun and paralyzed Cap'n Joe. So quick. Just like that. I mean, I was behind Cap'n Joe and I thought Jimmy was just punching him real fast but then the big guy stopped moving and I knew exactly what'd happened.

That was it. Only him and Dermoody then. It wasn't even a fair fight. Dermoody, all bleeding from his cheek and squinting, kept lunging forward and trying to grab Jimmy. But my cousin was too quick, skipping to the side and unloading on his kidneys, chopping his neck. Jimmy dodged an awkward punch and swept behind Dermoody, kicking his legs out, dragging him to what was left of Melinda's body and smothering his face in her still-flowing blood like a dog owner would do to a puppy when trying to train it not to pee in the house.

He shoved Dermoody's nose in it and the warm liquid must've

gone up into his nostrils when he tried to breathe and he had to cough the flecks and lumps of bone or organ out. But the slightly metallic taste must've lingered on his tongue. Just like the taste of Cue's blood and spinal fluid cocktail surged on the crease in mine. How it seemed connected to the nightmares I'd had every night, and every morning I'd awaken with the same taste in my mouth. Like it never went away. But I couldn't let it take over me. I had to stay focused. Present.

Jimmy hauled Dermoody to his feet. It was still a sight seeing such a small guy drag people bigger than him around. Dermoody's last words before Jimmy froze him were aimed at me with big pleading eyes like he wasn't even the same person that pulled the trigger earlier: "Don't you want to be free, Jen?" And then he was a human statue.

I closed the distance between us and spat in his face. The mucus I summoned up dragged a path down his cheek, like a slug, revealing his mottled skin underneath Melinda's blood. This killer was going to get what he deserved. I pawed the shotgun up from the floor and lunged for Dermoody clumsily, fishing in his back pocket for the shells, the yellow ones. Then I cracked open the stock, tipped out the empties, and tried desperately to shove the new shells in just like I'd seen my beloved principal do. Took me four tries before I got them using the back of my numb left hand.

"No, Jenny, please." Jimmy's voice sounded so normal compared to the rest of him. His face was contorted all up and his knees and forearms were coated with a thickening mess of Melinda's blood. The cougar and the letters on his shirt weren't even visible anymore. For the most part, it looked like he was wearing a red shirt and red shorts. I couldn't believe it was the same person that had just mashed Dermoody's face into the reddest part of the floor.

"Dammit, Jimmy, you fuckin' heard him! How's he ever going to be punished? They're going to call him a hero for defending the school and he's fuckin' right." I was screaming the words, I didn't know where it came from, all of a sudden I couldn't stop the anger in me. "If Ridley's gone and he stays, the students'll be worse off than we ever were before! He's got to go!"

"You still can't do this," Jimmy said. He held up crimson palms. Like that was going to convince me.

"But no one else will!" My words were shrill, it didn't even feel like me talking, like something had been opened inside and was talking for me. "How can you fuckin' say that? Donnie is deader than a bucket of shit because of you, and probably a few more people too, and now one of the people that deserves it the most isn't going to get it? Fuck *that*, I'll do it myself!"

Jimmy swiped the gun from me so easily. I think I kind of wanted him to. With my hands the way they were, I could never have pulled the trigger. Not even with a thumb. It was physically impossible. All the drama wasn't strictly for Dermoody. I knew it. He was just a nice unmoving target. It was for everything, everyone. It would've been for never seeing my mom again, for never being able to see my brother again, for seeing my father having control over only half a body, for the storm of confusion that was Jimmy good and bad, for the stupid terrible fuck-up that was me.

That was when one of the doors to the quad opened behind us. Like a bad surprise. Like a fuckin' gameshow. And what do we have behind door number two? Why, the mystery guest, of course! He's head of the Whips! He's acting like a vulture, waiting for others to do his dirty work! He's cleaning up the mess, tying up loose ends, because Ridley told him to! Would those of you who can still clap please give a warm round of applause for . . . Bruiser Calderón!

Jimmy and I both jumped back at the same time, ready to defend ourselves. Jimmy pointed the gun at him but Bruiser just put his hands up.

"You goin' after Ridley? Good. Go right ahead, kids. Don't let me stop you. I got a feeling his time is up." He entered the cafeteria and held the door open for us to walk through and out. Into the snow.

When he saw we weren't taking him up on his offer, he backed off and let the door close with him inside. He left two wet boot prints on the tile.

"Don't worry, I'll take care of them," he said.

Jimmy must've believed him because he broke open the stock and dropped the shells onto the ground, kicked them away underneath a far table. Then he set the gun on the floor and we backed toward the doors. It seemed like a hell of a risk to me with Bruiser right there. But as soon as the gun was unloaded and down, Bruiser stopped paying attention to us. Besides, if he was gonna do us in, it sure as hell wouldn't be by gun.

"Yoo hoo." Bruiser dipped his shoulder as he said it to Dermoody. "Remember me? *¿Recuerda mi hermano menor?* Remember what you did to him? I know you can hear me, *jefe*. I could hear everything when I was like that too. That's why this is gonna hurt a whole lot worse. *¡Vas a sufrir mucho dolor y entonces una muerte fantástica!* Because you'll know it's coming."

Bruiser leaned close and whispered the last part right into Dermoody's ear just as Jimmy dragged me out the door and the air, below freezing, slid over my wounds, making me forget how hot they were for a moment. Like a clear plastic bag. Like that boy in the bubble.

ACROSS THE QUAD

WE TRUDGED OUT INTO THE SNOW, NEARLY A QUARTER- inch deep. We did it fast. Like we were running away. Not sure what to expect. What was Bruiser going to do? Was he going to come after us with the gun once he did whatever he had to do to Dermoody and Cap'n Joe? It didn't look like it. The second we left it was like we were never there. Bruiser was talking to them, those statues, moving his mouth, strutting as he picked up each shell that Jimmy had kicked. I could only look behind me as we made our way across the quad, at Bruiser as he put the shells in the shotgun and dipped his shoulder, threw his head back, laughed. I was a water skier cruising on the wake of Jimmy's speedboat. I didn't even turn around when I heard fighting in front of me. I couldn't look away from the scene in the cafeteria.

Jimmy punched throats. Jimmy kicked ribs. I could hear it. I could see the bodies fall past me like broken mannequins failing miserably at making decent snow angels. Jimmy froze them: ice sculptures. But I still couldn't tear my eyes away from the rectangular glass entryway. In the dark, it looked like a fluorescent strip of light boxes, all lined up in a row, pouring yellow out the cafeteria entrance and into the quad around me and illuminating the falling snow. Bruiser wiped the stock of the gun, then the barrel, then the trigger with his shirt. He was getting smaller as I got farther away. The whole scene was. I couldn't tell if he was smiling anymore.

I barely felt the snow on my skin, on my hair, melting and joining my sweat. The thought of running away, running home, only briefly occurred to me as the shrinking Bruiser twisted the gun into Dermoody's hand and aimed it right at Cap'n Joe. Then POW. Even through two barriers of bulletproof glass and some twenty yards or more of distance, I could hear it like a muffled sonic boom: Cap'n Joe went over on a right angle, a tipped-over nutcracker.

Bruiser wasted no time pointing the shotgun up, maneuvering it into Dermoody's mouth, still smoking, had to be. I winced, imagining a burning hot gun barrel in my mouth, blistering my lips immediately. It would sink into my gums like that hot knife and that butter. Some things had to be seen all the way through to the end. That was my thought when tiny Bruiser must've pushed his finger into tiny Dermoody's finger and pulled the tiny trigger that I couldn't even see anymore, just had to imagine was there, and then Dermoody lost the top part of his head and then rocked but just kind of stayed standing up like an inflatable bop bag. The gun dropped to the floor beside him. Then Bruiser sat down on the bench of one of the tables.

It was like watching a play. I expected the bright yellow rectangle of lights across the quad to go out, click off, or fade down so I could be a regular audience member and clap and thank god that the tour-de-fuckin'-force was over and I could go home and purposely not think about the shit I saw. But when I heard the sound of Jimmy throwing open the door to the theater building, heard metal slam hard against brick, I knew we still had one more act.

THE BRASS SECTION

I STILL HADN'T COMPLETELY REGAINED MY COMPOSURE when we entered the drama building. But then I got wrecked. My head caught a blow right above and behind my ear: right in my parietal, right in my Germany. It definitely rang in my ears, deep down, both of them. I must've been holding my head. I was probably on the floor. Didn't really notice the difference between up and down for a moment. Was just trying to find my Rhineland.

Then Jimmy was next to me. "You okay?"

"I'm okay." I shook my melon before I said it. Everything appeared to be in the right place. Checked my head. I wasn't bleeding. Nothing was loose.

Jimmy ducked a trombone. Some Blades had just emerged from the band room to our left and must've grabbed the only weapons they could find. The only things heavy. Slightly dizzy, I pushed myself up along the wall as Jimmy took a trumpet away from a Blade and then started whacking her in the legs with it, right on the kneecaps, and then he really started moving. His whole body was a storm cloud and his limbs were bolts of lightning. Seriously, there was no other way to describe Jimmy as he sped his movements up like the Bionic Man, as if everything he had done previously was actually Jimmy slow-mo: completely surrounded by five kids, he lashed out with a kick in front of him that smashed a pelvis, spun and slung out both arms in what I think were punches and both kids went down grabbing their throats, but as they were falling, before they even hit the ground, Jimmy twisted away from a lame kick like it wasn't even there and powered the Blade in front of him into the wall next to me before unleashing the most wicked roundhouse I've ever seen on the last one, fully bending the trombone into a forty-five-degree angle like it was a paper clip before kicking the kid to the ground with a speed not unlike Dermoody's shotgun blasts.

"Ready?" he asked.

I could only nod and hope that the twinge at the base of my skull wasn't about to become a gorilla-sized headache. Or worse, the old one coming back, the fist crammed into my brain stem. The tumor.

Jimmy pulled the door open and we entered the darkened

theater at the back, looking down on the seats and the stage. I made sure the door didn't make any noise when it shut.

The theater itself was as old as the school, but Ridley was having it redone. The carpeting once affixed to the outer concrete walls had been completely torn out and now it was just huge curved slabs with tiny chunks of said carpet still sticking to the wall where the glue was too strong. Eventually acoustic-friendly panels would get socketed in but not until much later, not until seats'd been torn out and boxes added.

As it happened, the seating was split into four sections, with two wing groups on the outsides, and one large middle section that was cut in half by an elevated wooden walkway. It stopped just short of the abbreviated orchestra pit and led to the light and sound booth, which could only be accessed by a ladder and basically looked like a diorama designed by a six-year-old: a spray-painted black shoe box stood on its end with a rectangular hole cut out at the top that had a big black table inside, filled with buttons and lights.

Looked like whoever was in there was just learning because the trio on the stage kept getting hit with alternating hues of red and orange lighting: on, off, on, off. The stage went blue.

"Enough with the fucking lighting! Let them act!" someone screamed from the front row, momentarily shocking the actors on stage.

It was Ridley.

THE FINALE

RIDLEY MUST'VE BEEN PRETTY CONFIDENT THAT EVERY-
thing was going to work out since he was sitting in the front row, just
watching the play rehearsal, when we walked in. Act I, Scene IV of
Hamlet, the very beginning of it, with Hamlet, Horatio, and Marcellus on the platform. But the platform in question was just an awful
twelve-foot-tall canvas painted with big gray bricks to look like the

side of an old castle but really it looked more like misshapen LEGOs. I didn't even need to see behind it to know that it was probably built like a tree-house landing.

Apart from an awful background painting of the castle throne room pushed slightly off to the side, the stage was bare. Made of the same black wood as the walkway and sound booth, it was a good-sized stage breadthwise. Lots of room for a sword fight. The actors were crowded together in the center of the stage, lit up in a wavering blue spotlight. The kid playing Marcellus looked like he was wearing plastic armor. Just fake.

The actors started the scene again. Right about the time the pain in my head reached official headache status.

"The air bites shrewdly; it is very cold," the kid playing Hamlet said. He was a Runner. I knew him. Heller, his name was, and he was actually an Uncle in his family.

"It is a nipping and an eager air," Fred said.

"What hour now?" Heller was overacting already, craning his neck and everything. He was sniffing the air too. No idea why.

"I think it lacks of twelve." Fred was real understated, just like a companion to a prince would be, I guess. He was stealing the scene.

"No, it is struck." Heller raised his voice too much, played with his gloves too.

"Indeed? I heard it not: then it draws near the season wherein the spirit held his wont to walk." Fred's last word hung in the air.

Then the actors stopped, waited. Fred did a great little improv where he put his hand to his ear and got a silly look on his face. He knew the scene was blown.

"Trumpets! Fucking Trumpets and Fucking Ordnance!" Ridley screamed at the booth behind him. "Sound effects! Actors need cues! So does the audience!" Funny thing though, at that point, he was the only one in the audience. Apart from us.

Looked like Ridley had taken over directing duties. Or at least thought he had. He didn't throw the script down or anything, just sat there, waiting. He probably knew we were there. But it was Mock that spotted us first. He'd been leaning against the fire exit by the right wing of seats, dragging on a cigarette and blowing the smoke out the slit in the door but he didn't waste any time tossing it away.

He came at us, right up the aisle. I've got news for you though, if you're not fast enough to dodge an attack coming from someone above you, then don't go after someone higher than you on any staircase, ever. Gravity just isn't on your side when fighting upward on a slope. The consequences are pretty much disastrous and Mock learned them all firsthand. Never even had a chance. He caught Jimmy's full leaping kick in the throat and tumbled down the stairs backward making cracking noises that echoed around the theater. I swear I saw Ridley put his hand on his head when Mock flopped onto the concrete beside him.

A few stragglers followed, all three repeated Mock's mistake. Bodyguards working as shop monkeys, set designers, carpenters, whatever. Ridley had put them all to work. And they might as well have all been named Jack, because each one fell down the hill, broke his crown, and wouldn't be getting up in the morning. I slung one into the seats to my left. This Jill wasn't going tumbling after.

People jumped out of the lighting booth and ran for the exits as I followed Jimmy down the stairs. Marcellus ran for it too, scraping his plastic armor together the whole way.

"Your lucky day, huh?"

Ridley got up and walked through the orchestra pit and took the side stairs up to the stage. He was in no hurry. He was wearing a blue, white, red, horizontally striped polo shirt that changed to square lines of purplish red and all-over blue as he passed under the stage lighting.

"You forced my hand. I wasn't quite ready to go ahead with everything today but I had to, didn't I? You and your preemptive strikes. So how *is* Melinda? Is she well?" Ridley walked to the back of the stage, behind the throne room painting. "All the same, I had a feeling it would end this way. It's what I get for being disorganized. Perhaps a little bit greedy."

Jimmy and I didn't need to say anything. We crossed the pit and got up to the stage, taking up fighting positions side by side.

"Freddy, please go to the dressing room right now." It was Ridley's firm voice and Fred scooted off stage right, leaving a mushrooming of swept velvet curtain behind him.

Then the other actors emerged, forming a barrier between Ridley and us. It was pretty clear that we had to go through them to get to him. So be it. They must've been doing a costume fitting or something, because they were all dressed up. I don't know, maybe it was a full dress rehearsal. They did only have a week until the opening. King Claudius, Queen Gertrude, Heller Hamlet, Laertes with his sword, Rosencrantz and Guildenstern were all going to get it about four acts too early, all for real on a big, empty, black stage.

Quick and messy: I saw legs in alternating colors of tights fly up into the air of my peripheral vision before I even threw a punch. There went Rosencrantz and Guildenstern. I kicked Gertrude in the belly and then swept her legs out from under her. Her hooped dress billowed as she fell. I stomped her in the mouth and felt her jaw give underneath my heel. Strangely satisfying. Her crown rolled off as she jerked, gurgling for air. It got crushed underfoot by Laertes backing up from one of Jimmy's furious combinations. Also trying to avoid Jimmy, Claudius got my nasty boot in his ear and then a chop to the throat for his trouble. He raised his face to me from where he fell so I smashed him in the eye with my elbow. He brought his head up again so I kneed him in the ribs and kicked him in the solar plexus, then the neck. After that, he didn't move. The nails sunk in all the way to the rubber of my sole both times, taking bits of flesh out with them like little shish kebabs. Laertes's dull metal sword snapped in two and the other half was sticking out of his leg when he fell to the floor with a hollow thud. The stage wasn't solid.

Heller Hamlet was no better a fighter than an actor. Jimmy beat him with the flat of his own blade before knocking him out with the hilt in the back of the neck. Next to Heller Hamlet was the face of a sixteen-year-old made up to look like he was sixty with a dark gray painted-on mustache and greasepaint wrinkles staring up at me without drama, not closing his eyes because he couldn't anymore. Stupid Polonius. I had no idea where he came from. Jimmy must've really got him good. I wished I'd seen it.

And then it was just me and Ridley, with Jimmy standing directly between, warning me off, trying to be the hero and protect me. Everything was lit up in the blue light. That hue that was supposed to tell the audience it was nighttime, that something dramatic was about to happen, and the only recognizable sounds in the whole theater were the wheezes of half a dozen injured people cursing and struggling to breathe.

THE BIG BOSS

WITH JIMMY IN FRONT OF ME, I NEVER SAW RIDLEY PULL
the gun. But then Jimmy disappeared, just gone. Like he did against
The Bulgarian, must've, there was no other explanation, but there
was an explosion and I was the absolute center of it. It was so much
louder than I thought it'd be, not bang. BOOM. Like an old cannon,

and then again, BOOM. Then there was a flash and everything went white, then black. I didn't know it was a bullet at first.

The wrenching shock wave hit me in the right arm just as the sound fully reached my ears. Then I could feel air there, an actual hole. It felt like my whole body got kicked down with a giant boot, leaving its imprint from head to toe with its ridges and valleys of hard rubber sole. Supposedly I was already falling backward when the second bullet hit me but I didn't feel it, didn't feel pain, just another full body earthquake, an aftershock. The epicenter was underneath the side of my rib cage, with the fault line torn lengthwise somewhere inside my chest.

I thought I was dead. I wondered who would give Dad his meds with me gone. I heard my mom's voice. It was very clear.

She said, "Don't climb there."

It was the exact thing she'd told me when I was five. I climbed the stacked-up railroad ties at the back of our old house anyway. I fell hard on my back and knocked my wind out, then lied to my mother about how it happened. I told her I'd been stung by a bee. I didn't want her to know I'd disobeyed.

When I got hot, I knew I was still alive. I swear I could smell my skin burning as I opened my eyes and stared at the ceiling of the theater, the alternating lines of visible girders painted black. I clawed at my side, at my arm, at the bullets that had burrowed inside me. They were lighting me on fire. I scratched harder and harder but I couldn't even come close to it with my fingers still taped to my palms.

"Look, my lord, it comes!"

Still in character, Fred must've yelled it from his hiding position behind the curtain. Guess he hadn't gone to the dressing room as Ridley had commanded. The show must go on.

Enter the ghost. I pushed my head back, to look behind me, upside down. A trapdoor in the walkway had opened and this glowing white thing came out, raised itself up. Great special effects, I thought before I looked at the empty light and sound booth behind the ghost. It looked so much like Cue. I couldn't believe it. I probably smiled when I said, "Hey, Mister Cue."

It had to be him. It had his nose. He was looking at me and it was real quiet. I thought maybe the explosions had damaged my ears, broke my eardrums out because they weren't ringing. I'd heard Freddy though, his projected voice. I'd heard Freddy. The words banged around in my brain: I'd heard Freddy.

But then Ridley responded to Fred, maybe he'd studied Fred's lines with him so much, always being Hamlet to his Horatio, that it just came out of him: "Angels and ministers of grace defend us!" And I heard fast footsteps as he took off running through the backstage area for the exit doors. Beyond them was a strip of sidewalk and then the parking lot. He must've thrown them both open with outstretched hands because the stage got flooded with lights. White, red, and blue threw themselves all over the theater, through Cue's body. Cop cars, had to be, because I could hear a siren too. Then nothing as the doors sprang back and closed heavily. Everything was back to blue.

I knew I was bleeding, but I couldn't feel it going out of me, just my back getting wet. My chest got heavy. Like someone sitting on me. Cue was next to me then, putting his hand on my forehead and my headache went away. The fist unclenched. The tumor shriveled. Like he took it with him, pulled it out of me when he stood up and walked forward. I could move my neck so I raised it a little and saw Jimmy standing there. He had his head down. He was facing away from me.

I wanted to tell Jimmy that I was okay, but I couldn't. I could barely breathe. Maybe he thought I was dead and it was his fault for dodging, for disappearing. But, I wanted to say, Jimmy, it isn't your fault I'm so slow. I didn't feel as hot anymore, but it felt like I had two basketballs implanted underneath my skin and they were stretching too much from being pumped up. That I was going to pop soon. It isn't your fault, Jimmy. Never was your fault that I'm so slow.

Cue's ghost walked forward, disappeared into Jimmy's back. Like he stepped into him. That was when Jimmy's head came up. He ran toward the doors and jump kicked them open so hard that they groaned and I saw only the darkness of Jimmy's outline connect with Ridley's hands-up silhouette, like a cut-out shadow with his arms held high against the lights, and then Ridley fell forward, pretty much busted in two. He didn't put his palms down to keep himself from going headfirst into the sidewalk. And he didn't move after that.

"Jesus!" screamed somebody outside. It was a male voice.

"He's fucking killed him!"

One of the doors stayed open. Jimmy must've broken the hinges. The other one shut but didn't latch.

"Get on the fucking ground, now! Right now!" The closest cop was yelling at Jimmy. He had his gun out, real straight. I think he was scared and surprised. He hadn't expected someone to come flying out the doors maybe.

Another cop came up beside the first one, and he hit Jimmy with his gun. They made Jimmy get on his knees and put his hands on his head. Then they put the cuffs on him, bent his arms back, and locked his wrists together with steel, nice and tight. Cuffed his ankles together too. Then they dragged him to his feet, out of all those lights. Out of the alternating blue and red, and the harsh, continuous, headlight white.

I heard a car door close and I knew it was locked. Probably twenty cops spiraled in through the exit after that, with their guns and roving flashlights, but they waited for an ambulance before they moved me. I must not've looked so good. Two guys had to turn away and one looked like he was going to be sick. My tongue felt swelled against the roof of my mouth, and I had to work to get air in around it. But the worst part was that the taste had disappeared, the salt-blood, every last ounce of Cue, gone. The little girl was finally alone.

The last sound I remember was Fred's uncontrollable shrieking. The high moan that didn't sound all that different from the sirens but came in thick bursts of lung-emptying exhales. I recognized it. I felt it reverberating in my ear canals and shaking down inside me and matching something. It was the exact same sound I would've made for Cue, if only I'd given in that night I lost him. It was a noise, a pitch, that played in me too. Like both Fred and me were instruments with a single string encased deep in our flesh, deeper than bullets could go, tuned to play a long monotonous note from one plucking. I tried to move my left arm. It was stuck to the floor. I closed my eyes, tried to keep my breathing going around my abandoned tongue, my sinking chest, as I waited for the gurney. I didn't need to see anything else. I knew he'd found Ridley. I knew he was crying. Good night to that sweet prince.

CONSE-QUENCES, A.K.A. THE EPILOGUE

THEY BLAMED ALMOST EVERY DEATH THAT DAY ON JIMMY.
Well, except for Dermoody and Cap'n Joe. Those two got blamed on
Dermoody, but that got kept real quiet. Every other death got pinned
on Jimmy though, all thirty-six. It didn't matter that they had very
little hard evidence. He was an easy target. So they found witnesses,
and lined them all up against him. The kid with the reputation, that

big old outsider. That slant-eyed kid with a different last name who would kill you as soon as look at you. See, the blond girl on the news didn't say it but her eyes did. And then she flipped her hair.

So even though he was seventeen years old, Jimmy was tried as an adult and got handed seventeen consecutive life sentences, one for each year he'd lived. He got incarcerated at a maximum-security prison and had to be isolated from the other prisoners because of his skills. He isn't allowed any visitors. He didn't appeal. During the trial and sentencing, Auntie Marin moved into our house. After all the drama ended, she was unable to move out. Guess she couldn't face the prospect of an empty home on top of everything. I wasn't able to convert Cue's room for her right away even though I had plans: new bed, new everything. She mostly slept in Dad's room with him. They got real close through the whole ordeal. She'll never be my mom though.

As for our cozy little family funeral, I don't feel like talking about it. I told Dad to sell all of Cue's old comics to pay for his burial and the body went right into Dad's plot next to Mom. Out of Cue's stash, I had Dad keep #337 and #394 of *The Mighty Thor* for me. I just liked the covers.

Things are real different. Dr. Vanez and a team of other doctors fixed me up and the victims' relief fund that got collected paid for everything, which was great, because otherwise I'd've been paying them off for the rest of my life. That really surprised me, so many people reaching out and donating money for us just because they heard what happened. I'm still grateful.

On a good day, a day that isn't cold, I have only 60 percent mobility in my hands. That pretty much means I can't really bend them at the third knuckle because of all the scar tissue across the middle. Had to have a graft on each palm. They look like smoothed-out funnel webs from those spiders. Flesh was harvested from my ass for that. They also gave me the option of lower back, but decided against it when they saw my tattoo. That whole thing was fun. They'd said it was going to be relatively painless. But I couldn't sit down for a week afterward, and when I could sit, it was on a big foam donut like the kind people with bad hemorrhoids get, and now I have huge scars where my legs connect to my butt. Like missing patches. All I know is that I'm real lucky. At one point, the doctors were considering amputating both hands supposedly. A nurse told me that more than three ounces of glass shards got removed from my head, neck, and shoulders. She said they actually weighed it before throwing it in the medical waste bag. She also said it was kind of weird because she'd never seen any doctors actually weighing stuff that came out of someone before so I guess they were just curious. Serious though. I was such a mess when I got to the hospital that it's possible they didn't get all of the chunks out when paying attention to my more immediate injuries and some of those wounds healed over and I still got some in me. I don't know. I do have some weird bumps on my head. And all those stitches? They aren't even worth counting anymore. For real. Turned out Donnie broke my shoulder blade with that kick. I had to have surgery for it. Pins got put in to encourage (doctors like to say that word a lot) the scapula to fuse back to itself. But there were complications, so I had to have another surgery and have the pins taken out and screws put in instead. Seemed like I was in a sling forever. I got real depressed. My arm motion still isn't back to normal thanks to me losing a little chunk of triceps in surgery and I've still got radial nerve damage pretty bad. I can't give a hitchhiker thumbs-up sign because I can't move my thumb so much or extend my wrist. A few muscles in my forearm don't really work anymore either. They took the bullet out though. It sits in a jar of marbles by my bed now, right on top of the one they took out of my ribs. The one from my arm looks like a bullet, you can tell, but the one from my ribs just looks like a melted-down bolt. They would've thrown them both away if I hadn't half screamed for them in the ambulance. I still can't believe they were inside me. The paramedics had to reinflate my lung and the doctors had to reconstruct my other two ribs that the bullet broke with a bone graft from my hip and some metal to keep them together. Like I got welded on the inside. Like my rib cage is part birdcage. I don't even know how many transfusions I got, at least two that I know of. So I have plenty of someone else's blood in me now. Got a bone graft from my other hip on two knuckles because the doctors said I punched them into dust and ruined the joints. No fluid in there. Nothing. Just desert. So I can't really use the index finger and middle finger of my left hand. I guess it's fuckin' ironic that it looks like I'm making a gun sign with that hand all the time. Do you have any idea how hard it is to eat and drink when you can't hold a glass or bowl properly without using both hands? Even a spoon or fork is tricky. I got to balance it between two fingers like chopsticks because my index and middle fingers won't reach my thumbs. A knife? Forget about it. Auntie Marin has to cut everything on my plate before I can eat it. I appreciate it more now. Putting a tampon in was fun too. I once had my time down to three minutes for that because I was too proud for a diaper-y maxi-pad. Fuck it, though. I use 'em now. I use my palm and a flat surface like my dresser to press them hard and flat into the little bridge of my chonies, a little defeat. They make crinkle sounds when I sit funny. I still get "lag" on my vision when I get up too quickly or get too tired and my brain can't process what my eyes show it. Like vertigo, but worse. I puke if it gets to be too much, that's happened a few times. Every night there's a big kitchen bowl next to my bed. Sometimes I forget it's there and tip it over. That's only happened once when it was full. Every so often my head feels like right after I've been hit: I get all loopy, with motion trails across my vision like comet tails attached to anything moving and sometimes stuff that isn't. It happens randomly. The doctors say this condition could go away at any time. They just don't know. I'm still doing physical therapy. Probably I'll be doing it for another year and a half. I've basically come to grips with the fact that I'll never be normal again. At least, I think I have. I had to leave school for six months to heal. Before you go thinking that that's just two words, "six" and "months," put together and it's supposed to be a long time but doesn't mean anything, I'll just tell you that's about one hundred and sixty-eight days, give or take an afternoon or two, and roughly four thousand and thirty-two hours. That means one hundred and twenty days of daytime television, five hundred and four meals that came from a cafeteria that smelled like disinfectant, and only thirty-three visitation days when I was "taken out for a walk" but really, for the majority of 'em, I was just pushed around in a wheelchair that lapped the sidewalk skirting the manmade pond in the back of the hospital. The average number of laps Auntie Marin and me could do was sixteen in twenty minutes. Once, when she was mad about something, we did twenty-four. For the rest of that time, I was in a stupid bed, pretending to read but mostly just writing about things I could remember or drawing things I didn't want to forget. There was nothing else to do. Had to beg the nurse to help me tape the pen to my fingers with the same tape they use for IVs. She got used to doing it. Sometimes it was like I had a fingernail that I could write with. I asked for red pens only so I could pretend it was written in blood. I know, morbid. Slept all the time in between. The intensive care ward, long-term section, was where I turned sweet sixteen. I blew out all my candles from a reclining position. The nurse wouldn't let me eat any cake though, I wasn't allowed due to dietary restrictions. Doctor's orders. Had to watch Auntie Marin and Dad eat little bites in front of me and look sad and embarrassed at the same time. I lost a lot of weight, a lot of muscle. Had loads of vitamins and drugs pushed through my IV. Your veins can get tired of taking an intravenous line for too long. I got deep bruises and lots of swelling. Like a big, man-o'-war jellyfish died under my skin. The nurses had to switch mine a bunch of times, from arm to arm, up and down. By the very end, I had an IV in my leg and my whole body looked like a patch of sea for a school of spawning jellies.

I go to North High across town now, started in the fall semester. Remo helps me with my homework. The school board buses me to the new school. They changed the zoning after everything happened. I can wear dresses if I want to, but I never do. I stick to my flannels. They hide a lot of what's wrong with me. Auntie Marin trimmed up some of Cue's so I can wear them. She takes better care of Dad than I ever did, and he's improving, walking on his own more now, painting often. I want to graduate and move away to somewhere real sunny. Somewhere that doesn't make my joints feel like they're being squeezed every time I take a step or try and pick up the phone.

All in all, it's okay but sometimes, I can't feel things. Not just in my arm or my head or anywhere else but deep down. Like I don't have many feelings. Like my cousin pushed my numbness into me and I'm not so much cold anymore, just numb from the inside out. Still have all my ice though, frozen solid, going nowhere. If Jimmy was here to talk to, face-to-face, I'd ask him if he had ever learned anything about fighting damaging not only your body but your soul too. You know, just to see if they taught him anything like that in Hong Kong. Or maybe if what we did had anything to do with it. I guess I figured that the priests would talk to him about stuff like that, rules of life or something. How to stay pure in matters of karma, I don't know. I can't put that kind of stuff to him in letters either. It just looks wrong and stupid when I scratch it into the paper, so I don't. I'm pretty sure he'd never write back anyway.

I think about Cue's ghost though. My psychiatrist—nearly everyone has an appointed psychiatrist since that day, it's paid for by the victims' fund—says it was a hallucination, a product of extreme stress and shock because of my getting shot. I don't listen to her.

Even though I can't explain it, I'm sure it was real. That it was his goodbye. I haven't told anyone else about it, especially not Dad or even Auntie Marin.

The Good Reverend Doctor Martin Luther King High School, a.k.a. Kung Fu High School, got closed down. They tried to clean it all up but it just didn't work. So it was bulldozed and the city built a community center on the old foundation. Sometimes, I walk by just to see the old place, even though it's weird as hell to see kids playing there. My new school is so much different. It actually matters how you look at North, just like it matters what car you drive and who you're going out with. I don't know. Seems to me that it was so much more simple at Kung Fu. At least there I didn't have to remind myself on a daily basis that I'm "not allowed" to clock that blond bitch for staring at me, for calling me a poor, retarded Mexican when she thinks I can't hear her. She's got the impression my brain doesn't work because I get dizzy spells and my hands are funny looking. I still want to use them, though. To hit her. Right in her pretty little nose that leads to the brain that thinks anyone who speaks a little Español is Mexican. If I could make a real fist, I would. I'm not half anything to her. I'm certainly not white. I'm all different.

My psychiatrist says I'm still trying to figure a lot of things out. Find comfort in new, safer boundaries, she says. She also goes on about how I have reentry stress from the "real world." I don't know much about that, but I do know one thing. I know what happened to the little girl now. That little girl once captured by the Sand Witch. I figure Cue would've wanted me to finish the story for us, so here goes:

See, one day, the Sand Witch said, "All that I own is now yours. It is time for me to pass on." So she packed a small bag and took two very important possessions, her diary and her pillow, kissed the little girl on her cheek, and flew away into the clouds. For some time, the little girl was very lonely in the big temple and she tried very hard to be the new Sand Witch, but she couldn't do it with a clear conscience.

She couldn't continue to eat the little boys that traveled along the road at dusk. It just didn't appeal to her. So she climbed down from the corrupted temple and she left everything behind: the spell books and the cauldrons, the potions and the magic recipes. The only thing the little girl took was a picture of the Sand Witch, who had been like a mother to her. When the little girl got to a city, she found a simple job, started a simple life, and blended in with the people that lived there. It was what she had convinced herself she'd always wanted. And though she gazed out the window sometimes, at the hills to the east where the corrupted temple was almost certainly being buried by the great sandstorms of the region now that no one was there casting spells to protect it, she did not miss her old home. In fact, she didn't miss flying ever again. Yet this knowledge did nothing to damage the little girl's persistent and reluctant craving for the sky. To her mind, it was a different matter altogether.

APPENDIX

HOW TO MAKE A KINFÉ (BLADE)

1. Get 4 knives. Use metal shears to cut each knife in half.

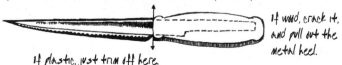

If plastic, just trim off here.

If wood, crack it, and pull out the metal heel.

NOTE: The blade'll probably be bent when it comes out. Pound it with a rubber mallet on a hard surface. You can find them in a hardware store pretty easily.

Stick it down the front of your loosest khaks. Tuck it into the waistline and wear a belt so it doesn't shift. Pull your shirt down over it. Generally, it's easier for girls to steal these than guys.

2. Pound with mallet.

3. Sharp, small, flat blade. Don't worry about edge. Can be sharpened later.

4. Put 2 blades back to back, weld or use industrial glue to stick them together.

5. Similar to Step #4, but this time create an 'X' shape with the four blades together, sharp edges out. Use dowels or molding to hold in place, rubber band it tight.

TOP VIEW (LOOKING DOWN)

6. Let it dry. If it's right, it should look roughly like an elongated Phillips head screwdriver except with four cutting edges and not as perpendicular.

7. To make the hilt: you can drill holes and use wood (A) like most people, or you can dip it in hot plastic (B) which is too damn messy, or glue a crude hilt on and tape it up tight (C).

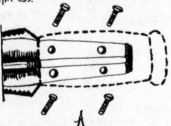

A.

Most any old drill will do so long as you have a good bit. Make sure to clamp. You don't want warped or crooked holes. Wear safety goggles for Christ sakes.

B.

Use tongs or wear gloves. Be careful not to make it so hot it bubbles because that's dangerous and a bitch to clean up.

C.

Seems like everybody has their own way of taping. Top to bottom, bottom to top, certain types of grip. It's all personal preference.

8. Sheaths are made by having two old ones torn apart and sewn back together to accommodate the new shape of the blade.

Shorten two old belts and slide them through the loops sewn on the back of the sheath.

HOW TO MAKE THROAT PROTECTION

1. Steal molding plastic from hospital supply closet, the kind used for casts and shit. Trace a curved shape resembling a boomerang. Cut it out with an X-Acto knife or jigsaw. Make sure to trace two small, vertical rectangles on the outside edges. Boil the cut-out piece in water to soften it up.

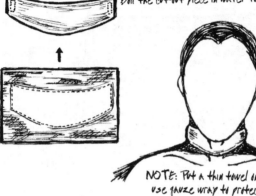

2. Place the piece on the throat to create a mold of the front neck. If it's for a male, make sure he swallows in order to create a big enough pocket for adam's apple when it hardens.

NOTE: Put a thin towel on skin or use gauze wrap to protect from burning.

TOGGLES

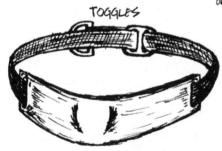

3. After it has cooled and hardened, punch out the holes on both sides and slide the strap through, securing plastic toggle(s) at the same time to ensure that it is adjustable when worn.

4. Remove neck portion from intact turtleneck using a curved cut. Be slow to avoid tearing. Use pinking shears if you have them.

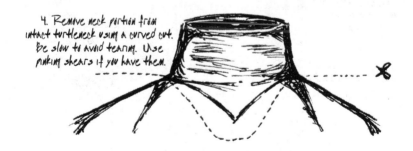

5. Either grab a sturdy t-neck dickey or do your best to re-use the previous cut turtleneck. Seems simple, but make sure colors match exactly. Everybody wears black without exception. Turtlenecks are stupid enough pieces of clothing as they are, any color but black would be ridiculous.

NOTE:
don't be stupid.
ALWAYS double
stitch with only
BLACK thread.
maybe even
triple if
you got the
dexterity
for it.

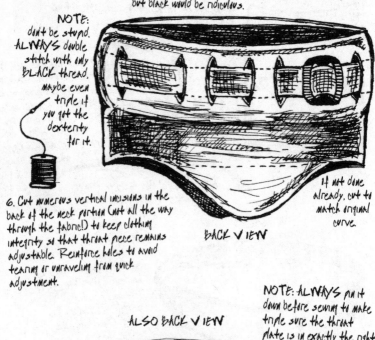

If not done
already, cut to
match original
curve.

BACK VIEW

6. Cut numerous vertical incisions in the back of the neck portion (not all the way through the fabric!) to keep clothing integrity so that throat piece remains adjustable. Reinforce holes to avoid tearing or unraveling from quick adjustment.

ALSO BACK VIEW

7. Sew the piece back onto the original open-necked turtleneck with BLACK thread.

NOTE: ALWAYS pin it down before sewing to make triple sure the throat plate is in exactly the right place! One that doesn't fit perfectly is not only as good as worthless armor-wise, but it's a damn liability if you get hit because it will compound injury or could even end you.

Do best to mimic original line of the turtleneck when sewing back on. If you screw up, don't sweat it. Most collared shirts and flannels will hide it if you keep 'em buttoned.

HOW TO MAKE SHUNTS & STRIP ARMOR

A.

B.

C.

Ideally, buy/steal sheet of aluminum, use metal shears and cut to fit. Definitely wear gloves. Most of the time though, just recycle whatever you got. Grab a few empty beer cans, remove tops and bottoms (A), cut vertically down the sides (B), open 'em up (C), pound out that metal 'til it's flat (D), layer them for higher tensile strength (E), solder 'em together (F), score and cut to fit.

NOTE: Soldering is no joke. Like all torch work, it takes patience and mad skill. Most families had someone to do this work for everyone.

D.

E.

F.

No one in our family was ever big enough for a full KEV vest, so we cut apart the few we could get our hands on.

1. Remove ballistics panels/trauma plates, use those similar to shunts to protect vital organs.

2. Cut into whatever segment sizes work for you.

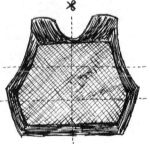

Remember: 1/4 inch thick weighs 1 pound per sq. foot. 1/3 inch thick weighs 1.3 pounds per sq. ft

HOW TO CONCEAL SHUNTS & ARMOR

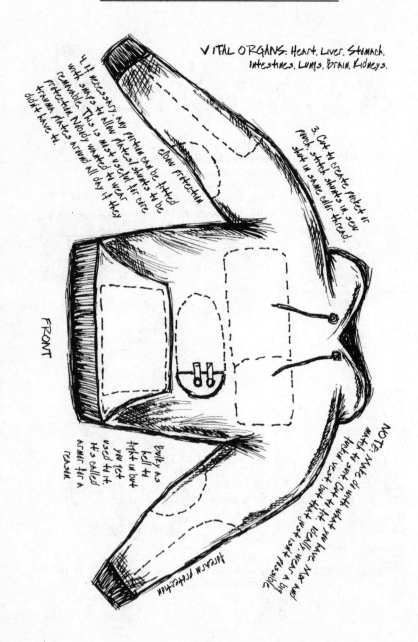

ACKNOWLEDGMENTS

Katy Follain

David Forrer

Brandon Gattis

Pamela Gattis

Robert Gattis, Jr.

Hugo Hutchison

Jenna Johnson

Lizzy Kremer

Harriet Moore

Byrd Leavell

Gustavo Arellano

William Peace, M.D.

Angie Reynoso

Paul Tan

James Davis

Paul Baggaley

Simon Lipskar

Daphne Durham

Sara Birmingham